DEATH BY D
The Sixth Grace

"Fans of cozies with a paranormal twist will be rewarded."

—*Publishers Weekly*

BABY, TAKE A BOW
The Fifth Grace Street Mystery

"...readers seeking a cozy, feel-good mystery will enjoy this outing to Grace Street. The delightful characters navigate their worldly and otherworldly challenges with affection and humor, and Tesh maintains a whimsical tone that doesn't detract from the serious subject matter."

—*Publishers Weekly*

"North Carolina PI David Randall and his psychic sidekick Camden contend with a missing baby and surly ghosts in Tesh's fifth book in the series. What seems like an open-and-shut case of a purloined newborn mushrooms into a run of investigations for Randall and Camden, whose talent for seeing the undead leads to a string of misadventures."

—*Library Journal*

"The fifth in Tesh's psychic series is again more enjoyable for the odd mix of characters."

—*Kirkus Reviews*

"...the main plot is solid, and the characters remain the chief source of appeal."

—David Pitt, *Booklist*

JUST YOU WAIT
The Fourth Grace Street Mystery

"Fans of lighter mysteries will welcome the adventures and misadventures on Grace Street."

—*Publishers Weekly*

NOW YOU SEE IT
The Third Grace Street Mystery

"Randall's investigations turn up some amusing characters among the flamboyant magicians and stagestruck wannabes, and the Grace Street residents contribute their share of quirkiness to the proceedings."

—*Publishers Weekly*

"This is the third Randall mystery, and readers who have yet to try this series should be encouraged to crack this one open."

—*Booklist*

MIXED SIGNALS
The Second Grace Street Mystery

"Randall's second appearance combines a solid mystery with a plethora of suspects and quirky regulars."

—*Kirkus Reviews*

STOLEN HEARTS
The First Grace Street Mystery

"Tesh brings a gentle touch to her new series featuring a psychic, his PI friend, and a houseful of intriguing cast members. These young men have suffered great losses in their lives, but together they are poised to solve mysteries. Definitely partner this title with Mark de Castrique's *The Sandburg Connection* for regional interest, music history, and world-weary characters."

—*Library Journal*

"A P.I. and a psychic team up to solve a series of crimes...Tesh gets her new series off to a promising start."

—*Kirkus Reviews*

"This is a good choice for southern-cozy fans who don't mind paranormal elements in the mix."

—Barbara Bibel, *Booklist*

Death by Dragonfly

Books by Jane Tesh

The Grace Street Mysteries
Stolen Hearts
Mixed Signals
Now You See It
Just You Wait
Baby, Take a Bow
Death by Dragonfly

The Madeline Maclin Mysteries
A Case of Imagination
A Hard Bargain
A Little Learning
A Bad Reputation
Evil Turns

Death by Dragonfly

A Grace Street Mystery

Jane Tesh

Poisoned Pen Press

Library of Congress Control Number: 2018931990

ISBN: 9781464211126   Hardcover
ISBN: 9781464210525   Trade Paperback
ISBN: 9781464210532   Ebook

Poisoned Pen Press
4014 N. Goldwater Blvd., #201
Scottsdale, AZ 85251
www.poisonedpenpress.com
info@poisonedpenpress.com

Printed in the United States of America

*This book is dedicated to a brand new Camden,
my great-nephew, Camden Ryan Andrew Tesh,
born March 2, 2018.*

Chapter One
"Art is Calling For Me"

When I became a private investigator I assumed all my clients would be alive.

I was wrong.

Besides breaking up an illegal baby ring, I'd recently caught a murderer and solved a big case involving the mayor of Parkland's wife. I'd also helped Camden free a ghost from a mirror. Here's where things get peculiar. The ghost, Delores Carlyle, had been a restless spirit whose only wish was to see her daughter one last time. Apparently happy with my work, she told all her dead pals in whatever spirit world they inhabit to contact the Randall Detective Agency for all their undead needs. Already, one spooky message had appeared on my own mirror saying "Delores Sent Me." There was no way to predict how any of this was going to turn out.

This hot Thursday morning in July I had an actual living client sitting in my office in the gracious old home renting rooms to an unusual collection of residents at 302 Grace Street. Leo Pierson was big and overly theatrical. With his large protruding eyes and mane of dark red hair, he looked like the leading man in a seedy acting troupe, the guy who always plays the kings and generals, and in fact, he was an actor. He'd driven up in a pearl gray Mercedes and parked next to my white '67 Fury. I was already tired of talking to him. But not only was he alive, he had money. So I sat forward in my chair and put on my most attentive face.

"How many items were stolen from your collection, Mr. Pierson?"

He reached into a pocket in his jacket and brought out a piece of paper and some photos. "Here is a list and pictures, Mr. Randall. The police have been completely useless. They simply do not appreciate the value, the mystique, the sensuality of Art Nouveau."

The items on his list were written in gold ink, all swirls and curlicues. The photos showed a set of silver spoons with twisted leaf-shaped handles, a glass dragonfly with rainbow wings, a poster of a woman surrounded by black and gold flowers, a brass ashtray decorated with a mermaid and flowing flowers, and a bright blue vase stenciled with birds. Okay, so not your usual missing items, but I didn't mind a challenge.

When I looked up, Leo Pierson fixed me with a goldfish gaze, a goldfish that would very much like a piece of bread. "These are very distinctive," I said. "I'm sure someone will have seen them."

Pierson set his silver-headed cane on the floor with a firm tap and placed both hands on top. "The poster and the ashtray are worth around twelve thousand dollars each, but the Lalique peacock vase is worth at least forty thousand dollars, the silverware I last had appraised at two hundred thousand, and the dragonfly is priceless, at least to me. It's my favorite piece. My father inherited them from a relative of his, Isabelle Duvall, whose great aunt was the model for the poster. They used to decorate her parlor, so they have sentimental value, as well." He leaned forward. "There is cause for haste, Mr.

Randall. My greatest wish is to have my own theater, and one has become available here in Parkland. Now, the dragonfly is worth more than all those other items combined, plus at least another hundred thousand more, but I would never sell it. I am willing to part with my other treasures in order to procure this theater. The seller is open to my offer, and I have a buyer for the items, but I must have payment by the twenty-third."

I glanced at my desk calendar. Ten days! "I'll get started right away."

"Yes, well, where's the psychic?" He looked around as if expecting someone to crawl out from under my desk. "I understand you have a psychic on your staff who can find lost objects. Camden, I believe his name is, and his wife runs the Psychic Service Network."

Camden owns this home. Usually, he is at his job as a salesclerk at Tamara's Boutique, but he wasn't needed there every day, so he practicing with his church softball team. I wouldn't call him "on staff." Camden becomes involved whether he wants to or not, thanks to his considerable and erratic psychic ability. "I'm sure I can find your items, Mr. Pierson." I turned to my laptop to make notes. "If you'd give me the details of the robbery."

"It happened this past Saturday night. Someone managed to dismantle my alarm system. It's quite a good one, or so I thought. The alarm is up in my bedroom, and if someone tries to break in, I should know immediately. Only this time, the alarm didn't work. I didn't hear a thing. The next morning, I found a window broken and my treasures gone. Of course, I called the police, but they were of no help whatsoever."

I typed this in. "They didn't get any fingerprints, tire tracks? No clues of any kind?"

"No." He took out a gray silk handkerchief and dabbed at his eyes. "By now, my treasures could be anywhere."

"What kind of alarm system do you have?"

"A Guardian Electronic, for all the good it did."

I also typed this information in. "Who knew about your collection?"

"A few friends and acquaintances from the art world. Lawrence Stein, who's on the board of the Parkland Art Museum; and Nancy Piper, who also works there in the finance department; Richard Mason, who runs the Little Gallery here in town; and Samuel Gallant, curator of the Princeton Art Museum in Madison."

"Any problems with these friends?"

"Oh, no. In fact, I had them to my house for luncheon and a private viewing a week ago."

The perfect opportunity for any one of them *to case the joint*, as we hard-boiled gumshoes like to say. I added this to my list. "Anything else I should know?"

"Nothing comes to mind at the moment. This reminds me of my role as Inspector Trumpet in *Railway to Murder*, Mr. Randall. There's a wonderful speech at the end of Act Two." He stood, shook back his hair, and pointed one finger toward the sky. "'The fewest clues I've ever assembled, but by far, the cleverest. No mere criminal shall deter me!' He fixed me with his large eyes as if I were responsible for this imaginary crime. "I'm sure you've seen the play."

"I've missed that one, sorry."

"Unfortunately, real life can't be solved in three acts. Get back to me as soon as you can."

Pierson hadn't been gone five minutes when I heard another car drive up, and Jordan Finley from the Parkland Police Department soon filled my office doorway. And by filled, I mean *filled*. Jordan's as large and square as a pro fullback. His short black hair bristled and his little blue eyes fixed me with a piercing stare.

"Did I see Leo Pierson leaving your house?"

"He hired me to find some missing artwork."

"I don't suppose he mentioned he's a suspect in a possible murder investigation?"

What the—? "No, he left out that part."

"Gee, I wonder why?" Jordan squeezed himself in the office chair. "What did he tell you?"

I indicated the photos on my desk. "He said his house was broken into and several valuable Art Nouveau items had been stolen. What's the deal? Did he kill the burglar?"

"Samuel Gallant is missing. Pierson was the last one to see him, and neighbors report hearing a quarrel between the two men the day before Gallant disappeared."

Gallant had been at Pierson's luncheon and viewing. "When did this happen?"

"This past Saturday, and it looks like the break-in happened late Saturday night or early Sunday."

Why didn't Pierson tell me about this? "Does Gallant have any sort of criminal record? Does Pierson?"

"Gallant, not even so much as a traffic ticket. We've searched his home and his place of business. As for Pierson, his record's clean, too. For now. You need to back away."

"I can't do that. Pierson just hired me."

Jordan's eyes narrowed. "Look. Right now we don't care about his artsy little doodads. We want to find out what happened to Samuel Gallant. I'm only sharing this info with you so you'll drop Pierson and let us handle this."

"How about this? You hunt for Gallant. I'll hunt for the doodads. I doubt our paths will cross."

Jordan gave a snort and pushed himself up. "Our paths always cross. But not this time. Do you hear me?"

I heard him, but that didn't mean I was going to listen.

As soon as Jordan left, I called Pierson. "You left out a few important details. Samuel Gallant's missing, and you're suspect number one. What's going on?"

Pierson heaved a huge theatrical sigh. "I don't see the relevance to the robbery. He wouldn't have taken my treasures. He had no interest in Art Nouveau and made that perfectly clear at my party. I have no idea where he is. He's very indecisive. He's probably standing in the middle of an airport somewhere trying to decide where to go."

"Neighbors heard you arguing with him the day before he disappeared."

"Of course I was arguing with him. He owed me money, and he was very late paying me back. Then he had the nerve to ask to borrow more, and I refused. That's what our quarrel was about. The fact I was the last one to see him is irrelevant."

"The police don't see it that way."

"I can't help that." There was a pause. "This isn't going to affect our working relationship, is it?"

"No, but you should have told me up front. Got any more secrets I oughta know?"

"I sincerely promise there are no more secrets."

I sincerely doubted that.

● ● ● ● ●

I went online and found some information about my theatrical client. He was independently wealthy and spent most of his time acting with theater groups here in North Carolina, as well as taking part in regional productions in neighboring states. Many pictures of Pierson in costume showed his face contorted with emotion, his large eyes bulging. I didn't recognize the plays, except *Arsenic and Old Lace* and *My Fair Lady*. I never had much interest in theater—aside from dating a very attractive theater major in college—but a previous case had involved actors and those very plays, so I'd learned enough to know that actors could be extremely needy and jealous. Leo Pierson didn't fit this mold—yet.

I wanted sustenance before I went on what would probably be a wild goose chase for Pierson's treasures, so I crossed the foyer and headed for the kitchen. We call the center of the main room "the island," a cluster of worn comfortable Goodwill chairs and a sofa where everybody sits to relax, read, watch TV, whatever. Kary's piano stands in the front left corner, a battered upright she can make sound like a concert grand. There are lots of plants, books, and the usual clutter. By the back bay window is a large round table and chairs for group meals. Separating this area from the kitchen is a counter and stools if you want to perch and snack.

Our home, 302 Grace Street, is in the older, greener part of what used to be Parkland's ritzy section. The house is an old yellow three-story structure with a big front porch and a yard full of huge old oak trees. It also has a leaky roof, unpredictable plumbing, and all the other charming quirks of a house built in the late Thirties. With its big windows, clean bare floors, and informal furniture, the place reminds me of a beach house or a well-kept frat house, but it's actually a boardinghouse. You've heard of halfway houses for runaways, flops, and failures. Well, this is an all-the-way house for Camden's refugees.

One of our latest tenants was a skinny would-be rock star named Kit who'd recently found success with his band, Runaway Truck Ramp. Kit and his attitude had been a real pain in the rear until Camden discovered the young man was also psychic and didn't know how to deal with the constant stream of unwanted information bombarding him all day. Once he'd shown Kit how to keep the worst of the visions at bay, Kit had become almost normal. He usually slept during the day, preparing for his nightly gigs at local clubs.

Our other new tenant was a woman named—I promise—

Vermillion. She'd been wandering in the neighborhood and sleeping on a park bench. The local women's shelter was over-crowded, so Camden told her she could stay a few days. A few days had stretched into a couple of weeks.

Vermillion was a wannabe flower child in her late thirties. Her hair looked like something you'd find clumped in the loft of an abandoned barn, but dyed tomato-soup red. Everything about her was tie-dyed and fringed. Everything she said was full of peace, love, and harmony except when she was hungry or got up too early. Then she was grumpy like a regular person. I didn't see her anywhere and figured she was probably over in the park having a sit in with her fellow hippies and smoking some illegal substances.

With Camden's wife, Ellin, at work, our regular extra-large tenants Rufus and Angie visiting Angie's sister in South Carolina, Kary rehearsing for a music festival at the Performing Arts Center downtown, and Camden at a softball game, I had the whole house to myself. This was not necessarily a good thing.

I got a Coke out of the fridge. I filled the water dish for our housecats, Cindy and Oreo, and made a few peanut butter crackers to hold me until supper. I took my snack out to the front porch and sat down in one of the worn wooden rocking chairs. Cicadas sawed away in the trees, and the sparrows and cardinals argued over the seeds in the feeder. A few cars went by, but this was a quiet neighborhood, and everyone else was inside to escape the July heat. We can't afford central air, but we have air conditioners in the bedrooms and ceiling fans, and the big house is usually cool enough, thanks to all the oak trees. A slight breeze stirred the thick leaves that shaded the porch. I'd almost gotten used to summers in the South. There wasn't much you could do this time of day except sit and think.

This wasn't how I'd planned things. I'd had a wife, a child, and a home. We ate dinner around the table every night and talked about what we did all day, as nice and normal as any family could be in this century. I was going to find lost things and solve crimes and clean up the world. Barbara was going to lead the Women's League and Garden Club, win tennis championships, and climb mountains. Lindsey was going to—well, Lindsey never had the chance to discover what wonderful things she could accomplish when a car accident killed her and Barbara left. But something wonderful had happened lately, easing my grief. I now looked forward to my dreams of Lindsey. Safe and happy in a celestial playground, she often reminded me of the many spirits that needed my help. I was beginning to believe she and Delores had their own investigation service going on over there.

Enough sitting and thinking! I had a list of names and ten days to find Pierson's artwork. I started down the porch steps when a horn beeped, and a red Ford pickup pulled up out front, full of laughing men in blue-and-white tee-shirts. Camden hopped out and waved good-bye as the truck sped away. He came up the walk, tossing a softball into his glove, his cap on backwards like some twelve-year-old, which is pretty much what he looks like.

He threw me the ball. I caught it and tossed it back. "Did you win?"

"Five to three. Emmanuel Baptist is history." He took off his cap and wiped his face with the edge of his sweaty tee-shirt. His pale hair was beyond tousled. I've seen many a brave comb commit suicide rather than make the attempt. "We could use another outfielder. The guys asked if you were interested."

"I'm surprised they let you play. Must be a real challenge for you."

He flopped down on the porch swing and grinned. "I only use my powers for good. You know that."

That grin is one reason every female within fifty miles thinks he's, in their words, "cute." The blue eyes are another. Someone once said the eyes were windows to the soul, or something Hallmarkish like that. If that's the case, then Camden's are cathedral style, floor to ceiling. When he wants to, he can give you a look that peels back every layer of your brain. You'd swear he was flipping through the synapses to find the info he needed. It's damned annoying. He could sit there, looking as innocent as he pleased. I knew he'd read the pitcher's mind and the catcher's and everyone else's on the rival team. Emmanuel Baptist didn't have a chance.

He smacked the ball in his glove a couple of times and then gave me one of those long eerie blue stares. "Something on your mind, Randall?"

"You tell me."

Another long look. I swear I could feel little fingers picking around in my brain. Camden and I have a strange psychic link. This link can be useful when I need to find him, but I'm not exactly sure how it works. It's not useful when I'd rather keep my emotions to myself.

I leaned on the porch rail. "I really thought this last case would do it. I expected to be on top for once. But every time, it's like I'm starting all over. Like things never change. I want change. I want something to happen. I'm stagnating here. I'm circling the drain."

"Damn." Camden looked impressed. "That's poetic."

"An indication of how low I've sunk."

"But you have a new client."

I straightened. "And a deadline. A two-for-the-price-of-one special named Leo Pierson. Not only did someone steal articles from his Art Nouveau collection, he's a suspect in the disappearance of art museum board member Samuel Gallant. Jordan delivered his standard warning, and Pierson insists he's not a murderer, so there you are. I'm on my way to hunt for all his little stuff, and I might do a spot of investigating into Gallant's disappearance, purely by accident. Want to come along?"

Before he could answer, the screen door squeaked and Kit came out, blinking in the daylight. He wore his usual tight black jeans and black vest studded with safety pins over a white tee-shirt that clung to his rail-thin body. His hair stuck up like a patch of stubby weeds.

"You're up early," I said.

He scratched his chin where all attempts to grow a goatee had failed. "Yeah, I gotta go see about an amp. Fella said he'd be at Foster's right about now. He was going to pawn it, but he might cut me a deal." He paused to give Camden a searching look. "You still thinking about that girl? I told you there was no way you could've stopped her."

"I know I could've done something to help."

The two of them obviously conversed on another plane. "What are you talking about?"

"My drummer's sister committed suicide," Kit said. "She wasn't gonna let anybody help her, no matter what. We both saw it coming, but Cam thought he could prevent it. Told him he couldn't. It was a pretty bad scene."

Since Camden can't see his own future, Kit makes a handy early warning system, but he can't keep the worst incidents from replaying. Camden had taught Kit what he called a "Shut the Door" technique to halt unwanted visions. It sounded to me like it didn't work this time.

"You couldn't shut the door on this one?"

Camden rubbed his forehead. "No. I've had quite a few intense visions lately. I hope I'm not headed for an upgrade."

"I got your back," Kit said. "I'll let you know if anything really bad comes up." He ran down the porch steps to his gleaming black motorcycle parked under one of the large oak trees. In a few moments, he roared down Grace Street, rattling the trash cans on the curb.

Camden watched him go and then turned back to me. "You know, I've only now gotten used to the telekinesis. Extra visions are not what I want."

"You don't want change. I want change. Same song, second verse. We're not going to sit around moaning about it. I've got ten days to find Pierson's treasures. Kit reminded me about Foster's. We could check there for Pierson's stuff."

Camden pushed himself out of the swing. "Yeah, I could use a diversion."

"Okay, partner, let's ride."

Chapter Two
"*Whither Must I Wander*"

While Camden took a quick shower and changed clothes, I called Lawrence Stein's office at Fishburn, Capra, Miles, and Stein on State Street and was informed that Mr. Stein had gone on a weekend fishing trip and wouldn't be back until Monday. Would I care to make an appointment? Yes, I would, and did. Next, I called the Parkland Art Museum and asked to speak to Nancy Piper. She was unavailable, but the secretary connected me to her voicemail. I left a message that I needed to meet with her as soon as possible. Richard Mason's contact information was on the Little Gallery website, but he was unavailable as well. I gave my desk calendar a worried glance as I left a similar message on his voicemail. This was Thursday. I had a week and three days to track down Pierson's artwork. It was vital I talk to everyone on his list.

The website for the Princeton Gallery in the neighboring town of Madison had a picture of Samuel Gallant, a tall willowy-looking man with a bored expression in his light blue eyes and a sneer in his smile. He was indeed curator, as Pierson had said. No one answered the phone. Okay, enough phone calls. The Princeton Gallery would be our next stop after Foster's.

Foster's is a big generic-looking box in one of Parkland's older shopping centers, a clean brick building with lots of windows, a far cry from the dim cluttered holes you see on TV. Kit must have made his deal for the amp because we didn't see his motorcycle in the parking lot. Inside the store, more amplifiers and banks of shiny guitars and other abandoned musical instruments lined the walls. CD and DVD players, toaster ovens, cameras, and other discarded appliances sat on clean metal shelves. Toward the back were glass cases filled with watches, rings, bracelets, and more costly items. Bilby Foster, owner and fence, hunched behind the counter like a troll guarding the king's treasure. I showed him the pictures of Pierson's lost articles and received a snort.

"Nothing much useful there." His short brow furrowed into a single line. "Don't do much trade in fancy artwork. Smartphones and tablets, now, there's where the money is. Bring me something tried and true."

"You'll let me know if something like this shows up?"

"Yeah, yeah, sure. This connected to some big jewel heist?"

"I don't think so."

"Thought maybe after all the hoopla with that murderer you caught, you'd be moving on to bigger stuff."

Why did the world need to know this today? "Yeah, well, I thought so, too. It hasn't worked out yet, but it will. Maybe this will be the case that does it."

Bilby's little brown eyes surveyed the pictures of the frilly spoons and flowers skeptically. "Don't count on it."

Camden had stopped before an array of mirrors. I'm through with mirrors and the things that lived behind them. Fortunately, nobody was home. Camden moved on past the chainsaws and flat-screen TVs and paused beside an old-fashioned baby stroller.

"When did this come in, Bilby?"

He peered up over the counter. "The pram? That's a nice one, isn't it? Somebody found it in their grandma's attic. You interested?"

"Maybe."

"Check it for vibes."

He'd already touched the handle. "It's okay."

"No evil devil babies or nothing? I'll give you a good price on it."

Camden was ready to be a father. He gave the stroller an experimental push. "I'll have to check with Ellie. She might want something more modern."

If she wanted anything at all. Ellin was not thrilled by the prospect of three children Camden had seen in her future. "Bilby, you know anything about a man named Samuel Gallant? Missing, possibly foul play involved?"

Bilby's features wrinkled in thought. "Gallant. Tall fella, looks like he smells something smelly?"

"Good description."

"In here all the time pawning stuff. One of those guys always needing cash." He shrugged. "I figure he's in deep to a gambling den, so somebody might have bumped him off."

That sounded too *noir*. "Any idea who?"

"No, but you could ask his niece. Her name's Rainbow. Works part-time for Janice."

I'd planned to head to the Princeton Gallery, but Janice was one of my best sources, and if Gallant wasn't at his museum, perhaps his niece knew where he was. A quick side trip and a hot dog wouldn't take much time.

● ● ● ● ●

Janice Chan's hot dog restaurant was one of the last fast food restaurants left in downtown Parkland. The little building burst with fragrant steam and the aroma of chili and French fries.

I had to wait a while, then wade through the crowd before I caught Janice's eye. She had two drinks balanced in one hand and a container of slaw in the other. Slaw on hot dogs. It's a Southern thing.

Janice gave me a nod as we slid onto a couple of empty stools at the counter. Last month, the restaurant had been haunted by the ghost of a young girl whose treasured possessions were buried underneath floorboards in the kitchen. Thanks to Camden and Kit communicating with her to discover her problem, the Hot Dog Ghost's items were transported to a better resting place in the park. A grateful Janice paid us with free hot dogs. In a few minutes, she returned with my usual order: two dogs all the way, fries, and a Coke, and the same with extra cheese for Camden.

"Got a minute?" I asked.

She blew a strand of fine black hair out of her eyes. "I'll be back."

She took several more orders from customers, plopped hot dogs into buns, wrapped them, and slipped them into white paper bags. People shouted out orders, tossed money on the counter, and rushed in and out. I sensed heartburn on the horizon. Someone spilled a Coke, and Janice's long-suffering partner, Steve, heaved a sigh and got out the mop. Finally, the rush of customers moved on, causing a lull in the action.

Janice peeled off her mustard-and-ketchup-stained plastic gloves and tucked the wayward strand of hair behind one ear. Her beautiful dark eyes were opaque, as usual, but she smiled.

"What's up?"

I reached for the ketchup. "Couple of questions. Do you have someone working for you with the colorful name of Rainbow?"

"Yes, Rainbow Gallant. She should be here in a few minutes."

"Her uncle Samuel Gallant is missing. Has she said anything to you about that?"

"She doesn't say much. Sort of drifts about. She's a good worker, though. Are you on the case?"

"Yes, and I'm looking for some stolen Art Nouveau." I showed her the pictures of Pierson's missing artwork. "Anybody been bragging about stealing some leafy spoons?"

She gave the pictures careful consideration. In her busy little restaurant, Janice overhears a lot of useful information, but after a few minutes, she shook her head. "No. Sorry."

"It was stolen from a home on Amber Street this past weekend."

"Looks like museum pieces. I've seen posters like this before in art appreciation class." She handed the pictures back to me. "Wish I could be more help, but the only thing I know about art is it's something I can't afford. Who's your client, can you say?"

"Leo Pierson."

She smiled. "Big guy, too much hair, eyes like a carp?"

"That's him. How do you know?"

"He stopped in here, looking for directions to Grace Street."

"So you're the one who gave me a glowing recommendation."

"I do what I can. If I hear anything about his artwork, I'll call." Motion outside alerted her. "Oh, here's Rainbow. I'll send her over."

Rainbow Gallant arrived in a Geo Metro, a car about the size of Turbo, Kary's Ford Fiesta. She held a brief conversation with Janice, who motioned to us. Rainbow did indeed drift over. She was tall and willowy like her uncle, and like her uncle, she had pale blue eyes and a bored expression, but her smile was pleasant. She wore her long pale hair tied in two braids, a plain green tee-shirt, and a long multi-colored skirt in some gauzy material that reminded me of crepe paper.

"I'm Rainbow. How can I help you?"

We stood and offered her a seat at the table. "I'm David

Randall and this is Camden. We're investigating the disappearance of your uncle."

"Oh, don't bother." She gave a little dismissive wave as she sat down, her skirt billowing. "I may have overreacted when I notified the police because he's probably on the run from his creditors. Such a goof. But he's never been out of touch for this long, so I thought they'd better find him."

"When's the last time you saw him?"

She rearranged the many bracelets dangling on her wrists. "Sunday afternoon. I stopped by his house to help him with the laundry. He's hopeless with the washing machine. My aunt used to do all that before she died. I was supposed to come back Monday and help him move some furniture, but he wasn't there, and he didn't show up here at Janice's for lunch Tuesday. That's when I called the police, but it's probably nothing."

"The police say he quarreled with Leo Pierson. Did you hear their argument?"

Rainbow was now interested in untangling her hoop earring from one untidy braid. "No, I don't know who Leo Pierson is. Uncle Samuel most likely owes him money."

She was right about that. Maybe I should take Bilby's suggestion seriously. "Are you concerned one of his creditors may have decided to end his gambling ways?"

"No, like I said, he does this all the time. Only he's usually pretty good at letting me know if he can't come to lunch."

"Would he take someone's artwork to sell to pay his debts?"

She stopped playing with her jewelry. "Steal it, you mean? Oh, no, I can't see that. He said something Sunday about a sure thing and if the deal came through I wouldn't have to work at a hot dog place anymore. He's had sure things before that never panned out, so I didn't believe him."

"Did he give you any details about this deal?" I didn't think I would get anything useful from Rainbow, but her answer made me sit up and take notice.

"No, he showed me this weird little spoon and said, 'This is going to make me rich.'"

This had to be one of Pierson's treasures. "Did he tell you anything more about this spoon, like where he got it?"

"No. I thought he was crazy. Who'd want an old bent spoon?"

I took out my phone and showed her Pierson's silverware. "Did it look like this?"

She pointed to the spoon. "Oh, yeah, that's it."

I showed her the other photos. "Did your uncle have any of these things?"

"Nope, just the spoon."

"Did he mention Leo Pierson or Art Nouveau?"

"No."

"Let me forward these photos to you, and if you see any of these items in your uncle's house, would you contact me?"

She regarded me suspiciously. "You think my uncle stole this stuff?"

"I'd be curious to know where he got it."

"Okay, and I'll give you his number, too. Maybe you'll have better luck reaching him."

We exchanged numbers, and after I sent Rainbow the photos of Pierson's treasures, Camden complimented her on one of her rings.

She held out her hand. "Do you like it? It's one of those mood rings from the Sixties." She tugged it off and dropped it into his hand. "Try it."

He slid the ring onto his little finger where it immediately went black.

"Oo, I've never seen it do that," she said. "You must be having a bad day."

He looked pensive, as if this was another bad sign. "Or my hand is cold."

"That's true." Once back on her finger, the ring changed to blue. "Do you want to try it?" she asked me.

"Maybe later. Do you know of anyone who might want to harm your uncle?"

She flipped both braids back. "He's really not the kind of guy people notice. That's why he runs off. He just wants attention." She glanced over to the busy counter. "I'd better go help Janice. Was there anything else?"

"No, thank you."

"No problem."

She drifted away. "Anything from the ring?" I asked Camden. "You looked like it bit you."

He pushed his hair out of his eyes. "Everything she told you was true, and that's definitely one of Leo's spoons. She's much more concerned about her outfit."

"Well, now that we are fortified and have an honest-to-God clue, let's take a short trip to Madison and see if Gallant's hiding out at his museum."

Chapter Three
"In This Dark Tomb"

Madison, like Celosia and Burnley and Tillson's Corner, was one of the many small towns in North Carolina that replaced fading textile mills with a growing wine industry. Madison was forty minutes away, past strip malls, clusters of fast food restaurants, and acres of lush vineyards. When we got to the gallery, I parked beside a fleet of U-Haul trucks. One truck was backed up to the museum door. A dark-haired young man with a clipboard directed two workmen carrying a very large painting of a three red triangles and a big black dot. Two more workmen waited on the sidewalk. One held a statue of an oddly shaped black dog. The other had his hands full of iridescent blue-green tiles.

"That's it. A little more to your left. Yes, slide it in next to the cabinet. Perfect." The young man made a check on his clipboard list. "Okay, *Wandering Dog* goes next, followed by *Uniform Tiles #650*. Fill in the rest of the space with the paintings I showed you." He turned to us. "Can I help you?"

I didn't want word to get back to Jordan that I'd been snooping around, but fortunately, Camden usually dresses like a starving artist. "I'm John Fisher and this is my client,

J. Michael. You may have heard of his work, *The Other World Collection*. We'd like to speak with Samuel Gallant about possibly holding a show here at the gallery."

He shook my hand. "Andrew Winston, assistant curator." He had an open, friendly face with dark eyes behind tortoise shell-framed glasses. "Sorry, friend. Mr. Gallant isn't here and even if he were, it wouldn't do any good to talk to him about a show. The gallery's closing, due to lack of funds." He indicated the trucks. "We have to return everything we borrowed, which is almost everything in the museum."

"Do you have any idea where he is or how to get in touch with him?"

"I can give you his number, but he may not answer. I don't mind telling you, he's a man who's easily distracted."

"Is that one reason you have to close?"

"No, we were in financial trouble long before that." He made another mark on his list and called over his shoulder to one of the workmen. "Don't forget that stack of frames in the hall. Oh, and did somebody get that pair of red vases? Be sure you double-wrap them in bubble wrap."

The workman assured him the vases would be double-wrapped. Another one approached carrying a bright yellow fire hydrant complete with a gush of plastic silver water. "Is there room for *Hydrant Amarillo* in this truck?"

"That goes to the Museum of Modern Art in Parkland," Winston said. "Truck five."

Hydrant Amarillo was hauled off to its new home.

"Too bad we couldn't buy that for Rufus as a memento of our last case." I said to Camden. When Rufus borrowed a bulldozer from his construction site and attempted to flatten a realtor's office, he'd managed to run over a hydrant. Fortunately, Angie had been on hand to straighten him out.

"Anything else, gentlemen? I'm really very busy."

Time to come clean. "Mr. Winston, my real name is David Randall, and I'm a private investigator. Were you aware that Gallant's niece filed a missing persons report on her uncle, and the police consider his disappearance suspicious?"

He blinked, startled. "What? Suspicious? What do they think happened?"

"They're not sure. When did you last see Mr. Gallant?"

He gave his glasses a push to resettle them on his nose. "Last Saturday. I remember because it was crazy around here. We were trying to have a discussion about moving everything out and we kept getting interrupted. He had numerous phone calls, and three people stopped by who had to talk to him."

"Did you know these people?"

"One was Chance Baseford, and everyone knows him. Gallant had asked him to come have a look at the museum in the hopes of getting a good review in the *Herald*—like that was going to happen. I personally wouldn't give that old codger the time of day. He'd say I was off by ten minutes."

Chance Baseford was editor and art critic for the *Parkland Herald* and notoriously derisive of anything that didn't meet his impossibly high standards. I was surprised he'd bother to come to a small failing museum outside of Parkland.

"One other man was Richard Mason, who came to pick up one of his outdoor mobiles, and the other fellow I didn't know, but he was a large man with a booming voice and wavy red hair."

Leo Pierson. "What did he want?"

"I didn't hear their conversation. I was trying to get some work done." He gave his glasses another push. "Are there serious suspicions about Gallant's disappearance? I would bet you anything he's just wandering around somewhere."

"I hope you're right. Were there any Art Nouveau pieces in the museum?"

"Gallant wasn't into Art Nouveau. He was more interested in modern art, you know, squiggles and big splotches of paint. Which reminds me." Another call with instructions. "Make sure we got the top that goes with Mason's errant wind mobile."

One of the workmen called back. "Thought that guy was coming to get it."

"He forgot the top. I told him we'd bring it to Parkland." He grinned at me. "If I were Mason, I'd forget the whole thing. It looks like a pile of rusty leaves to me." Someone shouted another question. "Tell them to go ahead and load the statues. I'll be there in a minute. Sorry I can't be more help, fellas."

"You've been very helpful, thank you. Would you mind if we had a look around?"

Fortunately, his list held his attention. "If you think it'll help." He reached into his pocket and handed me a key. "We finished cleaning out the main building Tuesday. There's not much to see, but go ahead."

The museum was a modern gray stone building shaped like a horseshoe. I unlocked the carved wooden door. Inside, the curved walls were bare and the floors had been swept. Camden felt along the walls where pictures used to be and wandered through the larger hall and touched the empty pedestals.

"All modern art, as he said."

"So Baseford, Mason, and Pierson all paid a visit on Saturday. Three possible connections to Gallant's disappearance."

Camden stooped down to pick up something. "Here's a piece of wire."

"Special wire that will lead to the killer?"

"No, but I can use it to fix the screen door."

"Then I'm glad our trip to Madison wasn't a complete loss."

But as Camden straightened, he froze. "Major vision coming in fast," he managed to say before he started to fall.

I caught his arm and kept him upright. "What is it?"

"Damn, what's with these sudden attacks? They're so abrupt." He'd steadied himself, so I let go. He pushed his hair out of his eyes. "It's Gallant. He's here somewhere."

"Hiding?"

"Dead."

I looked around the empty hallways. Outside, the workmen continued to haul artwork to the trucks as the supervisor checked off each piece. "Where is he?"

Camden's cell phone rang, startling us both. He pulled it out of his pocket. "It's Kit." He answered and listened. "Yeah, it just happened. I know, thanks. That's what I saw. Okay." He ended the call. "Kit apologized for the late warning. Gallant's in the storage closet at the end of the hall."

The unmistakable odor of a dead body, rotten fruit, and a cabbage smell, hit us first. Even though we were expecting it, it was still a shock when I opened the storage closet door—a slack dead face and shiny brown shoes, right before Gallant's body toppled like an ironing board toward us.

"Look out!" I pulled Camden back, and we jumped as the body hit the floor.

Camden swallowed hard. "Good Lord."

It was Samuel Gallant, all right. I recognized the bored expression and the sneer, now permanent fixtures. His yellow short-sleeved shirt and khaki slacks were rumpled, but I didn't see any bloodstains, and he still wore his brown loafers. Out for a casual stroll, a last-minute inspection of his museum, or unsuccessfully hiding from an enemy?

Camden and I had encountered enough dead bodies to know not to touch him. I didn't see any stab wounds, gunshot wounds, or evidence of strangulation. The body didn't have the cherry-red color associated with carbon monoxide poisoning.

"He's been missing for three days, but his body is still stiff," I said. "What's the deal with rigor? Thirty-six hours?"

"Sometimes longer, but three days is pushing it."

"He was alive on Sunday when Rainbow did his laundry."

We looked around for anything that might give us a clue to his death. Now that the body was found, Camden's bad vibes had disappeared. "Randall, look at that." He stooped down and indicated an object lying behind Gallant in the empty closet.

The little leafy spoon gleamed silver in the half-light.

"The spoon he showed Rainbow."

"We'd better leave it right there," I said. "It's bad enough we found the body. We can't tamper with evidence."

Camden straightened. "Why didn't the workmen find him? They had to notice the smell."

"They finished in here Tuesday, remember?" I gave Gallant's body one more look. Although I couldn't roll him over for another view, there were no indications of a struggle. The closet wasn't airtight, so he wouldn't have suffocated. It was as if Gallant himself had gone into the closet and died. I'd been joking when I said maybe Gallant was hiding out in his museum. He'd played his last game of hide and seek. "Maybe he had a heart attack."

Camden looked skeptical. "That doesn't explain why he was in an empty closet. You want me to call Jordan?"

"Yeah, go ahead. He likes you."

Jordan may not have been exasperated at Camden, but he wasn't happy to find us at the scene of the crime. He took our statements and told us to get out. I wanted another chance to talk to Andrew Winston, but he was appalled by the discovery of the body and in earnest conversation with another officer. The workmen stood by the trucks, waiting their turns to be interviewed, smoking cigarettes, and looking unconcerned. When I started in their direction, another policeman warned me away.

"At least one of the spoons has been found," I said as we walked to the Fury. "If Gallant showed the spoon to Rainbow and bragged about becoming rich, he must really be the thief, but where did he stash the rest of the artwork? Too bad you couldn't hold the spoon for a minute."

"The way my visions have been lately, I'd be afraid to."

We got into my car and sat for a while, decompressing. Since starting my own agency, I'd seen more dead bodies than I liked, and Camden has a long list of horrors he says he'll never forget. Add one more to the nightmare file.

"You okay?" I asked.

He took a deep breath. "Yeah." His phone rang again.

"Is that Kit? Maybe he saw what happened."

"It's Ellie."

I could hear Ellin's voice, but couldn't quite make out the words. I wasn't surprised when he ended the call and said, "Red alert. Crisis at the PSN. We'd better get over there before Ellie implodes."

Chapter Four

"If My Complaints Could Passions Move"

Before heading to the TV studio, I called Pierson to tell him Gallant's body had been found and so had one of his spoons.

"The police will want to talk to you, and so do I."

"He's dead? I can't believe it!"

Before he could launch into dramatics, I said, "Why did you go to Gallant's museum Saturday?"

"To talk about showing my artwork, of course. Why else would I go?"

To check out closets big enough to store a body? "Didn't you know his museum was closing?"

"I thought an exhibit of my Art Nouveau could help turn the tide."

In a museum devoted to modern art? "Did you leave one of your spoons to hold your place?"

Pierson's voice was loud enough to reach the highest balcony in the theater. "What are you talking about? No, I did not! If the police found one, does that mean *Gallant* stole my treasures? Then who killed him? Why? Was the dragonfly there? The poster? The vase?"

"After you talk to the police, give me a call."

Camden didn't have any details on the PSN emergency. Apparently, Ellin's signals were too scrambled. But I knew we'd learn all about the problem in full stereo sound and high-definition. The Psychic Service Network is Ellin's reason for living.

Ellin was holding a meeting on the light-pink and blue set of *Ready To Believe*, one of the PSN's popular shows. The set was decorated with two pink chairs and a low white table set with flowers and an array of healing crystals, as well as pictures of swirling stars and planets hanging on the pale blue walls. The soothing psychic colors and healing crystals were not working today. Waiting along with her were Bonnie Burton, Teresa Perello, and Reg Haverson. Bonnie and Teresa were the two very attractive women who hosted *Ready to Believe* and *Past Forward*. Bonnie had feathery blond hair. Teresa was a brunette. Both had soft voices and a soothing manner, off-stage and on. Reg was the emcee, announcer, and warm-up man. All three were standing a safe distance away, not surprising, since Ellin was in one of her killer moods. I could practically hear the hum of radioactive anger.

Ellin Belton Camden was a stunning woman with short golden curls, big blue eyes, and a great figure. Seeing her, you think, "Wow, what a doll." Get in her way and you realize you're about to become part of the pavement.

Camden and I had entered the side door of the small brick building and had passed the rows of seats for the audience, the cameras, and stepped over a fat row of cable on the floor when Ellin came at us in full force. "Cam, you will not believe what Matt Graber has done now. He's stolen one of our best potential sponsors, and he has the gall to say he wants to be on the *PSN Hour*."

Matt Graber was the host of *Cosmic Healing*, another show that dealt with the paranormal. I'd caught an occasional glimpse of the program while channel surfing. It looked so boring, I hadn't been interested enough to watch more than a few minutes. "Why don't you want him as a guest?"

She spared me a glare. "The only reason he wants to be a guest is so he can turn up his nose at our operation. He thinks he has the only format that works. Standing in front of an audience and answering their questions for an hour is not a format. It's a snore-fest. We had the Tinkle Time Ice Cream account all sewn up, and now they say they're going with Graber's show."

Teresa looked anxious. "Graber is always so intense. You can never tell what he's thinking."

I found this remark amusing since Teresa works for a psychic service, but she's not psychic, and neither are Bonnie and Reg. Ellin's even less psychic, if that's possible, but she's extremely protective of her network and always ready for battle.

"I'm going to have a word with Tinkle Time, and they'd better have a damn good explanation for why they changed their minds." She turned on Reg. "You met with them initially, didn't you, Reg? Did they say why they were going with Graber?"

Reg Haverson had the looks and the tan of a playboy tennis pro and spent more time grooming himself than a pack of baboons. He's usually all over these staff meetings, pushing for his ideas and his choice of guests, but today he seemed distracted. Probably didn't have his brand of super-styling hair gel at the Drug Palace.

"Ellin, the Tinkle Time Ice Cream advertising department is two scoops short of a banana split."

"I don't care if they're stupid. I want their business."

He sighed as if she'd told him to roll a boulder uphill. "I'll talk to them again."

Bonnie wrung her hands. "I'm really worried. What if Graber comes on our show and brings those snakes? I'll faint, I know I will."

"He can bring whatever he likes," Ellin said. "He's not getting on any of my shows. I need more information on Graber. Randall, he doesn't know you. Make yourself useful and go to the next taping of *Cosmic Healer*."

Was she actually asking a favor? "I can do that."

"Cam, you go with him and get the real inside story."

His eyes went wide. "Ellie, the man has two huge snakes."

She ignored his concern. "You don't have to be anywhere near them. I really need some dirt on this guy. I don't know why I didn't think of this before."

Bonnie clutched his arm. "Please, Cam. Teresa and I are really worried he may try to take over our show."

With three women pleading—well, two pleading and one demanding—Camden didn't stand a chance. He made one last attempt to change Ellin's mind. "You sure you don't want to send Reg?"

That was the last thing Ellin wanted to do. "Graber knows Reg works for me. I don't think he's met you. He may not even know we're married. I'm Ellin Belton at work."

I wanted to say, what kind of psychic is this guy if he doesn't know, but stopped myself. Ellin had said, "Reg works for me," and Reg had let that remark about his standing in the PSN pass without debate.

Ellin gave Camden one of her X-rated looks that means good things are in his future. "If you do a little spying for me, I could probably let you skip a couple of visits to the studio."

In order to keep the Earth spinning safely on its axis, I occasionally take Camden to the PSN. He refuses to take part in any of the shows, but it satisfies Ellin to have him stop by. I think she figures eventually he'll miss the spotlight and want to host a program. He and Ellin are forever bartering over his studio time.

"How many?" he asked.

"Oh, I don't know. Four?"

"Six."

"Five."

"Okay. But I'm only spying one time."

"Deal." She knew one time would be all he needed.

This problem solved, Bonnie and Teresa thanked him and chatted on about guests they wanted to book for the next season of *Ready to Believe* and the big psychic fair they were planning to hold at the Ramada Inn.

Reg wandered over to another part of the set. I followed, curious about his mood.

"So, other than the takeover threat by Graber, how are things going at the network?"

The old slick Reg was back. "Not bad. Of course if Ellin would listen to some of my suggestions, things would run smoother. I have all kinds of ideas for spicing things up. I think a psychic Olympics would be a real ratings-grabber."

"Long-distance readings, mental gymnastics, synchronized visions?"

I was kidding, but Reg took me seriously. "Exactly. If Ellin wasn't so fired up about Graber, I'd have a chance to present my better ideas."

Ellin doesn't need an excuse not to listen to Reg. "Camden and I will find out his evil schemes."

"Honey says my ideas are wonderful."

"Honey?"

His face got all goofy. "That's what I call my girlfriend. You should see her, Randall. She's perfect."

Oh, now we were getting to it. "Congratulations."

Reg waggled his eyebrows. "You know what I mean. You're in the same situation."

I glared till he stepped back. "If you're comparing my relationship with Kary to one of your little flings, you're sadly mistaken."

He put both hands out to ward me off. "Take it easy, Randall. I meant she's a younger woman, that's all. I thought you'd understand."

"How old is your little Honey?"

He straightened his tie. "Twenty-one. Perfectly respectable. I'm twenty-nine."

"Plus ten."

Offended, his face turned red under the perfect tan. "You can check my bio."

The best lie I'd heard all day. "Give it up, Reg. Camden's the only one around here who can get away with looking younger than his age. I don't care if you've got yourself a little tootsie, but don't insult my intelligence."

"I'll have you know I am twenty-nine years old."

"You know, sometimes when you've gone too long without sex, it scrambles your brain."

Reg huffed and decided this wasn't worth a reply. He probably couldn't think of a snappy rejoinder. If he had a new girlfriend—a new young girlfriend—he'd be a lot happier. He sulked through the rest of the meeting and left before the others. I said good-bye to Bonnie and Teresa while Ellin gave Camden one of her special extra-long kisses. I think it would almost be worth listening to her complaints to be kissed like that. Almost.

Camden decided to stay for a while, and I certainly couldn't blame him, so I returned to the Fury and checked my phone. Nothing from Richard Mason or Nancy Piper. I drove to the Parkland Art Museum and discovered Ms. Piper had left for the day. Too busy to check her messages, or avoiding me? The same thing was true at the Little Gallery, which was closed and locked. Had Mason skipped town with the dragonfly in his pocket?

Discouraged by my lack of any further clues, I drove home. When I arrived, Kary was sitting on the porch, and my mood immediately improved. As usual, she looked fantastic, even in jeans shorts and a pink sleeveless blouse. Her long silky blond hair was pulled back in a graceful ponytail. Gold hoop earrings dangled from her perfect ears. She raised her can of diet soda in greeting.

I leaned in for a kiss. "How was the workshop?"

"Extremely boring. Do you know how hard it is to sit in a meeting for four hours on such a beautiful day? Now I know how my students feel. Let me get you a drink."

"No, that's fine. Don't get up." I pulled another rocking chair up beside hers and slid into it. "I had a snack at Janice's."

I know what I see when I look at Kary, and I know what she sees when she looks at me, besides a damned good-looking man, that is. I'm six years older, twice divorced, with little or no prospects—in other words, a real catch. However, our relationship had recently taken a giant leap forward. "So, when are you moving in with me?"

She set her soda can down by her chair. "We need to talk about that."

"If you're concerned about your reputation, marry me. I'll make an honest woman out of you."

This teased a smile from her. "No, it's not that."

"If you think I took advantage of your fragile mental state, think again. You started it."

Another smile. "I wouldn't have, if I hadn't wanted to. I'm not sure where this leaves us."

"Better than ever."

"You still want to get married, though."

What's the problem? "That would be the next logical step, yes. The fact that the honeymoon came first spices things up."

"I know we joke about it, but I'm not comfortable with the idea."

I'd run into this before. Kary's sheltered ultra-religious

upbringing had prevented her from experiencing a normal childhood, and her disastrous teen pregnancy and subsequent health issues had taken two years out of her life. That one rebellious act and the depression that followed almost killed her until Camden took her in.

I did not want her to have any reservations. "We don't have to get married. We can continue to live in sin as long as you like."

This, as I'd hoped, made her smile again.

"But you want a family, David. So do I."

That's what Lindsey wanted for me, too. "Then we'll find a way to do that. We can do like Camden does and pick family members off the street."

"We could." Kary picked up her soda and took a sip. "Here's something else I'm thinking about. During that boring work-shop, I had an idea. As much as I love working with the little ones, I want to take some classes in guidance and become a counselor. I think I'm qualified to help other girls avoid the mistakes I made."

"That sounds like a great idea."

"This doesn't mean I'm giving up on my adoption plans, but for now, I need to channel all my baby issues into something useful. Plus it will keep me from going after Rufus."

"We must save Rufus at all costs."

"On a lighter note—and do not laugh—I'm going for Miss Panorama."

"Why would I laugh? I love seeing you in a tiara."

"I know I said I was through with pageants, but there's plenty of prize money in this one if I win."

I knew what she meant. Every extra cent she made went into a special adoption fee bank account.

"You will." I couldn't believe she didn't win every pageant she entered. As good as she looked in jeans, in an evening gown, she could stop your heart. In a bathing suit, forget nine-one-one. You'd already died and gone to heaven. "How's the music festival coming along?"

Kary had been invited to accompany several of the performers. "Pretty well. I know some of the art songs, but I'll have to work on the others."

Art Nouveau, art songs. We were getting pretty arty around here. "Is an art song different from a regular song?"

"They're musical settings of poems in a classical style, usually written for one voice with piano accompaniment. 'Oh, Promise Me' is one and 'O Perfect Love.' You've heard Cam sing those for weddings. 'The Last Rose of Summer' is another fairly well-known song. These folks are going for the hard-core stuff, though. Brahms, Beethoven, Scarlatti. So I'll be practicing a lot."

I always enjoyed hearing her play, no matter what type of music. "I don't mind that."

She changed the subject. "You're cooking tonight, I believe. What're we having?"

"Chicken pie."

"Sounds delicious. How about your cases? Anything happening?"

"My latest client, Leo Pierson, has an extensive collection of Art Nouveau objects. This past Saturday night, someone disabled his alarm system and stole several objects." I showed her the pictures. "That's not all. Pierson's the main suspect in the mysterious disappearance of Samuel Gallant. Mysterious, no more. Camden and I found his body at his museum in Madison." Recalling Gallant's dead face and the sickening thud his body had made on the floor gave me a sudden shiver.

Kary stopped rocking, eyes wide. "Oh, my God. What happened?"

"I don't know. There weren't any signs of a struggle or the

use of a weapon or poison, and it's doubtful Jordan is going to tell me the cause of death. One of Pierson's Art Nouveau spoons was on the floor behind Gallant's body. On Sunday afternoon, he showed that spoon to his niece and hinted his money troubles would soon be over, so looks like he's the culprit, but the deal went south."

"Did you say Samuel Gallant?"

"That's right. Do you know him?"

"If it's the same man, he's supposed to be one of the pageant judges. Hang on." She took out her phone. "There'll be some info on the pageant website." In a few minutes, she read, "'The Miss Panorama Pageant welcomes new judges Allison Carter, owner of the Your Best Look Salon; Gina Anderson, former Miss Tidal Basin; and Samuel Gallant of the Princeton Gallery in Madison.'"

"That's the guy. Is there anything else about him? Maybe he riled one of the other judges."

She tapped her phone. "No, but the pageant director might know more. I'll find out."

"As long as it doesn't interfere with your pageant doings."

"I think this is a little more important. Plus you know I love it."

"We could make it a full-time job."

"There would be quite a few disappointed second-graders at Parkland Elementary next fall."

"Oh, they'd get over it. Kids are tough." I got up. "I'll get started on my pie."

I'm a decent cook, which had surprised the ladies of the house. "Think about it," I'd told them that first night they were treated to one of my famous chicken recipes, Chicken Kiev a la Randall. "Two wives, two kitchens, two sets of cookware. It was inevitable."

Since we're on a strict budget here at 302 Grace, there're

always lots of stews and casseroles involving leftovers in creative ways. Camden's specialty is lasagna, which is always delicious, and we finally convinced Kary to stop making tuna casserole.

I had sprayed a baking dish with cooking spray and was rolling the dough for the crust when Kary came in with her laptop and sat down at the counter.

"I sent a message to the pageant director. He'd heard that Gallant was missing and said the committee was going to have to replace him, anyway, because he insisted on being paid. Judges usually don't get paid for these pageants. Maybe on a national level, but not for Miss Panorama."

"Gallant was desperate for money."

"I'd say so. The director said they had a big argument about it."

"Did Gallant have any family other than his niece?"

Kary was way ahead of me. "No, I Googled him and found practically nothing. Oh, and here's a little something about Art Nouveau. It was an artistic movement that was very brief, only twenty years or so, at the turn of the nineteenth century. The artists emphasized flowing lines and plant forms, all curves and waves. It was sort of a back-to-nature rebellion against all the other more formal styles."

She turned the laptop so I could see the pictures of little curved spoons and the flowing hair on the mermaid's head. "That's it, all right," I said.

"There are all kinds of plant and insect designs. People had furniture, stained-glass windows, even homes made in the Art Nouveau style. Here are some good pictures from the *All Color Book of Art Nouveau.*"

The *All Color Book of Art Nouveau* was a tall, slim red book with an artistic swirl of black on the front. I checked out the gold vase with shiny blue flowers growing up its sides, a stylistic stained-glass window depicting a young woman dressed in a flowing gold-and-blue gown with butterflies on the sleeves and pearls on her fancy headdress, a leafy staircase that appeared to melt around the corner of the stairs, and swirly doorways that shared pages with sloping spindly chairs and women's serene white faces growing out of lamps and ashtrays. There was even a picture of a glass dragonfly, a lifelike creation with clear veined wings, a long shiny body, and two large Pierson-like eyes.

"This must be one like Pierson's prototype."

Kary took a closer look. "It's beautiful."

"According to the book, it's called a car mascot and it's designed to change colors the faster you drive."

"I wouldn't mind having one on Turbo." She took back the laptop and showed me another page. "Here's the newspaper account of the robbery." She clicked a few keys. "It says here that Mr. Leo Pierson of 1411 Amber Street was robbed on Saturday night or sometime early Sunday morning. Missing are several valuable objects from Mr. Pierson's extensive collection of Art Nouveau. Police found a broken window at the back of the house and the alarm system had been disconnected."

"Disconnected. I'm going to have to find out more about that."

Kary glanced at the cow-shaped clock above the sink. "How long does your pie need to cook?"

"About an hour."

"Then get on your running shorts and chase me around the block. I need to get in shape for the pageant."

Chapter Five

"Are You With Me?"

By the time Ellin and Camden came home, not only had Kary and I run around several blocks, we'd had time to enjoy ourselves in the shower and the chicken pie was perfect—golden brown and crispy. We also had green peas, peaches another friend of Camden's had brought back from the eastern part of the state, and the usual gallons of iced tea. I never drank much tea until I moved South, and I can never drink it as thick and sweet as Camden does, but I'd learned to like it a lot, especially on hot days like this. I'd learned to like ham biscuits, too, and collard greens and sweet potato pie.

Vermillion wandered in and pulled up a chair. She had leaves in her red hair and her love beads and bells made a jangly noise as they hit the edge of the table.

"I had a super groovy day in the park. There's this guy who says I can crash at his place, but he wants forty dollars. You got forty dollars I can have, Cam?"

"I think you'll be better off here."

"You see some radical thing happening in the future?"

Even I could foresee that a random guy met in the park and in need of cash was all about free love and no consequences.

"Yes," Camden said. "Drugs for him and jail for you."

"Oh, then maybe I oughta stay here. Oh, man, is that chicken pie? I was going vegan, but that smells too good."

Camden passed the pie. "You can go vegan tomorrow."

She dug out a big chunk and plopped it onto her plate. "Solid." She gulped down her dinner with annoying smacking sounds. Ordinarily, Ellin would have plenty to say about Camden's boarders, but tonight, she complimented me on the meal. She didn't even fuss at Camden for passing little pieces of chicken down to Cindy and Oreo, who waited patiently under his chair.

Vermillion wiped her mouth with the back of her hand until Kary handed her a napkin. "Thanks. I heard this amazing poet in the park today. I can't remember everything he said, but one poem was called 'Living in Harmony,' and one of the lines was 'Peace for these troubled times starts with the few and ends with the many.' Isn't that profound? I love poetry. Maybe he'd let me move in with him."

Camden tried to dissuade her from another disastrous choice. "Poets usually live alone so they can create."

She took another chunk of pie. "Oh, yeah. Forgot about that."

Vermillion forgot about a lot of things. I got up, my hands full of dishes. "More tea, anyone?"

Kary stacked her empty plate on top of mine. "None for me, thanks. I'm heading upstairs."

Ellin gathered the napkins. "No, thank you. I've had a long day. I'm going out on the porch for a while to rock and relax."

Camden got up to hold her chair. "I'll come with you."

Vermillion gazed into the distance. "I must sit in the sunset. The rays are far more beneficial."

That meant she was going to the backyard. Fine by me. I put the empty dishes in the sink and ran the hot water, hearing an ominous groan of old pipes. When I came back to the table for what was left of the chicken pie, Vermillion was counting out a row of tiny pills.

"What's all this?" I asked.

"Don't worry, they're legit. I got high blood pressure."

She showed me the bottle. The label had the jaw-breaking name of hydrochlorothiazide. "Are you taking all of them?"

"No, man, counting them out for the week. I want to have enough. Kary gave me this plastic box to keep them in. See? It's got a little compartment for every day of the week. Cool, huh?"

"Very cool. How many people hang out in the park with you?"

"We got quite a few. Time to bring back the Summer of Love, you know? Man, I wish I'd been around then. We all do."

There were worse things to do than imitate the flower child culture of the Sixties. Looking at Vermillion's peace sign tee-shirt and tattered skirt reminded me of another retro hippie. "You ever meet a young woman named Rainbow?"

"Oh, yeah, she's around. Knows all the words to every Janis Joplin song."

"She ever mention her uncle, Samuel Gallant?"

"Don't remember that."

"Ask her about him the next time you see her."

"Sure, man."

I didn't have much faith in Vermillion's memory, but it was worth a shot. I was also curious about Rainbow's reaction to Gallant's death. After I cleaned up the kitchen, I gave her a call. When she answered the phone, she sounded more resigned than upset.

"Thanks for calling, Mr. Randall. I suppose you heard the news."

"Yes, I'm very sorry about your uncle."

"Yeah, well, that was sort of a surprise, but not really. He had a weak heart, and his pacemaker gave out on him."

"Is that what the police told you?"

"They said it looked like the pacemaker failed and he had a heart attack, so what else could it be?"

Lots of things, I wanted to say. A rare poison. An air bubble injected into his bloodstream. A sudden shock. People don't go into empty closets and have heart attacks. Or maybe they do.

"It's really too bad," Rainbow said with a sigh. "He always said the house would be mine, and he did leave a will, as hard as that is for me to believe. While I'm cleaning out his stuff, I'll look for that artwork."

I thanked her and then called Pierson. My call went right to voicemail. Were the police still questioning him? That didn't seem likely. Maybe he'd been charged with the murder and used his one phone call to call a lawyer. While I waited to hear from him, Camden and I decided to forgo our usual science fiction movie to watch *Cosmic Healing*.

I went to the island and sat down in the worn blue armchair. Camden took his usual seat on the green corduroy sofa, reached for the remote, and clicked on the TV. He found the right channel, and Matt Graber appeared in the middle of an impressive set decorated with stars, moons, and comets. Graber was an ordinary-looking man in his mid-forties, medium height and build, with short brown hair and a slightly pinched look around dark eyes. His mouth turned down at the corners.

Camden set the remote on the coffee table. "Looks serious."

"Communing with the cosmos is hard work. You oughta know that."

Graber moved along the first row of the audience, keeping up a steady stream of talk.

"Someone here with chest pain or pain along the left side, possibly the ribcage or stomach."

"That covers the entire body," I said.

"Someone with an 'S' in his or her name. Steven or Sam or Sidney. Or an 'S' sound, like Phyllis, Doris, Agnes."

A dumpy woman with fried hair suddenly came to attention. "Agnes."

Graber paused before the woman. "Is that your name, or the name of someone who needs psychic healing?"

"My grandmother."

"Is she with you today, or has she passed on?"

I was interested now. "Camden, is he planning to heal from beyond the grave?"

"That's something I'd like to see."

The woman answered, "She's in a rest home in Asheville."

Graber hadn't changed expression. "Your grandmother suffers from some sort of chest or stomach pain?"

I gave Camden an expression of my own. "What are the chances of that?"

"Pretty good, I'd say."

"And you don't even do psychic healing."

The woman was watching Graber with almost pathetic eagerness. "She has stomach cancer. If there's anything you can do to help—"

Graber held out his hands, palms forward. "What is your name?"

"Arlene."

"Place your hands on mine, Arlene. I'm going to summon all my healing power and send it into you. When you go to your grandmother, put your hands on hers like this, and the power will be transferred to her. You'll see remarkable results."

He breathed in deeply and pressed his hands to Arlene's. She shook and fell back into her seat.

Camden was delighted. "You are now heeeeled! Go and sin no more."

To me, Graber was only an entertainer and more likely a con artist. "What do you think? Should Ellin be worried about this guy?"

"Ellie worries about everything."

On screen, Graber continued his spiel. "Anyone suffering from headaches, migraines. Someone with a 'B.' Bobby, Billy, Betty—"

"Bobby," someone called from the audience.

"They're giving him the answers," I said. "He's got this cold reading thing down cold."

Camden agreed. "Throw out enough suggestions and something's bound to be right."

Graber cured a headache, a toothache, and a bad case of nerves. Then he moved back to a table. On the table was a glass case. Inside the case were two large snakes.

"Oh, wow, are we in luck," I said. "Not only does he heal, he handles snakes."

Camden was looking everywhere except at the TV. "You can turn it off now."

"Can you stand it for five minutes? I want to see how snakes fit in."

"No snakes."

"Go in the kitchen."

He retreated. I don't mind snakes, but they make Camden jumpy. He says he can trace this fear to a night he slept in someone's barn and a huge king snake decided to snuggle up next to him where it was nice and warm. As he ran screaming into the dark, he fell and upset a nest of baby snakes that slithered like water all around and over him. He said he practically turned inside out getting away.

On screen, Graber picked the larger of the two pythons out of the case and wound it around his neck. As he approached the audience, some people drew back. Graber smiled his first smile of the day, a thin, tight smile that was more of a grimace. "There's no need to be afraid. I rescued these two beautiful animals from a pet shop where they were crammed into a small dark cage with barely enough room to turn around. Now they are healthy and happy. Another amazing example of the healing power of the cosmos." He turned to address his viewers. "If I can bring health and wellness to the lowest of nature's creatures, think what I can do for you. Don't forget your health is a gift that should never be wasted or taken for granted. I'm Matt Graber, and I wish you wellness."

I changed the channel to *Mission to Mars*. "All clear."

Camden came back to the island. "If he wants me to have health and wellness, he'll keep the snakes in their cage."

"Have to admit it's kinda eye-catching. Maybe Ellin needs to get a cobra or something."

He flopped back on the sofa. "Ellie needs to relax. I don't think Graber's a threat. He has a completely different approach, that's all."

"You know she won't be happy until we go over there."

"Maybe I could wait in the car." He reached for the remote and muted the sound. "Have you noticed the pipes making a grumbling noise?"

"Yeah, you might want to get them checked—unless that's something you can fix."

"I'm going to give it my best shot."

I decided I needed to know something. "Are Rufus and Angie going to keep Mary Rose?"

"I hope so."

"But you don't know."

"Contrary to popular belief, I don't know everything." He gave me one of his intense blue stares. "How do you feel about a baby in the house?"

"I'm okay with it." I turned my attention to the TV. The

screen had dissolved into wavering gray lines. "Oh, brother. Here's something else for you to repair."

Camden's eyes reflected the gray light. "It's not broken. Someone's trying to come through."

"Someone or something? If you say, 'They're heeere' in a spooky voice, I'm leaving."

He turned up the volume. "It's for you."

"Must be Delores."

Words appeared on the screen. I had just enough time to read my name before the TV crackled with static and the movie popped back on screen.

Camden looked puzzled. "That's odd."

Odd! "Which part?"

"I thought—"

He paused for such a long moment, I wondered if he'd fallen into another vision. I turned down the TV. "You thought what?"

"It was a message for you, but it stopped."

"I don't have a problem with that. If it's really important, she'll call back, right?"

"Right." He didn't sound convinced, and he didn't say much during the rest of the movie and went to bed as soon as it ended.

I thought Kary had gone to bed, too, but she was awake, propped up on the pillows, her face glowing by the light from her laptop.

"David, I've signed up for online classes in guidance counseling through the college."

I sat down next to her. "Not wasting any time, are you?"

"The only problem is how to pay for these classes. I can afford two each semester, but that means it'll take me longer to finish. The other option is to use my adoption fund money. I'm going to have to think long and hard about that."

One silky strap of her short nightgown had fallen off her shoulder. I slid it back on. "I can help you out if you'll let me."

"I'll have to think about that, too." She closed the laptop, set it on the nightstand, and began undoing my shirt. "What were you and Cam watching?"

"*Cosmic Healing.* But I am much more interested in watching what you're doing."

The shirt was off and tossed aside. Kary tugged at my belt. "How was it?"

"Graber is your usual phony psychic. His snakes are the real stars of the show. Good heavens, woman, slow down. Have you no shame?"

She chuckled. "Try and stop me."

Two quick pulls and her nightgown was history. "Challenge accepted."

Chapter Six

"If You Die of My Death"

My dreams were nice and steamy until around three a.m. After a blurry glance at my digital clock, I went back to sleep and dreamed of Lindsey. She had been on the swing set in the playground and slipped off her swing to walk toward the edge. As usual, she wore her white lace dress and a ribbon in her long brown curls. Flowers swayed at the border to the playground, and I could hear the far-off calls and laughter of other children. Lindsey waved and smiled.

Hello, Daddy.

"Hello, baby," I said. "Were you or Delores trying to reach me?"

No. It was someone else. She couldn't get through. It would be easier if Cam could see her, but I think I can show her the way.

"Why can't he see her?"

He needs your help, Daddy. He's going to do something he shouldn't do.

Oh, I didn't like the sound of this. "Can you tell me what it is? What's causing the problem?"

The Dragonfly, she said and abruptly faded away.

The Dragonfly? Pierson's dragonfly? What did that mean?

• • ● • •

The odd dream made me oversleep, so the next morning, I missed the chance to talk to Kit about the TV message. I still hadn't heard from Pierson. Camden was under the sink in the downstairs bathroom looking at the pipes, and I asked him if he'd heard from Lindsey. He can always tell if I've had a dream of her.

He climbed out of the cabinet. "She started to come through, and then things got blurry. Could you hear her? What did she say?"

"She said someone else was trying to reach me. She also said you were going to do something you shouldn't. What aspect of your wild secret life haven't you told me?"

He opened his toolbox, which was on the floor beside him. "Something I shouldn't do? I have no idea."

"It has to do with Pierson's dragonfly."

"That makes even less sense."

"I would certainly like to hear from him."

I left Camden deciding whether or not to tackle the plumbing and drove to the City Cab office downtown. Cab driver Terrance "Toad" Hall, another good source, had heard of Gallant's death, but only what he'd read in the *Parkland Herald*. He was also familiar with Art Nouveau.

He leaned against his green-and-white cab, lit a short black cigar, and took another look at the photos Pierson had given me. Toad's a tall elegant man who favors long-sleeved shirts and ties even on the hottest days, but he drives like that crazy frog in *Wind in the Willows*, hence the nickname. "There isn't a gallery in town showing Art Nouveau this season, and Baseford hasn't said a word about any traveling exhibits."

Besides the regular museums, the city had a fairly large art gallery adjacent to the university, plus many smaller galleries, and Baseford knew everything that was in them or likely to be purchased. "I might have a word with him, then." A couple of words, including, why would you travel to Gallant's museum when a phone call would've answered his questions?

"Yeah, sure. Can't be too many people around interested in this. I'm an Art Deco man, myself. Not as sissy. But you could get some real money out of these things." He pointed to the photo of the leaf spoons. "Now this set of spoons is worth a quarter million, easy."

"Yes, Pierson said around two hundred thousand."

"And this poster by Mucha. He was one of the premier artists of the Art Nouveau movement. At least ten thousand." He indicated another photo. "This dragonfly, for instance. It's a hood ornament, if you can believe it, real classy. Designed by Rene Lalique. As your car moves, that disc underneath the dragonfly revolves and sends colors though the wings. The faster you go, the faster the colors change. Lalique created lots of different ones. Called them car mascots."

"Yeah, so who'd want to steal it? Who knew it was in Parkland?"

Toad shrugged. He handed me the photos. "Your best bet is an APB to all museums in the country."

I took out my list. "Know anything about these folks?"

Toad took a few puffs on the cigar. "Lawrence Stein's no saint. Stepped over quite a few people on his way up the corporate ladder, so he's got plenty of enemies. Mason's an electronics whiz and makes really strange sculptures. I don't know much about Nancy Piper, except she was recently hired on at the museum."

"Thanks. Keep an ear out, will you?"

"Sure. Let me see the pictures again." He looked through the photos, a slight frown creasing his face. "Seems like I heard something about these particular things. Did they all belong to the same person?"

"Pierson's distant relative, Isabelle Duvall."

"Duvall," he repeated thoughtfully. "Nope, not coming to me. If I think of it, I'll let you know." He glanced at my car. "Still driving the Fury? I thought after you solved that last big case, you'd get yourself some real wheels."

That's what I thought, too. "Can't give up the Fury. She's my inheritance."

"Yeah, well, you get attached." He patted the cab's fender. "Let me know when you find that dragonfly. I could use it on old Betsy here. Make her Cab Nouveau."

Old Betsy already had three sets of Mardi Gras beads, feathers, and wind chimes dangling from her rearview mirror, swaying hula girls in the back window, and a plastic statue of Snoopy playing golf on the dashboard. "The finishing touch," I said.

● ● ● ● ●

My next stop was the *Parkland Herald* office.

Wasn't I lucky? Chance Baseford was willing to give me a few minutes of his precious time. I'd forgotten how I can't stand the supercilious jerk. He was properly shocked about the theft, but there was also a disgusting gleam in his eye that made me feel he and Leo Pierson had gone a few rounds before, and Baseford was all too happy about his rival's misfortune. Then again, Baseford thought of everyone in Parkland as his rival.

When I asked him about Samuel Gallant and the theft of Leo Pierson's Art Nouveau pieces, Baseford's broad fleshy face went all crinkly with fake distress. "My, this really is too sad." He sat back in his swivel chair, his full head of white hair a stark contrast to the rows of colorful books on the shelf behind him. Even though he was now editor of the paper, he hadn't given up his position as art critic. I caught a glimpse of collections of movie and TV reviews by a nationally known critic, as well as commentaries on *How The Media Affects Our*

Lives, and a couple of thick biographies on artists and musicians. Framed certificates and plaques decorated the walls of the narrow office. Over the door hung a grinning caricature of Baseford gleefully skewering a hapless dancer on his pen.

Baseford crossed his fingers over his ample stomach. "According to our own excellent reporting, what happened to Gallant is considered suspicious, but there isn't a clear cause of death. As for Pierson's items, of course, if I hear anything at all, I'll be sure to let you know, Mr. Randall."

He wasn't going to dismiss me this easily. "If you'll recall, I'm the reason you're now editor of the *Herald*."

"Are you speaking of that unfortunate mishap with our former editor who liked to create his own sensational news by murdering people?"

"That's the one."

Baseford smirked. He had enjoyed getting the best of his former employer.

"So what you're saying is I owe you one?"

"A reasonable exchange of information isn't too much to ask. Why did you leave your ivory tower here and go to Gallant's museum? One phone call and he's destroyed. You wouldn't even have to set foot in the backwoods."

"I'd heard it was closing and wanted to see for myself. Gallant has always been an irritating presence, a poser, and a nuisance. Always short of money and pestering people to lend him some. Easily led, as well. The man would bet on whether the sun would rise. I knew he'd run the Princeton into the ground."

"Irritating enough to get rid of?"

"Only in theory, Randall. You can't possibly believe I'd do something so mundane as murder."

True, it was hard to imagine Baseford making the effort to stuff a dead body into a closet. "You could pay someone to do it."

"What exactly is my motive? Many people irritate me. You irritate me. But I'd much rather use my words and my artistic reputation to destroy my enemies. The revenge lasts longer."

"Any idea who might want to kill Gallant the old-fashioned way?"

"No." He gave me a long measuring look. "I believe I saw your name in our paper not long ago connected with a certain realtor's unfortunate dealings in illegal adoptions. You certainly attract interesting cases. I don't have enough information to solve Gallant's murder for you, but as to the theft of Pierson's artwork, I'll be sure to write an editorial urging our museums and galleries to update their own security systems."

"How many people were aware of Pierson's collection?"

"I was aware of it, of course." Because nothing artistic could exist without his knowledge. "I'd never seen his collection, but then, I never travel to the suburbs if I can help it, unless there's something I must see, like the demise of the Princeton Gallery. I imagine most of the people at the museum have at least heard about it."

"You know everything about the art community." I was rewarded with a regal nod. "Is there anyone who had a grudge against Pierson? Anyone who'd like to set up a scheme, possibly hire Gallant to steal his stuff just to thumb his nose at the guy? Not everything was taken, which leads me to believe the mastermind behind this job knew his Art Nouveau and hit where it would hurt most."

"As for a grudge…" He narrowed his eyes, thinking. "…I really don't know Pierson well enough to answer that. The man could have dozens of enemies. Lord knows he makes enough noise."

I would've used the word theatrical. Baseford's face had turned an odd shade of pink, as if thinking about noisy Mr. Pierson had unsettled his artistic soul.

"Aside from all his wearisome dramatics, Pierson hasn't a clue about the true value of his collection."

"What would that be?"

"I suppose he told you some nonsense about his second or third cousin once removed, Isabelle Duvall?"

"He mentioned her."

Baseford gave a short bark of what might have been a laugh. "He didn't say anything about the feud or the mysterious treasure?"

"Only that he had a buyer for all the items except the dragonfly, which wasn't for sale, and the money would bankroll a theater he wanted to purchase."

Baseford sat back, exasperated. "Good Lord, the man's a fool."

I'd had enough riddles. "What are you talking about?"

"Pierson's family and the Duvall family have been feuding for years over ownership of this Art Nouveau. One accused the other of stealing it, and they've been stealing it back and forth forever. What did he tell you it was worth?"

I checked my notes on my phone. "Not counting the dragonfly or sentimental value, two hundred and sixty thousand dollars. He said the dragonfly was worth much more."

He made a dismissive snort. "Pocket change."

"I take it this 'mysterious treasure' comes in here?"

Baseford was all too willing to enlighten me. "Oh, this is the best part. Separately, these pieces are worth a paltry two hundred thousand dollars, but somewhere along the line, a Pierson or a Duvall took specific marks and letters from the pieces, which, when put together, lead to a hidden treasure supposedly worth over twenty-five million dollars."

Was he pulling my leg? "Marks and letters?"

He rolled his eyes as if I were too stupid to be believed. "On the bottom of the ashtray and the vase would be a mark for the artist's name. On the poster would be letters."

"How do you know all this?"

"Of course I know all this! Leo Pierson definitely doesn't. Tell him. I'm sure he'll be amazed." He made a great show of turning back to his laptop. "Was there anything else, Mr. Randall? I have several reviews to finish. The Parkland Symphony's concerto last night was a complete disaster, and I can't wait to share my findings."

I'd had enough of Baseford. I've always hated the idea of some fat pompous ass deciding what movie I should see, what book I should read. Who died and gave him control of the remote? Now I'd found out he was too arrogant and mean-spirited to let Pierson know the key to a possible fortune. I took out one of my cards and put it on Baseford's desk. "Thanks for your help."

Another royal nod and I was free to leave his presence.

It was now lunchtime, and I was no further along than before. No return calls from Ms. Piper or Richard Mason. I called Pierson again and once more, the call went to voicemail. Where was he? Had a rogue band of feudin' Duvalls come down from the hills to wreak revenge on their sworn enemy? Did he know about the feud and the hidden clues?

Damn, I thought as I drove home. Day two of my search and nobody wants to talk to me except Baseford. Maybe I'm not cut out for this. Maybe I'd be better off selling insurance or fighting forest fires. Even the Black Eagles whomping through the boisterous "Short Dress Gal" couldn't cut through my current gloom, and I can always count on jazz to shake me out of a mood.

I pulled into the driveway alongside a large van that had "Wally's Plumbing" on the side in large dripping letters.

Uh-oh. This did not bode well for our strained finances. When I walked into the house, I heard loud clanking noises and creative swearing that led me up to Kary's bathroom. I found Camden and a large unhappy individual in coveralls wedged halfway under the sink surrounded by lots of soggy towels.

I asked the obvious. "Pipes finally break?"

Camden emerged, wet and rumpled. "Nope, but we've got a leak." More clanking and subterranean swearing gurgled from Wally. "What's the damage, Wally?"

Wally came out, shaking his sparse hair and looking like a mole who'd accidentally tunneled into a lake. He was a portly fellow in his sixties with thinning gray hair. He wiped water from his eyes, pulled his glasses from his shirt pocket and placed them on his short nose. "Okay, Cam, here's what we're looking at. You got to replace all these pipes and the pipes in the other bathrooms, all of them. I don't think they've been replaced since the Flood, you'll excuse the pun. I can give you a price for the whole deal." He named an amount that made Camden gulp. "I can get started on it today, take me maybe, oh, three days at most. Otherwise, you're gonna have these nice little surprises every day. Cost you even more to have them done separately."

Camden looked as if he were going under the waves for the third time. "Go ahead and fix this one. I'll check my savings."

"Sure." Wally disappeared under the sink again.

I followed Camden as we walked out into the hallway. "What savings?"

He sat down dejectedly on the steps that led to the third floor. "I haven't got a cent."

"I've still got a chunk of cash from my last case."

He shook his head. "The house is my responsibility."

"Yeah, but I'm living here, too, and I don't want to wake up underwater."

"But that's your money. You need it for the agency."

"Have you thought about asking Ellin to cover expenses? Of course, you know you'll end up paying in PSN time."

"Worse than that. She'll have more ammunition for her Let's Move Out campaign."

"Didn't you sense this was coming on? Didn't you have a vision of us floating out to sea?'

He put his head down in his hands. "No, I did not."

Okay, this was serious. "What's going on?"

He didn't answer for a long time. Then he raised his head. "I was in my teens when I finally figured how to control the visions, shut them off, or sort through to find the important ones. They're pushing in harder now and I don't know why."

I had no idea what he needed to do. "Have you talked to Kit about this?"

"A little. But this is something I'm going to have to take care of myself, like the telekinesis."

"Okay, so you're having power surges. Maybe you're going through the change."

He grinned reluctantly. "Change. My favorite thing." His grin faded. "I don't want to lose control, Randall. I don't want to see what happens if I do. I waited a long time to have a family, and I don't want to ever jeopardize that. There's Ellie and the children when they get here, and Kary, Rufus and Angie, Vermillion, Kit—even you."

Sounded like he was taking on way too much responsibility. "I will keep you in line." The doorbell rang. "I'll get it."

I ran down the stairs and saw the pearl gray Mercedes parked in our driveway. Leo Pierson peered his big wide face in the screen door. Well, it was about time he showed up.

"Hello? Anyone about?"

As soon as I opened the door, he launched into impassioned speech.

"The police believe Samuel Gallant stole my treasures! Do you have any clues as to the whereabouts of the rest of my artwork? The police do not. Has Gallant's house been searched? I need an update on your progress."

"I have some more questions for you, too. Come in."

Pierson entered the house, still declaiming. "They say they found proof that he's the thief. But he didn't like Art Nouveau! When I showed him the dragonfly, he said it looked like a shiny rock with eyes. He must have been set-up."

That had occurred to me, too. "Other than the spoon, do the police have any proof Gallant's the thief?"

"No. The idea of Gallant stealing from me never crossed my mind. The police are calling his death suspicious. I mean, they said the man had been dead two days! Then where are my treasures? Do you have any suspects?"

Rainbow had seen her uncle on Sunday, and the workmen had finished cleaning the main area of the Princeton Gallery on Tuesday. Camden and I found his body yesterday, which was Thursday. Had he been attacked at the museum, or murdered somewhere else and then put into the closet? "Where were you two days ago?"

He drew back with a theatrical gasp. "Good heavens, I didn't kill him! If he stole from me and hid my treasures, why on earth would I kill him? I'd never find them. If the police have searched Gallant's home and his museum, then I can only believe he sold my treasures to someone else, or someone killed him and took them." His tone changed abruptly. "My goodness, who is this lovely little creature?"

Cindy had been watching from the safety of the piano bench. She hopped down to inspect this new visitor. Pierson bent to touch noses with the cat, who regarded him with a long amused stare.

"That's Cindy," I said.

"Charming!" He straightened and pointed his silver-headed cane toward Wally's van outside. "Plumbing issues?"

"A little leak upstairs."

He gave the ceiling a glance. "This reminds me of my role as Noah in *The O'erwhelming Flood*." He struck a pose, one hand over his heart. "'O, tides of misery and fate! The people cast about their boats too late, and all go under with a sigh, for lo, the end of all is nigh!'"

I wanted to stop this before he performed the whole play. "Pierson, there's something else you didn't mention. What's this feud between your family and the Duvalls?"

"Oh, that's nothing. A story my father told me once. That happened a long time ago."

"What about the marks and letters on your artwork leading to hidden treasure?"

He drew back, startled. "Now that sounds intriguing."

"I spoke with Chance Baseford today. He told me certain marks on the ashtray and vase—and I'm assuming on the silver-ware and dragonfly, as well—and certain letters on the poster could be put together to lead to twenty-five million dollars."

Pierson opened and closed his mouth like a goldfish encountering a side of the bowl he'd never explored. "What?"

"That would explain why only certain items were stolen."

"All the more reason to find them! And all the more reason to employ a solution you have not considered." He indicated the island. "May I?"

He sat down on the sofa. Cindy jumped up beside him and settled in his lap as if they were old friends.

I sat on the arm of the blue chair. "A solution?"

"Yes. I believe your associate, Camden, the owner of this house, is the psychic?"

Hadn't we covered this ground already? "If you'd feel better talking to someone at the Psychic Service, I can give you their number."

"Now, now. Don't take offense. I was only wondering if he'd be willing to 'tune in,' or whatever he does to seek out missing articles. One item in particular the thief will regret he stole. He's going to be very sorry he tangled with the dragonfly."

From the way Pierson said this, I envisioned him in a mask and cape, leaping from the rooftops, buzzing like an electric drill. "The Green Hornet's cousin, right?"

I got a major glare from those protruding eyes. "The dragonfly hood ornament. The centerpiece of my collection." His booming voice dropped to a stage whisper and his eyes rolled like a goldfish on its last drop of water. "That's another thing I had to tell you. It's cursed."

My first thought was, *Oh, this is getting better and better.* I couldn't make up stuff like this if I tried. Then I recalled Lindsey's warning. Was this what she wanted me to know? Was there any truth to it?

Pierson adjusted his cuffs and looked slightly embarrassed. "I know I should have mentioned this at our first meeting, but I saw no reason to alarm you."

Besides being a suspect in a murder investigation, hadn't I had a premonition Pierson was hiding more secrets? Maybe I was getting psychic. "I'm not alarmed." Except that you're walking around loose. I looked skeptical and he got huffy.

"Cursed jewels and *objets d'art* are not uncommon," he said. "The Regent Diamond, for instance, brought nothing but grief to Thomas Pitt, and we won't even go into all the problems with the discovery of the treasures in King Tut's tomb."

"I know the Hope Diamond was unlucky for some of its owners, but the Smithsonian seems to be doing okay."

"Exactly. Most curses are quite capricious. They'll skip a generation or lie dormant for centuries. The dragonfly I own is just such a creation. It's Lalique's first attempt, the prototype, if you will. Six previous owners have died sudden violent deaths, but four others have managed to survive unscathed, myself included."

"So we're looking for a dead thief with a dragonfly clutched in his hand."

I braced for another bulbous glare, but Pierson laughed. It was a full infectious laugh.

"You're an amazingly flippant man, Randall. I suppose one needs such a defense mechanism in your line of work. Gallant is dead, but he didn't have the dragonfly. So where is it? Is there any reason Camden wouldn't help me?"

I was about to say I can find your cursed dragonfly when Camden came down the stairs to the island and halted as if he'd heard someone call his name. He stared at Pierson. The man stood and extended a hand.

"Mr. Camden? I was hoping I'd get the chance to meet you. My name is Leo Pierson. I understand you can find lost items?"

As Camden slowly shook Pierson's large hand, there was a whoop and Kit thumped down the stairs barefooted, his tattered black clothes askew and his wiry hair on end.

"Cam! Don't shake that guy's hand—oh, damn, too late."

I could tell by the way Camden gasped and his eyes glazed over something dark and disastrous had burst into his mind. Uh-oh. This was a deep one.

Kit hurried to my side. "Make him let go, Randall."

I'd already decided that was a good idea. I pried Camden free from Pierson's hand and he stood, stunned.

Excited by Camden's reaction, Pierson reached into his pocket. "I've lost some very valuable pieces of Art Nouveau. I have some photos."

Camden didn't need photos. "I see them."

"See them? Already? Where? Where are they? Is the dragonfly there?"

Camden started shaking, a bad sign. I'd seen him go off like this before. He wasn't seeing Pierson's stuff in a neat row on a shelf marked "Lost and Found." Whatever he was seeing, it was bad news.

He gripped the top of the armchair for support. He spoke in an odd voice. "This isn't the last. This isn't the life you want."

I took him by the arm. "Camden. That's enough. Come on."

I didn't think it was possible, but Pierson's eyes bulged further out. Camden's eyes had gone blank. He started to hyperventilate.

I gave him a little shake. "Come on, come back. Back to Earth. Come on, Camden."

Fortunately, this wasn't one of his really deep trances, the kind that take nitroglycerin and a backhoe to dig him out. He took a few shuddering breaths and then relaxed. His eyes came back into focus.

Pierson took several steps back, mouth open. "Good heavens! I had no idea I'd cause such a reaction! I apologize."

Camden slowly let go of the chair. He rubbed his forehead. "It's okay. Some visions are stronger than others."

"Sorry about that," Kit said. "I was asleep and thought it was a dream. You okay? Too much death in this one."

"Yeah, thanks."

I made Camden sit down on the sofa. "I take it you saw Pierson's stuff?"

Camden looked up at the man. "I caught only a glimpse. There was a lot of interference. That dragonfly is one hot little item."

"It's cursed," I said.

"I got that."

Pierson was enthralled. "So the bad vibrations from the dragonfly are blocking your view? This is amazing! Could you pick up anything else? Where are my things? Who has them? What could you see?"

Camden rubbed his forehead again. His hand was trembling. "Nothing. I'm sorry."

"But you were in contact! Could you try again?"

There was no way in hell he was going to shake hands with this guy again. "Not today."

Pierson swirled around to Kit. "What about you, young man? You must be psychic, too."

Kit backed away. "Huh-uh, no way, man. I ain't shaking your hand."

Pierson was about to explode. "This is phenomenal! This is exactly like the beginning of Act Three of *Spellbinder* when the séance goes awry." He made a sweeping motion as if pushing something aside. "'Away, evil spirits!' 'But you have called us from our tormented sleep! We come with messages you must heed!'"

It was time for him to go. "Pierson, why don't I call you later?"

"But you have not one but two psychics here! Surely one of them can locate my artwork."

Kit retreated to the stairs. "I didn't see anything."

Pierson leaned over the back of the sofa. "Cam, perhaps if I brought another item from my collection, something Gallant might have touched and rejected, would that help you focus on the location?"

"It might." I could tell Camden wanted to get rid of the man. Just having him in the house was probably a major psychic distraction.

"I'll go right away!" Pierson dashed out of the house.

Kit returned to the island, his thin young face concerned, and perched on the arm of the chair. I sat down on the sofa so I could face Camden. "You don't have to do this. I can find these things on my own."

He sighed as if he'd peered too deeply into Leo Pierson's soul, and he probably had. "It's all he has."

"Okay, fine, it's all he has. I'll find it." I didn't like the look in his eyes, shocked and withdrawn, as if he'd witnessed some horrible disaster. "What did you see?"

He looked past me into some black hole of a vision. "Death. Six times. All violent. One right after another, like six shots from a gun."

Six previous owners have died sudden violent deaths, Pierson had said.

"Yeah, I saw that, too," Kit said. "Only mine was fainter than yours, Cam. I just saw shadows. I wasn't going to tell that crazy actor that. Sorry I didn't get down here sooner."

Camden swung his eerie blue gaze my way. "Don't take this case, Randall."

I felt the hairs on the back of my neck stiffen. "What do you mean, don't take this case? I've already taken it."

"There's too much death involved."

"You're seeing the past. Pierson told me about the curse. It's already happened. Six deaths. It's over, right, Kit?"

He rubbed his spiky hair. "Well, the past ones are over, but there might be new ones."

"That's what you see?"

"It's like I told you. Shadows. My vision wasn't as strong as Cam's because I didn't shake that guy's hand."

Camden sat up and reached into the pocket of his jeans. "And mine are too strong." He brought out a small bottle. He shook two pills out in his hand and took them with a swig of tea from the cup he kept on the coffee table.

I hadn't seen those before. "What's that?"

"Helps the headaches. That hood ornament caught me right between the eyes."

"Did you get those from Vermillion?"

"It's only aspirin." He propped his head down in one hand. "Don't take this case. Tell Pierson to get someone else."

"No, damn it. I can do this."

"Randall..." He lifted his head. "I have every faith in your detective skills, but I saw something extremely dangerous in your future. If you continue to search for these things, you're running into a lot of danger."

Camden's predictions are not to be taken lightly. "I always run into a lot of danger. It's one of the perks of this job. Your warning is noted, but I'm not giving up now. There are big bucks involved. And don't say money isn't everything, Mr. Leaking Pipes. Want me to call Ellin?" Ellin doesn't even have that mysterious radar called woman's intuition, something I thought all women were born with, but she can settle him down when he gets like this. He says holding her hand erases all the really tough visions.

"No, don't get her started. I'm okay. I just don't like dying so many times at once."

"You felt as if you were dying?"

He took a long drink. "Yes, and it scared the hell out of me. Something isn't right, and a big burst of negative energy from a cursed object did not help." His gaze went beyond me to God-knows-what. "Maybe I'm going crazy."

I turned to the only other psychic I knew. "Kit, what do you think it is?"

He shook his head. "Man, I don't know. I'm still learning to control my own visions. But I saw it coming. I can do that much, anyway."

Not a bad idea. "Okay, so we've got the early alarm system in place."

Camden thanked him.

"No problem. I owe you big-time for showing me how to deal with all this stuff."

Kit hopped off the chair and went back upstairs. Camden didn't want any lunch, and by the time I'd fixed a sandwich, he and Cindy were asleep on the sofa, the cat curled on his stomach. Maybe the dragonfly was the cause of his sudden increase in power and shaking Pierson's hand intensified its strength. All the more reason to find the damned thing.

Chapter Seven

"Now, O Now, I Needs Must Part"

My phone beeped with a message, and I stepped inside my office to answer it. Finally! A message from Ms. Piper at the art gallery, asking me to call, which I did.

"Ms. Piper? David Randall. Thanks for returning my call. It's about Leo Pierson's Art Nouveau."

Her voice was crisp, as if I'd interrupted an important meeting. "What sort of information do you need?"

"I'm trying to locate some pieces that were stolen from his home a few days ago. Any information would be helpful."

"I'm very busy right now, but I could see you around four o'clock, if that's convenient."

I checked my watch. One-fifteen. That would give me plenty of time to check out Matt Graber. "That would be fine, thanks."

I did some more work in my office, searching online for any sight of Pierson's treasures. I discovered that he could buy another dragonfly on eBay for around fourteen thousand dollars, but there was no guarantee this was a real Lalique. He could even buy a complete set of car mascots at auction if he had between eight hundred thousand and a million dollars. I did a little research on Lalique, as well, finding a photo of a surrealistic half woman-half insect pin all blue and gold called "Dragonfly Woman," that was exhibited at the 1900 Paris Exhibition, and another photo of an amazing gold-and-blue enamel necklace with a design of black swans. Lalique was also a success at the 1904 World's Fair in St. Louis and designed stage jewelry for actress Sarah Bernhardt. In 1925, he designed the first car mascots—*bouchons de radiateur*—if you want to get fancy, for Citroen and made others for Bently, Bugatti, and Rolls Royce, to name a few. Besides the large dragonfly, "Libellule Grande," Pierson's treasure, there were twenty-eight other designs, including a small dragonfly, a peacock head, an owl, a rooster, and the largest, called "Spirit of the Wind," a woman's head with stylized hair streaming back. I thought the Fury would look pretty spiffy with The Comet on the hood. The Guinea hen, not so much. According to the article, the actual number of existing mascots wasn't known and most were eagerly sought after and very rare. While the eagle's head was infamous for being fitted on Nazi officers' staff cars, there were no curses associated with any of the mascots.

By two o'clock, Camden was awake and feeling better. I waited while he put on his sneakers, and we were off to tackle some snakes.

Matt Graber filmed his show at the television studio on the west side of town. The set-up at *Cosmic Healing* was similar to the PSN. Camden and I took seats on the aisle in the fifth row, as far as possible from the large cage in the corner. The cage was covered with a black cloth sprinkled with glow-in-the-dark stars. Camden kept glancing at it.

Matt Graber stood off to one side, preening, until it was time for him to take his place center stage and welcome everyone to another exciting episode of *Cosmic Healing*. Camden and I watched with feigned interest as Graber healed audience members and those of you watching by TV of sprained knees, ingrown toenails, bouts of insomnia, and more serious diseases such as diabetes and arrhythmia.

But then he started in on something a little too close to home.

"Someone here has lost a child. A girl. The initial I see is 'L.' Lynn, perhaps, or Linda. A tragic accident. The pain is intense. Leeann, Linette, perhaps."

If this joker thought he could trick me by pretending to have heard from Lindsey—

Every now and then during the PSN programs, I have to keep Camden from jumping up and running down to the stage to set somebody straight. The presenters, for the most part, are harmless, but occasionally, one will give dangerously wrong advice. When the wife of a sponsor was hosting the PSN shows, telling diabetics to pile on the sweets and heart patients to scale the Matterhorn, I had to physically keep Camden in his seat. Today, it was his restraining hand on my arm.

"He's just fishing. He doesn't really know."

About that time, a woman said, "Lizabeth," and Graber rushed to her side of the stage.

"It was a tragic accident, unexpected."

The woman's voice trembled. "She drowned in the swimming pool."

"Yes, yes, I see blue waves and bright sun. It was a sunny day."

Graber continued to fabricate the tragedy, using the woman's responses and body language to make the audience believe he'd plucked his information from psychic vibrations. The audience was properly impressed, and Lizabeth's mother pathetically grateful for the message from beyond.

"Lizabeth says she is well and happy and with countless other children who have passed on before their time. They have everything they could want. She wishes you health and wellness." Abruptly, Graber turned away, as if hearing another spirit call. "There's someone here with a dislocated shoulder, or someone who had a dislocated shoulder. I'm getting an 'F' name. Frank, Franklin, Francis, perhaps?"

"I'll give you an 'F' name," I said sotto voce.

At the end of the program, Graber reached for his snakes. Camden got up. "I'll be at the car."

Graber went through his speech again about how he'd rescued the pythons from the evil pet shop owner and how all of nature's creatures were sacred and deserved health and wellness.

Afterwards, I went to shake the great man's hand. "Mr. Graber, I'm with the *Herald*. Would you have time to answer a few questions for our special Sunday supplement?"

"Why, yes, of course. Let me put my pets away." He placed the two snakes carefully into their cage and turned to face me. "Now then. What would your readers like to know?"

"Everything. How you got your start, when you first discovered your remarkable healing powers, how you rescued the pythons."

His thin smile still showed no trace of real humor. "How much time do you have?"

"I'd be grateful for anything you'd like to share."

"Please come have a seat."

We sat down on the set for *Cosmic Healing*. I set my cell phone to record and placed it on the table. Graber launched into what was obviously his Psychic Story.

"I can't have been more than eight or nine when I first realized I was different from the other children. If they fell and scraped their knees and elbows, I could put my hands on their wounds and take the pain away. Then I started hearing voices, their voices, their thoughts, scrambled at first, but gradually, as I learned the extent of my powers, I was able to discern threads of memory and dream, visions of the future. Of course, I kept all this to myself, sharing my newfound knowledge only with trusted family members, but it soon became evident I had a talent that cried out to be shared with the world. I now feel it is my mission to help heal as many people as I can, heal them physically, mentally, and spiritually."

I did my best to look impressed by this overblown speech. "That's wonderful. How do the snakes fit into your mission?"

"Through the most fortunate of chances, I discovered I could empathize with the animal kingdom, as well. Now, I'm not calling myself a pet psychic by any means—I can't tell you if your cat enjoys a particular brand of litter over another—but I do sense animals' feelings. It was quite easy to feel the pain and confusion of the pythons trapped in that sub-standard pet shop."

"You realize some people may have a slight aversion to your snakes?"

"Yes, but it does them good to face their fears. It makes them aware that the psychic world does have its dangers. I wouldn't want just anyone trying to do what I do."

I definitely agreed with that. "What are your plans for your program?"

"I'm glad you asked. I have every intention of expanding my audience. I'm in negotiations right now in the hopes of appearing on another network and reaching a wider audience. Since I'm self-supporting, they lose nothing by having me on their shows."

I knew he was talking about the PSN. "Self-supporting?"

"*Cosmic Healing* is paid for by the sales of my books and tapes, as well as consultation fees from satisfied customers. I am my own sponsor, and I bring along three companies who enjoy brisk sales: Manville Cleaners, Parks Hardware, and the recently acquired Tinkle Time Ice Cream. Perhaps that's an odd choice, but I'm hoping to entice more children to the program, and as that old saying goes, 'We all scream for ice cream.'"

It was a lame attempt at humor, punctuated by a real scream from one of the stage crew.

"Mr. Graber, your snakes are out!"

Graber frowned. "I must not have latched the pen securely. Don't worry. They won't hurt you. Would you excuse me? I'm afraid some stupid person will try to harm my pets."

For such large snakes, the pythons moved rapidly toward the exit. Stagehands and cameramen leaped out of their path. When one brave soul bent down to grab a snake's tail, Graber said, "Don't touch them! I'm the only one who's allowed to touch them."

Right outside the exit was a Coke machine, and Camden had the misfortune to be thirsty. True to snakes everywhere, the pythons headed right for him. In an attempt to run, he stumbled and fell. One snake slid over his foot. The other went so close to his head, I'm surprised he didn't implode.

Graber managed to snag one snake while the other slithered off toward the parking lot. He draped the captured python around his neck and hurried after snake number two. When I got to Camden, his eyes were open and he was taking in quick little panic breaths.

"It's okay," I said. "They're gone."

"I heard them. I heard them."

I sat him up. "Yeah? What did they say?"

He continued to gasp for breath. "Heard them."

"Yeah, you mentioned that. What did they say?"

He took a moment as if to assure himself he was safe. "The smaller one said, 'Excuse me.'"

"How polite."

"And the big one said, 'Coming through.'"

"I always like a snake with a sense of humor."

He put a hand over his eyes and rubbed his brow, wincing. "That's not all."

It definitely wasn't all if he was hearing snakes, but as weird and potentially alarming as this was, first I had to get him calm. "Settle down. It's over."

"They said, 'See you later.'"

"Oh, they're dropping by for tea?"

Camden glanced around nervously as if expecting snakes to burst forth from every side. "I thought, I'll go out to the car. I'll be safe there. The snakes are inside. I'm outside. After Graber shows them to the audience, he'll put them back in their cage. They can't get out, and even if they did, they'd find a nice dark corner of the studio to hide in. They won't come out to the Coke machine."

Now he was rattling. I hauled him up. "Come on. We'll find a snake-free zone."

He dug in his heels. "What if they're sitting in your car, or curled up in the trunk, or coiled in the glove compartment—?"

"They're way too big for that. Come on." I managed to drag him toward the car.

"They'll see your license number. They'll attach themselves to the muffler and ride home. Do you know how many places they could find to hide in my house, not to mention the trees, or the hedge?"

I didn't want to think about that. "Take it easy."

We were almost to the Fury before he stopped short, now shaking with anger. "'See you later'? What the hell do they mean, 'See you later'? I don't want to see them later! I don't want to see any snakes. Why am I hearing snakes?"

That was a very good question, one I feared was connected

to his new power surge, but I had to keep him focused. "You hear the cats sometimes, don't you? And there was that little fox in the backyard with her baby."

"I like cats. I like foxes. I want to hear friendly warm-blooded animals that have legs."

"Just get in the car."

I had to check the Fury before he'd get in. When Graber came up, draped with both snakes, Camden took a dive for the floorboard.

"Sorry about that," Graber said to me. I don't think he noticed Camden, at all. "Did you need any more information?"

I turned so he'd follow me away from the car. "I think I got everything. Could I come by tomorrow and take a few pictures?"

"Yes, of course. I'll see you then."

Both snakes kept their heads up. I could swear the big one winked at me. Graber took them back inside the studio. I returned to the Fury where Camden had almost managed to get under the seat.

"All clear," I said.

He slowly unwedged himself. "How can he stand to wear them like that?"

"All part of his charm."

I got behind the wheel. Camden turned around, sat down, and wiped his forehead with the back of his hand. "That's my limit for undercover work today." He fished the pill bottle out of his pocket. "Damn. First the dragonfly and now snakes. What next?"

I wasn't so sure he should be taking pills, even aspirin. He had a low tolerance for any sort of medication. "Are those pills helping?"

"I think I need a whole handful right now."

"Seriously."

"No, of course not. But they do take the edge off."

Hmm. The edge off what? "You going to take them dry?"

"Not if you take me by the Quik-Fry."

Chapter Eight
"As a Ray of Sun"

I took Camden by the Quik-Fry to get a milkshake and when he assured me he'd calmed down, dropped him off at Tamara's Boutique to talk to Tamara about adding more hours to help pay for the plumbing repairs. Then I went to the museum.

On the phone, Ms. Piper sounded pretty snotty, so I expected horn rims and an attitude. I was right about the glasses, but they were modern and bright red to match her short spiky hair. She wore a suit that looked like it was made out of yellow leather with five huge buttons, each one a different color. It was a wild looking outfit, but on her it looked great. I found it hard not to stare at the purple button situated happily above the cleavage, or the green button sitting above her trim knees. I was also right about the attitude.

One perfect red eyebrow went up. "Mr. Randall?"

"David." I wondered what my telephone voice had suggested to her. Doubtless I looked as tall, dark, and handsome as I really was. "Pleased to meet you, Ms. Piper."

"Please come in."

I followed her down a cool dim hallway of the art gallery to her office. In here, the lighting was bright, walls decorated with framed posters advertising art exhibits: huge water lilies, some kind of fancy bridge, a lady with a parasol, all soft watercolors, a sharp contrast to the very modern Ms. Piper. Her desk was a smooth clean slab of polished mahogany with a few flower-shaped paperweights and a lamp with a glass shade made of leaves and grapes. She sat down in a padded swivel chair and motioned me to an odd metal chair opposite the desk. It was as uncomfortable as it looked. Obviously, visitors were not encouraged to stay.

Ms. Piper put her fingertips together. "Now, then, Mr. Randall, what exactly can I do for you? I was very sorry to hear about the theft of Mr. Pierson's artwork."

"Were you invited to lunch at his house a week ago?"

"Yes, several people were there from the art community."

"Could you tell me who they were and what you know about them?"

She took off her red glasses and gave me a full view of her dark eyes. She was wearing purple eye shadow and lots of mascara. On her, it worked. "Let me see. Richard Mason was there. He runs the Little Gallery. Lawrence Stein, a member of the museum board. Patricia Ashworthy, another board member was invited, but she's eighty-seven and doesn't drive very far, so she didn't come. Samuel Gallant." She gave a delicate shudder. "Isn't that the strangest thing about him being found dead in his museum's storage closet? Do the police know what happened?"

"They're treating this as a murder investigation. How well did you know him?"

"Not well. I met him only a few times. He seemed quiet to me, but I understand he could be quite quarrelsome."

"His gallery is closed, did you know that?"

She shrugged this off. "Dwindling funds is something all art museums have to deal with, especially the smaller galleries. The Princeton has been teetering on the brink of ruin for months."

"Did any of the people who came to Pierson's house have an interest in Art Nouveau?"

"Gallant turned up his nose at Pierson's collection, and I know Richard doesn't care for it."

But they would if they knew about the twenty-five million.

Ms. Piper continued. "I've heard Lawrence Stein prefers African art. As for Patricia Ashworthy, you'd have to ask her." She sat back in her chair and folded her arms. The purple button rose dramatically. "Mr. Randall, I don't believe any of these people capable of such a crime."

But they could hire someone else to do the job for them. Someone easily led and always in need of money. Someone like Samuel Gallant. "Ms. Piper, have you ever heard of a feud or a mystery surrounding these particular Art Nouveau items, a mystery involving a large sum of money?"

There was a flicker of interest in her eyes I couldn't quite interpret. "No. What sort of feud? What mystery?"

"The feud is between Pierson's family and the Duvall family. The money is twenty-five million dollars."

She made a production of removing her glasses and polishing them with a tissue from her desk drawer. "A feud's quite an antiquated notion these days, isn't it? And twenty-five million? For those pieces? I don't know a lot about Art Nouveau, but that's excessive."

"It involves solving a puzzle, using marks and letters found on the pieces."

Ms. Piper leaned forward and settled her glasses back on her nose "Well, someone would have to know a lot about that, wouldn't they? I'm sorry to say I don't."

"Thank you very much for your time." I indicated a poster of a little girl holding a watering can. The little girl's dress was dark blue with lots of white lace trim; the soft flowers around her were all colors. "That's very nice."

"It's by Renoir. My favorite painter."

"Mine, too." Actually, I'd been drawn to it because the little girl's long brown hair and sweet expression reminded me of Lindsey.

Ms. Piper gave me a look over the top of her glasses. "Oh, really?"

"Really." I held out my hand. "I hope I can call on you if I have any more artistic questions?"

She gave me a long measuring stare. "If you have questions of any kind, Mr. Randall."

Uh, oh. I'd seen that look before.

● ● ● ● ●

I know I'd cooked supper the night before, but I was in the mood for a cheeseburger, and it wasn't any more trouble to toss another half dozen onto the backyard grill. There was a nice breeze this evening, and the smell of charred meat brought Cindy, Oreo, and a few of their feline friends out of the honeysuckle hedge to wind around my bare feet.

Camden was still at Tamara's store and Vermillion was still in the park. The wailing sound of an electric guitar from the second floor told me Kit was practicing before his gig, so that left Kary, me, and the cats. Perfect. Kary brought some paper plates and napkins out to the tray table where I'd put the buns, mustard, ketchup, and slaw. Then she sat down in one of the blue-and-white plastic lounge chairs under the trees. She had on white shorts and an oversized tee-shirt with a faded fish design. She sat up on the lounge and put her arms around her knees.

I turned the top row of burgers. "What have you been up to today?"

"Besides signing up for a few classes and applying for grants to help pay for them, I've been honing my pageant skills, choosing what song to play, what gown to wear, that kind of thing. I can't afford a new one, but fortunately, I have gowns left over from other pageants that, with Angie's help, can be recycled. Tried out some new makeup. Deep stuff." Cindy stopped begging long enough to jump up beside Kary. Kary took the cat in her lap and scratched her behind the ears. "What's the latest on your case?"

I draped a slice of cheese over each burger. "The police believe Gallant stole Pierson's artwork but have no real leads in his death. Of the wealthy art collectors in Parkland, Toad suggested I talk with Lawrence Stein, but he's out of town until Monday. Ms. Piper, Gallant, and Mason had lunch at Pierson's a few days before Gallant disappeared. I spoke with Ms. Piper this afternoon. Also, there's been a very interesting development, courtesy of Chance Baseford."

She wrinkled her nose. "I can't believe he was helpful."

"It came disguised as a lecture and a slam against Pierson, who didn't know these details." I cleaned off the platter for the burgers. "Seems there's an ancient feud between the Piersons and the Duvalls over the very pieces that were stolen. If you put them all together, they spell 'Treasure,' or at least a clue to a big pile of money. Oh, and Pierson stopped by here to tell us his missing dragonfly hood ornament is cursed."

"Oh, that sounds tantalizing. Is he sure?"

"Judging by Camden's reaction when he shook Pierson's hand, I'd say yes."

"Uh, oh. Is he okay?"

"He got worse when he had a close encounter with Matt Graber's pythons."

Kary swung both legs around and sat up straighter. "All right. Start at the beginning."

"Ellin's flipping out because Graber took one of the PSN sponsors. She asked Camden and me to spy on *Cosmic Healing*, so we went over there this afternoon."

"He heals people with snakes?"

"He uses them to illustrate the power of cosmic healing. Unfortunately, they got out of their cage and decided to go say hello to the one person who did not want to talk to them."

Kary shuddered. "I'm not really comfortable with snakes, either. Did you take him to Ellin?"

"He's at Tamara's hoping for some more hours at the store."

"It's about the leaky pipes, isn't it? Can we afford to get them fixed?"

"I told him we could all pitch in. I also mentioned that Ellin could probably cover the cost. I don't think he's discussed it with her yet." The cheese had melted nicely over the fat juicy burgers. "Burgers are done. How many would you like?"

"A little one, please. No bun." She got up and stepped over two cats. I chose one of the smaller burgers and scooped it onto her paper plate. She gazed at me intently, and for a moment, I wondered if there would be a little action in that lounge chair. I don't care how many cats were watching. Yes, she was definitely giving me a look.

"David, you've got mustard on your chin."

"Oh. Thanks." I wiped my chin with the back of my hand. The cats yowled at my feet. I busied myself cutting up another burger for them and then sat down in the other lounge chair.

Kary wiped her fingers on her napkin. "Rufus and Angie will be home tomorrow, won't they?"

"I believe so."

"Don't worry about me. If they left Mary Rose with Angie's sister, that's probably the best place for her."

"You know, if we were married, we might have a better chance of adopting. You could start by moving in with me."

She gave me a skeptical glance. "Is your room big enough to accommodate all my things?"

"Keep your old bedroom and use it as a closet."

She laughed. "Now there's an idea."

"So what do you say? Camden might cut us a deal."

She paused to consider this and became serious. "I'd like to leave things as they are for now."

It was going to take longer than I thought to convince her, but one of the many things I loved about Kary was her strong independent streak. "I hope that includes your nightly visits."

"Of course." She ate for a few moments. "Now tell me what I can do to help you on this case. How many days do you have?"

"Two down, eight to go. Do you feel like infiltrating the Love-In at the park tomorrow? Samuel Gallant's niece, Rainbow, might be there, and you can find out more about her uncle."

"That sounds far out, man."

I gave her a kiss. "Mmm, you taste like cheeseburger. What a woman."

She kissed me back and after she finished her burger, went into the house to practice. That left me and the cats. I had one more burger, gave Oreo another, and wrapped the rest in aluminum foil. Cindy purred and rubbed against my legs. I patted her head. I'd never cared much for cats, but Cindy was a reasonable animal. "Bet you could find a dragonfly."

She purred louder and bumped her head against my hand, happy to be with me until one of her cat buddies yowled from the bushes and she went off with him. Maybe the other cat was one of her grown kittens, stopping by to say hello. As active as she was, Cindy was bound to have family in the neighborhood.

"Yo, Randall!" Kit called down from his window. "You got an extra burger?"

"Got plenty."

In a few minutes he joined me in the backyard. He unwrapped the leftover burgers and piled two with cheese and onions. "Thought I'd grab a bite before heading over to the club."

He had on his traditional black, but this outfit was a step up from the usual tatters: tight black leather pants, heavy black boots, and a black vest over a white tee-shirt. "What's the occasion?"

He indicated his outfit. "What, this? Oh, we're playing The Other Side tonight. Thought I'd dress up."

During my last case, Camden had infiltrated The Other Side disguised as a teenager. Much to his chagrin, he'd been able to pass with no trouble. "I know the place."

Kit took big bites of his first cheeseburger and swallowed. "Cam doesn't like being psychic, but I do. I hope I get telekinetic, too. I wanted you to know I'm on the job, and if it looks like something big's about to blow, I'll call."

There was something I wanted to know. "Do you hear Lindsey or any of the other spirits?"

"Sometimes. Maybe since Delores started telling them to come to you, there's been more psychic activity around the house than Cam can handle. You add that dragonfly, and you've got overload."

I didn't like the sound of this. "What can we do about it?"

"Cam's gonna have to learn to go with the flow."

"He'd rather not be psychic, so he's resistant to flow."

He reached for his second burger. "Well, hell, I think it's great, especially since he taught me how to control it, and I've had tons of visions, let me tell you."

"So this overload isn't affecting you?"

"Maybe it's because I'm embracing my destiny." He said this with a straight face and then guffawed. "Going with the flow, man. Oh, here comes Lily."

Lily Wilkes, Camden's next-door neighbor, came through the hole in the hedge that separated their houses. I'm not sure how old Lily is. Her face is very young, but her hair is as white and fluffy as cotton in an aspirin bottle. I'd been curious enough to ask her about it, tactfully, of course, and she told me aliens stole her real hair, replacing it with white fluff. Lily claims to have been abducted thirteen times, experimented on, and impregnated. She always relates this with perfect composure, and I always have difficulty keeping a straight face.

Lily doesn't come over very often, and when she does, she's looking for Camden, wanting him to come listen to a bunch of local kooks who think they've had close encounters. Since she's cute and friendly and weird as hell, at one time I thought they'd make a great couple, but Ellin's the only woman in Camden's life, and why should Lily settle for one man when she has all those randy ETs?

It must have been Bag Lady Day on Planet Lily. She had on a blue, long-sleeved turtleneck tee-shirt, green-striped slacks, a yellow poncho with uneven fringe, and a pith helmet decorated with sequined hearts. As I said, Lily's really cute, but she likes to wear these ungodly hats that make her look like some kind of little forest animal peeking out from under a bush.

"My God, Lily, aren't you burning up?"

She wasn't even sweating. "My inner temperature has been permanently altered."

"Oh, sorry. I forgot. Get the aliens to reset it next time you're up there."

She peered out from under the helmet. A little wider brim and she'd be able to pick up signals from those distant galaxies. "I don't think that's possible. Is Cam home?"

"He's at Tamara's. Who's meeting tonight?"

"The ASG and the newly formed SWS."

ASG I knew was the Abductees Support Group. "SWS?"

"Sky Watchers Society. We're going up to Coldcrag Mountain later in the month and check out the meteor shower.

You want to come? We've started having monthly meetings. You're always welcome. You, too, Kit. This week, we're going to bathe our amethysts in the light of the full moon. You'd probably enjoy that."

"Sounds super cool, Lily," Kit said with a grin.

"I'm a little busy right now, but if things slow down, I'll take you up on that," I said.

"Okay, thanks. Tell Cam to come over if he wants to."

Lily pushed back through the hedge. Kit watched her go, still grinning. "Now there's somebody who embraces their oddness. 'Embrace the Oddness.' That would make a bitchin' song."

After Kit left, I sat in the gradually cooling shadows of the trees, listening to Kary play something complicated and melancholy. I didn't recognize the tune, but it must have been one of the art songs. Having glanced at her sheet music, I imagined this cheery tune was called something along the lines of "My Love For You Has Withered and Died." I prefer the more complex sound of a jazz band, but this, like everything Kary played, was beautiful. Occasionally, she'd stop and replay a section. I couldn't hear anything wrong, but she'd go over the part until she was satisfied and then play on.

After a while, Tamara brought Camden home. I told him Lily had stopped by. He pushed through the hedge and returned a few minutes later to report the Sky Watchers Society was standing in Lily's backyard doing what they do best. While they welcomed him, they didn't need his help staring up. He ate a couple of cheeseburgers and said he was turning in, even though I mentioned that *The Crawling Eye* was on Channel 27 tonight.

"It can crawl without me. I've had a full day. Did Leo ever

come back with another item? Not that I was going to touch it."

I realized my theatrical client hadn't returned with another piece from his collection. "Haven't seen him. That's odd. He was about to pop with excitement."

"You haven't seen any snakes, have you?"

"No snakes."

He dragged himself up to bed. Speaking of popping, Ellin was next to come out to the backyard, bursting with questions about Graber.

I offered her a cheeseburger, but she waved it away. "Tell me what you found out."

"Our undercover scheme is underway. Graber thinks I'm from the *Herald*, and I'm going to get the full story and pictures tomorrow."

"What did Cam get?"

"Full-blown hysteria."

"What? He didn't have to go anywhere near those snakes."

"But they wanted to be his BFFs. They're planning to drop by later."

She gave me a look. "I don't know why I even bother talking with you, Randall."

"Oh, and things might be a little damp in the hallway. I hope Camden told you about our plumbing crisis."

I didn't like the way she smiled. "I'll take care of it."

Normally I can't see the future, but I knew Camden's run-in with the pythons was going to be the least of his worries.

Chapter Nine
"Crabbed Age and Youth"

Saturday morning, I decided to visit Patricia Ashworthy. Ms. Piper said she hadn't been at Pierson's gathering, but I had a hunch she could be helpful. Let me tell you, she was one tough old bird. She lived in a large yellow Spanish-style house in the Forest Oaks section of town, also known as Cashville. The house took up three lots, a sprawling hacienda with a red tile roof, elaborate statuary, and rows of those skinny little trees that look like sticks.

Patricia Ashworthy met me at the door. She was covered with art: gaudy spiral gold earrings, a necklace made out of multicolored glass beads, jangling bracelets with hunks of colored stones. Rings clung to her stubby little fingers like brilliant barnacles. She was small and stooped and ornery as hell, but underneath all the bluster, I detected curiosity and a delight to have company.

She gestured with a knobby black-and-silver cane shaped like a tree branch. "Don't just stand there, come in. I'm very busy today, but I can spare you a couple of minutes."

Like Mrs. Ashworthy herself, every square inch of the house was covered with art. I couldn't see the walls for the paintings. Rugs of all kinds carpeted the floors, some on top of others, Navajo, Persian, patchwork, animal skin, all layered like international sandwiches. The antique tables had antique vases, plates, figurines, and photos. There wasn't a chair in sight that looked safe enough to sit in. I followed Patricia Ashworthy through this gallery to an enclosed back porch. She indicated a fairly sturdy-looking wicker chair and plopped herself down on a velvet sofa.

"Now then. This is about Leo Pierson's missing collection, is it? The man was a fool to mention it in such company. We're all vultures, you know, waiting to swoop down and grab a tasty piece of art." She laughed at her joke, and her earrings dangled like modern art yo-yos.

"Who else knew about his artwork? I can't imagine it being common knowledge outside the art world."

"You can't sell it here, that's for certain. Everyone knows the pieces. It'd be like trying to unload the *Mona Lisa*. Has any of it been located?"

"One spoon was found with Samuel Gallant's body."

She cocked her head. "Really? I hadn't heard about the spoon. I saw the news about Gallant, of course. It's a shame, but he did have heart problems, same as me. His pacemaker must have gone out." She patted her chest protectively. "I'm having mine checked tomorrow. Oh, as for who has the artwork, it's obvious Chance Baseford's your man."

I was surprised. "Baseford? Any particular reason?"

She looked at me as if I'd dropped her favorite vase. "Everyone knows he hates any sort of artist or collector."

I took a moment to change gears. "You're telling me Chance Baseford collects Art Nouveau?"

"No, no. But he can't stand to see Pierson or anyone get any sort of attention, especially for art. Haven't you talked to him? You know how he is. Arrogant beast."

I recalled the look of glee in Baseford's hard little eyes. What was the deal here? Baseford was pompous and superior. Somewhere along the line, had his artistic ambitions been thwarted, forcing him to settle for the position of art and theater critic for the *Parkland Herald*? But he couldn't blame Pierson for that, could he? Aside from having an art collection, no one had heard of Leo Pierson. He wasn't mounting a new production of *Hamlet*, or trying to fund the ballet.

Patricia Ashworthy leaned forward. "And if you ask me, Baseford had something to do with Samuel Gallant's death."

She was determined to blame Baseford for something. "Why do you say that?"

"Well, it's obvious the man can't stand competition. Gallant must have threatened him on some level."

"From what I understand, Gallant collected modern art. I don't think Baseford's into that."

"Humph! You keep digging, young man. You'll find out he's responsible."

For everything, her tone implied, including global warming. "What can you tell me about Samuel Gallant?"

She waved a hand dismissively. "Flip-flopped on every decision the board made! I don't know how he ever dressed himself in the mornings. I imagine it took him hours to choose which tie to wear."

"I've met his niece, Rainbow. Does he have any other family? Friends?"

"No family to speak of, except that niece, and as for friends, I suppose we were the closest he had. Always wanted us in on his silly money-making schemes that never went anywhere. Always scrounging for money." Talking about Samuel Gallant had Patricia Ashworthy all wound up.

I wanted to get back to the crime. "What did Lawrence Stein think about Pierson's artwork?"

"Lawrence Stein has more money than he knows what to do with. He wouldn't be interested in taking anyone else's artwork."

"Richard Mason?"

"Known him for years. A straight-shooter. Creates his own art, and certainly doesn't get the recognition he deserves. He's been very kind to me. When my last husband died and I needed help to keep up my house—well, you can see it's quite extensive—Richard found this fine young man to assist me. I couldn't do without Flynn."

"What about Nancy Piper?"

"A nice enough young woman. Hired to handle museum finances and doing very well."

"You weren't able to attend Pierson's luncheon and viewing. Had you seen his Art Nouveau before?"

"Yes, I'd been out to his house. As I recall, he had those pieces arranged exactly as they were in Isabelle Duvall's parlor. Made a nice picture."

It occurred to me if Patricia Ashworthy knew of Isabelle Duvall, she might know more about the feud. "Are you familiar with the Pierson/Duvall feud and the mystery surrounding those pieces?"

The earrings bobbed as she nodded. "I'd heard some story about a treasure hunt. You see, the blue peacock vase would have an 'L' on the bottom to denote Lalique. So would the dragonfly. The silverware, I believe, is by Hoffman, and the poster was created by Mucha. What else was there?"

"An ashtray."

She gave the ashtray a moment's thought. "I don't know about that one. Anyway, you rearrange the letters, including some off the poster, and supposedly you have a clue to vast riches. A tall tale, as far as I'm concerned."

So Pierson's guests would've seen the items together, and

if any one of them knew about the treasure, would have recognized this clue. But would they need the actual items to
figure it out? Two Ls, an H, an M, whoever made the ashtray,
and words off a poster they could take a picture of. No need
to steal the actual artwork.

I asked Patricia Ashworthy the same question.

"I have no idea," she said.

"What about the feud?"

"Oh, a Pierson killed a Duvall. Or a Duvall killed a Pierson.
I can't remember. Whatever it was, it was a horrible tragedy.
It happened a long time ago." She returned to her favorite
subject. "Now if you ask me, Baseford hired Gallant to steal
Pierson's artwork and promised him a cut of the profits.
Gallant was certainly foolish enough to go along with that
kind of scheme. Baseford has all those Art Nouveau trinkets,
I'll bet you anything."

She was determined Baseford was the culprit, and nothing
was going to change her mind.

I stood. "I appreciate your help, Mrs. Ashworthy. I've taken
up enough of your time. Thank you."

"Oh, come take a little tour of my house." With the help
of the cane, she hoisted herself off the sofa, and curled one of
her ring-heavy little hands around my arm. "There won't be
any Art Nouveau, I assure you. Hate the stuff. Too fussy. I like
my art bright and strong." She leered at me. "Like my men."

It was all I could do to keep a straight face. I escorted her
around her hacienda and learned more about art than I ever
wanted to know.

Once I was able to pry myself free from Patricia Ashworthy, I
got back into the Fury and gave Leo Pierson a call. "Thought

you were coming back yesterday with something else for Camden to try."

"My apologies. I got so caught up trying to decide on the right piece to bring, I completely forgot the time and by then, it was too late to call you. Besides, Cam looked as if he might need a break before handling something else. What a remarkable talent! But not without its disadvantages, I see."

"We can both save Camden a lot of trouble if you'll let me find your missing items without having to resort to using his psychic visions."

"Yes, but you have to admit that calling upon the powers of the supernatural is fascinating. It's exactly like a scene from *Forbidden Contact* where a young Spiritualist makes an actual connection to the spirit world. 'Knock again, and I shall answer! I realize now without hesitation that your voice is real!'"

I don't know where in the world Pierson got these plays of his, but they all sounded like cheesy melodramas from the turn of the nineteenth century. "I've just been visiting with Patricia Ashworthy."

He laughed. "She's a caution, isn't she? Who's her choice for villain?"

"Chance Baseford."

"Of course. She hates him and that's understandable. Everything we put up, he tears down. But I can't see him stooping to common burglary."

"Tell me more about Patricia. Would she be interested in your artwork?"

"Where on earth would she display my pieces? Her house is so crowded you'd never see them."

"I'm going to talk to Lawrence Stein on Monday. What do you know about him?"

"Not very much, but I enjoyed the parties on his yacht. He's really proud of that boat. He must have every kind of gadget: electric fishing lure, electronic fish-scaler, the latest fish-finder technology—you name it."

So would he have any use for a glass dragonfly? I listened as Pierson continued to sing the praises of Stein's boat toys. Finally Pierson paused for breath and I could ask a question. "I need to know more about your family and the Duvalls. If the feud's still on, a Duvall might be responsible."

"But I inherited my artwork from my father, who inherited them from Isabelle Duvall. Doesn't that suggest someone along the line made peace with my family?"

"I want you to check out your family tree and ask any living relatives what they know about this."

"Very well. I'll do my best. 'For what can be so caring in a desperate world than the love of one's family, the harbor that shelters from the strongest blast this cruel world has to offer?' That's from *The Endless Hours*, act three."

I didn't have endless hours to figure this out.

• ● ● ● •

I called Kary and asked if she'd like to meet me at Baxter's Barbecue for lunch. Turbo, the neon green Ford Festiva, pulled into the parking lot a few minutes after I'd arrived and she got out, swinging her large pocketbook onto her shoulder.

"Hi, David. I've got some information for you."

We went into the little brick building and took seats in a booth near the front windows. Baxter's doesn't have much in the way of atmosphere—plain brown tables and chairs, plastic red-and-white checkerboard tablecloths and booths with red plastic seats, but the restaurant more than makes up for lack of ambiance with its food. "Succulent" is the word I'd use. I ordered a barbecue sandwich, fries, and an order of onion rings. Kary ordered from the lighter side of the menu, plain barbecue and a salad. We compared notes.

Kary took out her phone and checked her information. "Lawrence Stein's pride and joy is his yacht, *The Wall Street Wanderer*, equipped with every shining little device known to modern man. Patricia Ashworthy is from one of Parkland's wealthiest families. She was married five times and inherited all her husbands' fortunes. Richard Mason is curator and director of the Little Gallery." She glanced up from her notes. "Anything useful?"

"That's what I found out, too, plus Mrs. Ashworthy thinks Baseford is the cause of all evil in the world, and Gallant's pacemaker may have given out."

"Hmm, or someone tampered with it. Criminal mastermind Chance Baseford, perhaps, or techno-wizard Lawrence Stein?"

"Where'd you get such a devious mind?"

"Hanging around with you."

Our food arrived, my barbecue spilling from a fat white bun and a pile of steaming fries heaped with crispy onion rings, Kary's leafy little salad and a smaller heap of barbecue on a wheat bun. For the next few minutes, we were occupied with deliciousness.

Kary set her fork down and wiped her mouth with a napkin. "Did you see Cam this morning?"

"I left before he was up. Did Ellin drag him off to the station?"

"She left before I did. I think he was still in bed. Have you noticed him taking a lot of aspirin lately?"

"It's the Curse of the Dragonfly."

"I've got to have one French fry." She took one from my plate and dipped it into a pool of ketchup. "He's had headaches before and said aspirin didn't help that much."

"Maybe it isn't aspirin."

Her fry paused in mid-dip. "What do you think he's taking?"

"Have you seen the walking pharmacy that is Vermillion?"

Kary got her Teacher Look. "I'll have a word with him."

"Speaking of words, are Rufus and Angie home?"

"Yes, they are, and they left Mary Rose with Angie's sister. Rufus told me he knew I was in a swivet, and I'd better not get my tail in a crack, or he'd cut my water off."

"Three bizarre Southernisms in one sentence."

She pointed the fry at me. "I told him if he thought I couldn't handle his decision, his cornbread wasn't cooked in the middle."

"Dueling Southernisms. Even better."

"I'm truly fine with them leaving the baby where she can get the best care. I know I had my moments, but if I let every baby reduce me to tears, I'm going to need serious therapy, which I can't afford."

"Not if you plan to become a counselor."

"Exactly. Then I can counsel myself."

The waitress stopped by to refill our drinks. When she'd gone, I asked Kary what she planned to do the rest of the day besides spar with Rufus. "Help you solve the murder," she said. "Maybe there's somewhere else Gallant used to go."

"I'm not sure where he liked to gamble. Do you feel like checking every casino?"

Kary set her sandwich down, wiped her hands on several napkins, and picked up her phone. "Maybe he belonged to a gym or another organization." Her fingers darted over the surface. "Is there a club for artists? Or a bar? You know, like the Blue Moon where all the PSN folks go to wind down. Oh, here we are. The Artists' Club. Can't get any plainer than that. Why don't I give them a try? Someone there might know him."

"I'll call and ask Pierson."

Leo Pierson said that yes, he liked the Artists' Club. He couldn't recall seeing Gallant there, but it was possible someone at the bar knew him. When I related this to Kary, she agreed to find out.

I paid for lunch and put some bills on the table for the tip. "Let me see if I can think of a Southern saying. I enjoyed our lunch as much as granny's canned peaches." She snickered. "As much as puppies rolling in the rose petals?"

She gave me a kiss on the cheek. "It needs work."

I was walking her to her car when a black SUV rounded the corner and barreled toward us. I yanked Kary back as the vehicle zoomed past, missing us by inches. I caught a glimpse of tinted windows and smelled burning rubber as the SUV screeched down the next row of cars, narrowly missing a Jeep on the end and careening out of the parking lot.

Kary's pocketbook had tumbled to the ground, and I helped her gather her spilled belongings. "You okay?"

She was more indignant than frightened. "That was close! There's no excuse to speed like that in the parking lot. What the hell were they thinking?"

A random speeder? Soccer mom late to practice? Or someone who meant to mow us down?

"David?"

I blinked. "Sorry. Having a paranoid moment."

"You think we were a target?"

"I don't know." The SUV was long gone, but my suspicions were growing. "I'll be glad when I have all the facts about this family feud."

● ● **●** ● ●

When I stopped by the set of *Cosmic Healing* for my second meeting with Matt Graber, I found him in his office, going over a schedule with one of his assistants. He saw me in the doorway, sent the assistant away, and motioned me in.

I sat down in the leather swivel chair in front of Graber's desk. His office was not very large and almost sterile in appearance. Besides the desk and two chairs, there was one file cabinet and the snake pen where the two pythons were curled in a ball. No pictures, no plants, and no papers on the spotless desk.

Graber leaned back in his swivel chair. "Would you like a photo in here, or on the set?"

"In here will be fine."

"Very well." He sat up, put his elbows on the desk, and assumed a serious pose while I took several pictures with my cell phone.

"Great. Thanks."

"My pleasure." He leaned back again. I could tell he was trying to appear relaxed, but was way too highly strung. "I apologize again for my snakes' behavior yesterday. I don't know what got into them. Is your friend all right? I could tell he didn't want to have anything to do with them. Perhaps he has a phobia?"

"Some bad snake experiences in the past."

"I see. I could heal him of this, if he's interested."

"I think he'd like to deal with it in his own way."

"It's hard to understand how we develop these unreasonable fears. I for one believe any fear can be overcome, if we train our minds in new paths."

Did this guy always sound like a New Age guru? "Our readers would probably like to know how to do this."

He smiled his grimace of a smile. "I've only begun to master the technique, but I'm willing to share it with others. That's why I'm trying to reach as many people as possible. Are you familiar with the Psychic Service here in Parkland?"

"Yes, I've done several stories on them."

"Then you know they have their own network. My plan is to go on one or all of their television shows and teach this technique to thousands of new viewers who may have missed *Cosmic Healing*. I see this as a way to expand my extremely beneficial form of psychic healing."

I jotted down notes in my notebook. "That sounds like a good idea. Have you approached them about this?"

"I have an appointment with Ellin Belton at three."

"Have you met her before?"

"I've not had the pleasure."

No one has. "I hear she's pretty tough."

"I hear she's a clever businesswoman. If that's the case, she'll recognize how I can improve the PSN."

This guy might as well splash on the gasoline and toss in a match. I wrote in my notebook, *Fireworks display at three.* "Do you have any particular plans for improving the shows?"

Oh, he had plenty of plans. He counted off his complaints. "To begin with, they don't need that blow-dried game-show host making a fool of himself before each program. Extra senses are gifts that should be taken seriously. The carnival atmosphere isn't necessary. It's outdated. Second, the two women who host are attractive, but they don't really add anything to the proceedings. I doubt if they even possess psychic ability. They seem to be merely window-dressing. And third, is the audience paid?"

"I think so."

"More nonsense. My audiences come because they believe, because they need my help and advice. You see, I have a great deal to offer."

Graber had probably looked into the Great Beyond and saw himself as King of Cableland. "Would you include your snakes in your presentations?"

"Naturally."

"You don't see that as a carnival thing?"

"No, indeed. My communication with my snakes is an example of psychic ability at its highest level."

I glanced toward the cage. "What are they saying now?"

"They're asleep."

Plotting their next breakout, I thought, which turned out to be prophetic.

Chapter Ten

"That Flame That Burns Me Up"

I returned home to my office. I still hadn't heard from Richard Mason. Ms. Piper said he never bought Art Nouveau. That didn't mean he never stole any. A new message on his answering machine informed me he was out of town for an art show and would be back Tuesday.

I was pondering my next move when I heard Camden's yelp of alarm.

"Randall!"

I ran out the kitchen door to the backyard. Camden had been repairing the rail fence that separated his backyard from the neighbors' yard, but he'd dropped the hammer and had backed up against a tree, staring in disbelief at the two pythons weaving up from the grass.

"They're here! They're here in my backyard. They said see you later and here they are."

Until now, I hadn't believed Graber's pets would really come visit, but here they were, two sleek black-and-gold pythons moving slowly and deliberately toward Camden. I edged my way around the snakes. They paused and regarded me with unblinking gold eyes.

"Are they saying anything now?"

Camden's voice quavered. "'Hello, how are you?'"

"Then they aren't going to go for your throat. What do they want?"

"How should I know?"

"You always know."

He kept his gaze on the snakes. "Trust me, Randall, for the first time in my life, my mind's a blank."

Even though I'm not afraid of snakes, the unexpected sight of these two large creatures in our yard was unsettling. I knew Camden could communicate with them if he'd calm down. "Okay, well, ask them what they want. They sound friendly."

He gestured wildly. "Come over here so I can get behind you."

As I took a step closer, the smaller snake turned its head toward the large oak tree. The larger one slid up to Camden and paused.

He froze. "Oh, God…oh, God."

"Calm down and listen to it."

"I can't."

"Close your eyes, then. Don't look at it."

"And have it eat me when I'm not looking?"

"I'm standing right here. Ask them what they want. If they don't answer, we'll both run like hell."

He closed his eyes and took several deep breaths. Then he opened his eyes, his expression puzzled. "They want to climb a tree."

"Okay, so let them climb a tree."

He frowned slightly, listening. "They say they miss climbing trees. They're stuck in that cage most of the time. That's what they wanted to do the other day when they got out." With a trembling hand he motioned to the tree. "Go ahead."

The snakes turned swiftly and went up the tree like two

big ripples of water. Camden put his hand to his heart. "I'm going to have a stroke."

The branches dipped and rustled and a few leaves fell as the pythons rolled around the lower limbs. "No, you're not. They only wanted to come play in the trees."

He was not convinced. "So they can drop down on me when I least expect it."

"The big one might. He's the practical joker."

Camden glanced up. The pythons wound about the branches like fat party streamers. "Now what's Graber going to say when he finds out they're over here? He'll accuse me of stealing them."

That had occurred to me, too. "I think those two are crafty enough to get back home before he realizes they're gone." I hoped they were.

Camden managed to catch his breath. "I thought, I'll fix the fence. Something nice and calm and ordinary. Then Slim and Jim show up."

"Oh, they have names now? Slim and Jim Python?"

He was still shaking, but managed to grin. "Graber calls them Titus and Hercules."

A tail curled down from the branches to tickle Camden's ear. He jerked in surprise and if I hadn't had a hand on his arm, would have leaped to the moon.

"Damn!"

"Let's go in and let them enjoy their tree."

Camden was immensely relieved to go inside. He sat down on one of the stools at the kitchen counter while I rooted in the fridge for a couple of Cokes. I handed him one and popped open another.

"Speaking of Graber, I was just talking with him. He plans to be at the PSN at three. Want to come along? It'll be fun."

He took another nervous glance toward the backyard. "Couldn't that wait?"

"They aren't going to come inside. Aren't they happy in the tree?"

"Yes, but, they're so big." He paled. "The cat door."

Even as large as they were, the pythons could get in that way. "I'll block it off."

He looked around frantically. "Where's Cindy? Where's Oreo? Are they outside?"

"Relax. They're on the window seat."

Camden looked over his shoulder toward the back bay window to assure himself the cats were basking in the sun. Then he reached for the pill bottle on the counter, shook out two and then two more.

I frowned at him. "You really need to take some pills?"

He paused to glare. "Two giant snakes have come to visit, and I can hear them. I think this screams major medication."

Snakes in the backyard was one thing. Taking too many pills was another, and in my opinion, more dangerous. "That won't make the problem go away."

"It will for now."

He took the pills with a big gulp of Coke.

I picked up the bottle and read the label. "'Tranquillon.' Where'd you get this?"

"It's just aspirin. If snakes are dropping by and my visions are increasing, I'm going to need something."

I moved the recycle bin in front of the cat door. "Your fear of snakes makes adrenaline kick in. Maybe that's giving your visions that extra zip. Maybe if you went outside and gave Slim and Jim a little pat on the head, everything would go back to normal."

"That's not going to happen."

"What, snake-patting, or going back to normal?"

"Why am I hearing snakes now, anyway?"

"Maybe it's the next step in your vision upgrade." I was

going to continue my argument, but a familiar chugging sound announced the arrival of Turbo. "I'd better warn Kary we have guests."

As Kary got out of her car, I was surprised to see she was in full hippie regalia from sandals and bell-bottomed jeans to her peasant blouse and peace sign necklace. She wore a bright yellow-and-pink paisley scarf around her head and a pair of round lavender-tinted glasses.

"Wow, you look outta sight."

She did a turn so I could get the full effect. "Like it? We had a pageant meeting this afternoon, so afterwards, I rooted through the costumes and borrowed all this finery from the theater. I told Vermillion I'd join her in the park. That way I can meet Rainbow if she's there and gather some intel."

"Did you go to the Artists' Club like this?"

She readjusted the headscarf. "Oh, yes. I created quite a stir and received many requests to paint me. I told the bartender I was interested in having an exhibit at the museum, and he told me all about our cast of characters. He said Lawrence Stein came to the club only once before putting his nose in the air and commenting it was too common for him. He said Leo Pierson was great fun, especially when he got a little sloshed and recited great chunks of plays no one had ever heard of. As for Samuel Gallant, the last time he was there, he was bragging that his money troubles would soon be over."

"What grand scheme would take care of that?"

She took off the lavender glasses and put them in her fringed purse. "The bartender didn't know. He remembers this only because Gallant always moaned and groaned about his financial difficulties, so this was a new song he was singing."

"Anyone else on our list frequent the club?"

"Richard Mason is a regular member."

"Nice work." We started up the porch steps. "Oh, and here's

a head's-up. Graber's pythons stopped by. They're up in one of the trees, in case you wander out back."

"I believe I'll stay in the house."

"After a brief encounter with Slim and Jim, Camden decided he needed to take more pills. Would you check on him before you go to the park?"

"Check on and lecture, if necessary."

I looked at my watch. "Graber has a meeting with Ellin in about half an hour. I'd better swing by the network and prevent another murder."

If Graber was surprised to see me at the PSN, he didn't show it. He stood at the front of the stage as the audience members filed in, observing with his usual distain. "Mr. Fisher, are you doing a story on the PSN, as well?"

"Just visiting."

Bonnie and Teresa took their places on set, and Reg arrived to greet the audience. Graber spoke to him in a condescending tone. "If you'd tell Ms. Belton that I'm here."

Reg took immediate offense. "She's on her way."

"I'd heard that perhaps she was relocating to Charlotte."

"You heard incorrectly."

"If that happens, you'll need a new producer."

"If that happens, I'll take over Ms. Belton's duties."

Graber made a dismissive sound. "I don't think so, Haverson. You may look good on camera, but you haven't the skills to run a network."

I'd never seen Reg so angry. He puffed up and actually balled a fist. "What do you mean, I haven't got the skills?"

Graber wasn't impressed by Reg's outburst. "Let's be honest. I know you're hurting for sponsors, and my audience is down. The smart thing to do is combine our resources. You and these lovely ladies can continue harmonizing with the cosmos, and I can bring my special brand of healing, as well as three more sponsors. Everyone wins."

Reg continued to fume. "There's no way you're going to work here."

"We'll see what Ms. Belton says, shall we? Mind if I look around?"

He didn't wait for permission, but strode off toward the set.

Reg smacked his fist into his palm. "Of all the nerve! When Ellin hears he's trying to move in on the network, she'll shed his skin for him."

Bonnie and Teresa had listened to this interchange, and Bonnie was the first to express her fears to me. "David, I can't stand the thought of that man as our boss, and I'm terrified of snakes."

"Me, too," Teresa said.

Both women looked at Reg for his opinion on snakes. "We're not having snakes in here."

I thought Graber was being a high-handed jerk, but I had to agree with one thing he said. "Reg, are you sure you could handle running a network? It's a lot of unglamorous backstage work. You're an on-camera kind of guy."

He straightened his tie. "Maybe so, but how will I ever find out if I don't get a chance?" He gestured to the people filing in to sit down in the audience. "Besides, my fans would revolt if I left."

"You have fans?"

Ellin arrived as Graber finished his inspection of the set, the cameras, and the microphones. I was ready for major explosions when another commotion caught everyone's attention. People gasped and clapped. Camden was on the set, waving and smiling at the audience.

"Hello, everybody! Are you '*Ready to Believe*'?"

Bonnie and Teresa sat down, stunned, on the sofa. Reg gaped from the sidelines, and Ellin was rendered speechless as Camden began choosing people from the audience. This was a lively, super-charged Camden, who chatted nonstop as he bounded from person to person, shaking hands and letting out a steady stream of psychic news.

"Hi, Lorena! You need to cut down on the carbs and watch out for Miles at the office. He's after your job, so don't forget all the details of the Parker account, or you're going under. Oh, and your grandma says hi. Hello, Miriam! Uncle Bart's will is behind the picture of Roby and her kids. Bill! Don't go to Washington tomorrow. Friday's a better day for you. And, yes, Stacie really loves you."

How did he get away from Kary? An even bigger question was how did he get to the studio? By now, people were clamoring for him to come over, shoving each other in an attempt to be next. Ellin jumped up and down in her own frenzy.

"Keep the camera on him! No, we're not going to commercial yet! Stay with him!"

"Brenda, you should've kept in touch with Rocky. He's going to be very rich very soon. Karen, your mother says it's okay. She forgives you. Jerome, don't buy the Chevy. Sid, Mr. Right is in Oklahoma. You'll meet him at the rodeo. I know it sounds crazy, but he's a rodeo clown. You'll be married for fifty years."

He must have been saying all the right things because there were cries of delight. Then he turned toward the set. "Hey, everybody, watch this!"

He made a sweeping gesture, and all the set decorations, the vases, the flowers, the picture of swirling stars and planets went dancing in a circle.

Okay, so the telekinesis was still in good working order. Bonnie and Teresa made squeaking noises of disbelief and scurried to get out of the way. Reg stood open-mouthed as his comb and pocket square zipped out to join the circle. Camden continued to direct the dance like a conductor with an orchestra of random objects. He kept everything moving until Ellin finally had to go to commercial. The decorations landed with thuds and crashes. There was thunderous applause.

I pushed through the crowd to snag his elbow. "What's going on?"

"I feel better!"

"I can see that." The lights in his eyes were flashing like fireworks displays.

He twisted away and grabbed Ellin in a fierce embrace. "How was that?" He gave her a long kiss and hurried off to kiss Bonnie and Teresa, leaving Ellin to rock back on her heels.

Camden finished kissing all the women and ran out the door. It took Ellin another moment to recover.

"Randall, catch him!"

"Catch him? He's probably halfway up the Amazon by now."

"Something's wrong!"

"I thought you'd say something's right, at last."

She pushed me toward the door. "Go get him! He's not himself."

I hurried out to the parking lot and looked in all directions. No Camden. But I did see Kary's Turbo parked sideways and taking up three spaces. So that's how he got here.

My phone rang, and I answered Kary's frantic call.

"David, Cam took my car! He was sound asleep when Vermillion and I headed for the park. We were almost there when Turbo went flying by. He must have grabbed my extra keys off the hall tree."

"Turbo is here at the TV studio, but Camden has taken off on his own."

"Did you see which way he went?"

"He's probably headed for home. You wait for him there. I'll tell Ellin not to worry. I'll search some of his favorite haunts."

"If he thought he got a talking to before, he is in for the lecture of his life."

When I returned to the set, Reg had stepped in front of the camera and taken charge. "That was a word from Kitty Kare Kat Food. If you care for your kitty, you'll feed him Kitty Kare. Now let's have another round of applause for our surprise guest this afternoon, Camden. Unfortunately, he had another engagement and had to leave, but we'll try and have him back again soon. Now, Bonnie and Teresa will take your calls."

The cameras switched to Bonnie and Teresa on the set. Ellin grabbed my arm. "Did you catch him? What was that all about?"

"Camden got into some happy dust. He'll come down eventually."

A brusque voice said, "Well, that was quite a demonstration."

Matt Graber. I'd forgotten about him. He stood off to one side, and even from a distance, I could see his eyes blazing.

When he approached Ellin, his voice was deadly calm. "Who was that man?"

Better men than Graber had tried to intimidate Ellin Belton. She looked him straight in the eye. "That was my husband, Camden."

"I take it he is not a regular on this show?"

"No, he surprised us all."

Graber's gaze took in the entire audience, still buzzing happily over Camden's revelations. "I can also safely assume he is quite accurate?"

"He's never wrong."

"I see. Then you wouldn't mind telling me what he was doing in my studio the other day?"

Ellin didn't even blink. "Cam's interested in all facets of the paranormal. I'm sure he enjoyed your program."

He turned to me. "As for you, you're not really from the *Herald*, are you?"

"You psychics," I said. "Can't hide anything from you."

He gave a snort of derision. "Amateurs. If you think you can dissuade me from being on the PSN's shows, you're mistaken." He snapped his fingers at Reg. "Haverson, show me the office area, if you would."

Reg looked to Ellin for permission and she gave a short nod. Graber strode off, Reg in tow.

I wasn't sure what annoyed Ellin more, Graber's insistence on hanging around, or Camden's odd behavior. "He saw right through my disguise," I said. "So much for being subtle."

"I don't care about him." Ellin said. "I've got the rest of this show to finish. You're sure you didn't see Cam anywhere?"

"I'll find him."

"What did you mean by happy dust? Why would he take any sort of drugs?"

"Two big old pythons came by the house earlier today."

She lowered her voice. "Not Graber's snakes?"

"They came to climb a tree."

One of the cameramen signaled to her. "I've got to take care of the show," Ellin said, "then I'm calling Jordan to help us locate Cam. Let me know the minute you find him."

Chapter Eleven
"The Call"

I drove around to Janice Chan's hot dog restaurant, to the Little Theater, to the Baptist Church where the chorale practices, and to Victory Holiness Church, but my link to Camden wasn't working. I cruised the neighborhood and up and down Food Row. No sign of him.

Must be the pills he's taking, I thought. Maybe they're blocking the signal. Or maybe I haven't been integrated into his new power grid.

At home, Kary met me on the porch.

"He isn't here, David. I looked in all the rooms and up in the attic and even under the house. Did you find him?"

I started to answer when her gaze went beyond me.

"Cam!"

Camden staggered slowly up the walk. I couldn't believe he'd made it home all in one piece. His shirttail was out and his shoes were missing.

Kary ran and took him by the arm. "Are you okay?"

"Yeah," he said. "Tired." He stared at her hippie outfit. "What year is this?"

I helped him up the steps. "She's in disguise for my case. When did you come back?"

"About half an hour ago. I was on top of the monkey bars in the park." He rubbed his forehead. "I'm seeing six of you."

"Want to lie down?"

"No, let me sit for a minute. I think everything will level out."

He sat down on the porch swing. While Kary gave him hell for running off and scaring her, I called Ellin. Then I filled a large plastic cup with iced tea and extra sugar.

When I returned to the porch, Kary was still giving Camden "what-for," as Rufus would say.

"This is absolutely the craziest thing you have ever done. Do you realize what taking too many pills can do to your health? Do you even know what you're taking? And then to take Turbo! You hate to drive."

I didn't think much of this was getting through. "Steady on. He can't comprehend half of what you're saying right now." I handed Camden the cup and he thanked me. "Remember anything?"

He took a drink. "Did I crash *Ready to Believe*?"

"You were sensational."

"Oh, Lord."

"Ellin was speechless, so you know you made an impact."

He put his head down on one hand. "I'll never get out from under this."

"Seriously, she's so concerned about you she might not push for a return engagement. She's out riding around with Jordan, looking for you."

"I should call—"

"Already did. She should be home in about ten minutes."

Jordan's car had barely stopped in the driveway when Ellin jumped out and ran up the steps. She hugged Camden so tightly I thought she might come out the other side.

"Oh, my God, I was so worried. Are you all right?"

"I'm okay," he said. "I'm tired, that's all."

"You were absolutely wonderful. People can't stop talking about you."

"Ellie, you know I can't do that again."

"Come inside. We'll talk about it."

She dragged him into the house. Kary followed, still fussing. Jordan paused at the bottom of the porch steps, frowning in concern. "Where'd you find him?"

"He made it home on his own."

"You want to explain what the hell's going on now? Ellin went on and on about one of her shows. Didn't make any sense to me."

"He was Super Psychic on there for a while, what she's always wanted him to be. He came on the program and blew everybody away. He does that when he's high."

Jordan's eyes narrowed. "Would you care to explain?"

"I believe you're aware of his low tolerance for any sort of medicine. He's been taking some pills for his headaches, and I think they may be a little too strong."

"Any particular reason for these headaches?"

"Aside from explosive visions, Ellin's demands, touching a cursed object, and a couple of pythons stopping by to say hello, no. Which reminds me."

"Pythons?"

Jordan followed me to the backyard where I checked the tree. Slim and Jim had enjoyed their Snakes Day Out and were gone. With any luck, they'd made it back home before Graber noticed his pets were missing.

Jordan peered up into the branches. "Whose pythons and why?"

"They belong to Matt Graber, master of *Cosmic Healing*. He's angling for a spot on the PSN."

"You think that set Cam off?"

I didn't want to tell Jordan that Leo Pierson's lost dragonfly car mascot was probably the real cause. "He has a problem with snakes."

"Then why were they in his backyard?"

"They wanted to hang out."

Jordan regarded me with barely concealed impatience. "I can't have pythons roaming the city. People don't like it. Tell Graber to keep them locked up, or they'll be taken to the zoo."

"No problem. While you're here, what's the latest on Samuel Gallant's death?"

"Looks like his pacemaker gave out."

That's what Rainbow had told me. "Any clues as to why he was in an empty closet?"

"That's still under investigation. Do you have anything to tell me?"

A black SUV had narrowly missed running over me and Kary. I had eight days to find Pierson's treasures and two more people to interview. A mysterious feud and a puzzle worth twenty-five million dollars had yet to be explained. "Nope."

Jordan took one last look up the tree as if expecting a snake attack. He'd driven away when Ellin called to me from the kitchen door.

"Are they gone?"

"No more snakes."

"Thank goodness. I didn't want Graber accusing me of stealing those things. What were they doing here?"

I came up the back steps. "I told you they stopped by to say hello."

"Cam heard them? I thought that only worked with cats."

That reminded me to unblock the cat door. "They met when we did our undercover operation. Of course, now we're busted."

She made a dismissive gesture. "That doesn't matter. Graber

is not going to be on the PSN, I don't care how many snakes he has."

We moved into the kitchen, and I took a soda from the fridge. "Well, you don't need Graber when you've got Super Psychic."

She sat down at the counter. "Not when he has to resort to pills. He says he's taking aspirin, but I don't believe aspirin could cause that kind of reaction, do you?" She gave me one of her long measuring stares. "What sort of case are you working on now?"

"Trying to solve a murder and recovering some stolen property. These two things are most likely related."

"Is it a horrible death that's likely to give him flashbacks?"

Six deaths. Not sure if they were horrible. "The murder appears to be related to a faulty pacemaker. That's about as ghastly as it gets."

"For now."

She had me there. My cases always started out as someone's harmless run-of-the-mill problem and ended in an avalanche of death, destruction, and general craziness. A dead songwriter taking possession of Camden, check. Amateur superheroes running amok, check. Magicians murdering each other over a Houdini box, check. Ghost trapped in a mirror, check. A cursed dragonfly fit right in.

Ellin fixed me with her steeliest gaze. "You don't need to say anything, Randall. We both know this isn't over. Why don't you find another office somewhere? Preferably in a city far far away."

"Why don't you find another job?"

She arched her eyebrows. "What exactly do you mean by that?"

I was careful to stay on the other side of the counter. "You're not psychic. You never will be. You could run any company you wanted to. Why are you staying with the PSN? You have to know it's all a sham."

"Because I'm fascinated by psychic ability. I want to know how it happens, why it happens, why it didn't happen to me."

I almost said, it didn't happen to me, either, but decided to keep my mouth shut. It's a struggle, but on occasion, I can manage. No matter how hard I try to deny it, Camden and I have the very link Ellin would kill to have. Plus I was now Detective to the Dead.

She gave me a suspicious glance as if wondering why I was so quiet. Lucky for me she can't read minds. "That's why I try so hard, Randall. You don't give up on your cases, do you? I'm not the type to give up, either."

"You don't have to give up. But don't be so intense about it. Lighten up. And cut Camden some slack. He's had a rough few days."

She stood. "Then keep him out of your business."

"Only if you keep him out of yours."

Stalemate. The usual outcome of our little talks. I got a glare that would've singed off my hair if I hadn't been Ellin-proof and she stalked out. I was surprised my soda didn't boil over.

•• ● ••

That night, I heard from the TV Ghost, but not in the way I expected.

I took Kary to retrieve Turbo, and fortunately, the little car was undamaged. Kary handed Camden over to Ellin to straighten out and came to bed pretty riled up, so I used all my considerable charm and expertise to take care of her stress-related issues. She'd used a scented shampoo, so her long silky hair smelled like strawberries, and her skin felt as soft as the pillows.

"You can't be angry," I told her. "You feel and smell too good."

"It's the feel and smell of anger," she said, but she giggled when I tickled her and soon wrapped around me with a contented sigh.

Afterwards, she curled up next to me sound asleep, but I was still wide awake. That's when I saw the pale shadow in the mirror over my dresser. Words formed on the glass.

David Randall.

Oh, man. Not another mirror! I carefully slid out of bed and approached my dresser. "Yes, that's me. Can I help you? Did you try to contact me the other day?"

Yes. I could not get through. My name is Isabelle.

Isabelle! Pierson's relative, the one whose great aunt had been the model for the missing poster, the one who had owned all the missing artwork. "Isabelle Duvall?"

More letters formed. *Yes. I have been on the other side for many years. I am an old shade and not used to this form of communication with the living. But Lindsey showed me the way. She wants you to succeed, as do I. Can you help me?*

So Lindsey had managed to help this spirit reach me. "Yes," I said. "I'll do whatever I can. All those Art Nouveau items belonged to you, right? What can you tell me about them? Is it true they can lead to a fortune? Do you know where they are?"

My beautiful things.

For a moment, I thought she was gone. Then more letters appeared.

I paid for them with my life.

There was another long silence. I waited. Then: *Some said it was the Curse of the Dragonfly. I was the victim of a bitter feud, a feud that still exists today. After my death, the families fought over who should own my belongings.*

"Your artwork came to Leo Pierson," I said. "He inherited it from his father."

Yes. Even though a Pierson killed me, I wanted the Piersons to have it.

I went cold. "Killed you? For the artwork?"

Yes. I wanted to end this ridiculous quarrel. I wanted to leave them my fortune.

"But somebody on your side of the family had different ideas."

Another long pause. *They wanted revenge. They wanted to keep the feud alive.*

"Miss Duvall, who are your relatives still living today? Is one of them responsible for the robbery?"

No answer. "Miss Duvall? Isabelle?"

No more words appeared on the mirror. Was that the extent of Isabelle's message, or was she unable to come through?

I went back to bed. I hoped Isabelle would return or I'd have a follow up dream from Lindsey, but the rest of my night was uneventful, and I managed to fall asleep without any other interruptions.

• • ● • •

Once we were all settled at the table Sunday morning for breakfast, I told everyone what I'd learned from Isabelle. Neither Camden nor Kit had tuned in to the exchange.

Kit reached for the butter. "I was cranking out tunes at The Other Side. I wouldn't have heard anything."

Camden took the butter dish from Kit. "I didn't hear anything, either."

With his powers increasing, I was surprised Isabelle hadn't registered. "She said the Pierson/Duvall feud is alive and well, so I'll be discussing Pierson's family tree with him today. There must be a Duvall in the mix."

Kary dug out another spoonful of grits and passed the bowl to Vermillion. "I'll see what I can find out about Isabelle."

Rufus and Angie Jackson filled up one side of the dining room table. Angie was a large woman with short brown hair and small eyes twinkling from her round face. She was neatly dressed, as always, in a flowing blouse and stretch pants. All six feet and three hundred pounds of Rufus was wedged into his traditional overalls worn over a tee-shirt covered with beer slogans and a baseball cap with a braid he called a rat tail hanging out the back. The ever-present cap had a picture of a squirrel drinking a beer. "Didn't think artistic types went in for feudin'," he said.

"They do when twenty-five million dollars are at stake," I said.

Angie's attention was caught. "Are those things worth that much?"

"No, but they hold clues that lead to that much. Whoever has the whole collection gets to figure out the puzzle."

"Reckon Isabelle set that up?" Rufus asked.

"Yes, and then got killed before she could tell anyone the answer."

"Kinda inopportune, wasn't it?"

"'Inopportune.' Twenty points, Rufus."

"Twenty? Hell, that's a thirty-dollar word and you know it."

Kit raised his hand. "Okay, what's with the vocabulary challenge? I've heard you guys doing it."

"Pass the jelly and I'll tell you," I said. He handed me the jar. "My second wife thought my vocabulary needed improvement, so she bought me one of those Word-A-Day calendars. When we divorced and she tossed my belongings out on the lawn, the calendar was one of the few surviving bits. When I moved here and set up my office, it was the first thing I put on my desk. The word for that day was 'intransigent,' which means permanent, persistent, unfailing. I took that as a sign. Camden and I have been trying to outdo each other ever since."

"Then I joined in," Kary said. "You can play, too. We don't really keep score."

"Speak for yourself, girl," Rufus said. "I'm in it to win it."

Camden tapped his fork on his tea glass for attention. "Since you're all here, I need to let you know Wally's going to start working on the leaky pipes in the second-floor bathrooms. You might have to share for a while till I work out a way to pay him. Eventually, all the pipes have to be replaced."

Vermillion shrugged her shoulders. Kit looked concerned. "I can contribute some, but my gigs haven't been paying too well lately. I need a big break, you know? Wish I had a really cool gimmick."

Before either Kary or I could speak, Ellin said, "I'll take care of it."

Uh, oh. Kary glanced at me.

Camden looked at Ellin warily. "Thanks, honey."

She calmly buttered another piece of toast. "There will of course be a fee."

Here it comes, I thought. Oblivious, Vermillion chewed on her toast, but Rufus and Angie exchanged a knowing glance. Kit sensed danger and moved his chair back.

"Cam, I want you to be the main attraction at the psychic fair."

He brought both hands down on the table and rocked back. "Ellie, for heaven's sake. Kill me now."

She ignored his dramatics. "All you have to do is show up for a few hours each day, a few handshakes, a few insights."

"A few breakdowns."

"This is a big deal for the PSN, a great opportunity for us to publicize all our programs. Plus you owe me. Didn't you tell me your telekinesis was gone?"

"It was! I don't know how that happened."

She pointed the butter knife at him. "Then what made everything dance around the studio yesterday?"

He knew when he was defeated. "Me."

"Because you took too many pills, which was stupid." Pleased she'd won the argument, she patted his hand. "You don't have to worry about a thing. I'll make the arrangements."

"You can make all the arrangements you like. I'll just curl up in a fetal ball now."

"It will not be that bad."

"Ellie, right now I don't know what's going to cause my head to explode. First Leo's cursed dragonfly, and then Graber's snakes coming after me, and—"

"You can handle it."

"I like to think I can, and then lightning strikes."

"Stop worrying. I'll be there, remember? Your eraser?"

"Umm, eraser?" Kit asked.

"If I have a really bad vision, holding Ellie's hand blanks it out," Camden explained.

"Wow, cool. How come?"

Camden wasn't going to say it, but I didn't mind. "Because Ellin's a blank. Psychically, I mean." I smiled cheerfully at her scowl.

Kit was intrigued. "So, Cam, maybe she can take care of the power surge."

"No, this is different." He leaned forward. "Look, everyone, I'll try to explain. Up to now, I've been able to control the visions, but this weird pressure keeps building. I don't know where it's coming from, or how it's going to affect me." He pushed his hair out of his eyes and rubbed his forehead. "I've never experienced six previous deaths at one time. I've never heard snakes before. I don't know what all that means. I realize I took too many pills yesterday, but it felt really good to let everything out."

"Before you crashed," I reminded.

"Yeah, there's that."

"Don't stress out," Kary said. "Whatever this is, we'll get through."

Kit nodded in agreement. "We're with you, right, guys?"

Vermillion surfaced from whatever psychedelic dream she was wandering in to say a few words. "Peace for our times."

Camden looked around the table at his mismatched family as if content to have everyone in place, and his expression relaxed. "Thanks."

He and Kary went to church with Rufus and Angie. Ellin stayed home to work on a promotion for the PSN. Vermillion said she was a practicing pagan, so she returned to her sunny spot in the backyard. Kit went upstairs to practice. I tagged along with the church crowd, mainly to sit with Kary. I'm not David Randall, Christian Detective, not by a long shot, but things have happened I can't comfortably explain, including my little chat with Isabelle in my mirror last night, so I'm playing it safe.

● ● ● ● ●

For lunch, Kary fixed one of her more successful recipes, pinto beans with ham and cornbread. Then she put on her Sixties attire and headed to the park with Vermillion.

Before Ellin left for the studio, she stopped by my office door and stood, arms folded, as if holding herself back from a full out attack. "You conveniently left out this cursed dragonfly yesterday. What exactly is it?"

"The stolen property I'm looking for includes an Art Nouveau glass dragonfly. When Camden shook the owner's hand, he short-circuited himself, so I think the dragonfly has a good chance of being cursed."

"You have no idea how ridiculous that sounds."

"You live here. You ought to be used to ridiculous by now."

I was ready for another lecture, but apparently she decided

I wasn't worth her time. She headed back to the studio, no doubt to see if Matt Graber had snuck in during the night and set up camp.

I called Leo Pierson to ask about his family. "What did you find out about the feud?"

"Oh, that's quite the story," he said. "It would make a wonderful play, actually. The Duvalls and the Piersons never could get along. The Duvalls were very rich and never wanted anything to do with the Piersons. They accused each other right and left of various crimes, theft, seduction."

"Your relative Isabelle Duvall was murdered by a Pierson. Did you know that?"

He spluttered. "That's impossible! If the two families were so at odds, and she was killed because of it, why did my father inherit the Art Nouveau? Why did I get it?"

"Isabelle wanted her artwork to go to the Piersons. She was trying to end the feud, but somebody on the Duvall side isn't happy with this decision, and it probably has a lot to do with the money involved. Do you know any Duvalls?"

"No. My parents died years ago, and I have no other living relatives. There's no one who could tell me." Pierson's voice held a plaintive note. "Are you any closer to finding my treasures, Randall? There are only seven days left."

"I'm talking to Stein tomorrow and Mason on Tuesday," I said. "With any luck, they'll have more clues for me." Or maybe, as much as this grated on my nerves, Chance Baseford knew more than he was telling, and I'd have to talk to him again.

After my phone call, I went out to the porch. Camden was on the porch swing and Rufus took up the top step. He flicked a leftover crumb from his scraggly red beard and leaned over to direct a stream of tobacco juice into the flower bed.

"Cam's been tryin' to get me up to speed. What's with Kary? She tryin' out for Miss Age of Aquarius?"

I sat down in a rocking chair. "She's on an undercover mission for me. We're hoping Samuel Gallant's niece is hanging out with the Sixties crowd in the park."

"Gallant. That's the guy you and Cam found in the closet."

"With one of my client's missing spoons."

"Maybe your client hid all his stuff to claim insurance money."

"No, he's too attached to it, even the cursed dragonfly."

Rufus looked at Camden. "That's what's knocked you catty-wumpus."

"It certainly did."

"What's this about snakes? You seein' snakes all of a sudden? That ain't good."

"Real snakes," I said. "Matt Graber, host of *Cosmic Healing*, has two pythons who've formed an attachment to Camden, but he doesn't want to talk to them. I think he ought to."

"I'll chop 'em up for you, Cam."

"No, no. If you see them anywhere around the house, let me know, that's all."

Rufus spit another glob into the bushes. "You know you can't ride two horses with one ass."

"No, I can't."

Did Rufus ever run out of these sayings? "Translation?"

"The way I see it, you need to find this dragonfly and shut it off, and Cam needs to get over his fear of snakes. No more wild visions. Easy."

"I hope so," I said. "I only have one ass."

Rufus dug his cell phone out of his overall pocket and checked the screen. "Angie's wanting to go shopping." His large fingers tapped a reply, and he heaved himself to his feet.

In a few minutes, Angie opened the screen door, a huge

purse over one arm. "See you fellas later." They got into his bigfoot truck and roared down the street.

I pushed myself out of the rocker. "Let's stroll to the park to see if we can get some free love."

Chapter Twelve
"What If I Seek For Love?"

Camden and I walked down Grace Street and took a left on Park and then another left on Willow. Between Grace and Willow was a park with a bike and walking trail, flower gardens, a slide, swing set, a jungle gym for the kids, and a duck pond. Seated on the expanse of green grass under oak trees was a group of people in brightly colored clothes swaying to guitar music and singing an uneven version of "Blowing in the Wind." Psychedelic patterns bloomed on shirts and blouses. The women and men had flowers in their hair and all were trying very hard to appear cool. I caught a glimpse of Vermillion's red hair. She leaned back against a tree trunk, eyes closed.

"Soaking up those positive rays," I said. "See Kary anywhere?"

Kary and Rainbow were seated on a patchwork quilt, their heads close together in earnest conversation.

"Is she scoring some weed? Maybe that'll help your headaches."

Kary glanced up, saw us, and waved us over. We sat down beside the two women on the quilt. "Guys, I've found out something very interesting. Rainbow says her Uncle Samuel just had the battery in his pacemaker replaced, so she doesn't see how it could've given out."

"Those batteries are good for at least six or seven years," Rainbow said. "And something else. The police said they found his cell phone in his shirt pocket. He would never have put his phone that close to the pacemaker. His doctor told him it could cause problems. He always kept it in his pants pocket." She was almost in tears. "Mr. Randall, when the lawyer read the will, I found out that my uncle left me enough money for my college education. I always wanted to go, but I couldn't afford it, and now I can. You said you were investigating his disappearance. I want you to find out what really happened to him. I can pay you."

I didn't want to take any of her college fund. "We'll work something out."

"I thought he was being stupid going to the casinos all the time and playing the machines and trying all these money-making schemes. Turns out he was saving money for me."

"Would it be possible to have a look in his house? There may be something that will give me a clue."

"The police said they'd be through tomorrow. I'll let you know."

As the group began to disperse, Rainbow thanked Kary, rolled up the quilt, and left with another girl. Camden went to retrieve Vermillion.

I linked Kary's arm in mine. "Excellent work. How did you bond so fast?"

"I said I'd heard about her uncle from you and wanted to express my sympathies. The rest of the time, I listened."

"Practicing your counseling technique."

"I knew you'd want to know about the pacemaker, so I asked about that, too."

"So now I want to know if the murderer purposely put Gallant's cell phone in his shirt pocket to make it look like an accident."

"Or if Gallant just forgot."

"Then what was he doing in the supply closet? The fellow in charge of cleaning out the museum said no one had seen him. My guess is he was killed somewhere else and then stowed in the closet."

"Here's hoping Gallant left a clue in his house. Hold on." I stopped and Kary stopped with me. "Is that the same black SUV?"

A vehicle very similar to the one that tried to run us over was parked near the duck pond. Sunlight glinted off the tinted windows.

"Looks like it." Kary started forward. "Come on. I'm ready to give that driver a piece of my mind."

I was, too, but I wanted to be cautious. "It might not be the same car."

"We'll find out, won't we?"

As we approached, the SUV took off. The ducks honked in protest, flapping their wings furiously. The car took the corner with a screech of tires and disappeared up onto Food Row.

Kary watched it go. "That answers that question. What do you suppose that's all about?"

I had an idea. "Somebody's spying on us."

"Does this mystery person think we had something to do with Gallant's murder?"

"More likely, they think we know something about the twenty-five million dollars."

Camden came up with Vermillion. She was scowling.

"Uh, oh," I said. "Did they run out of peace and harmony?"

She crossed her arms and sulked. "They said there was going to be food, but there wasn't any. I'm really bummed."

"Camden, we'd better take our hippie chicks home and feed them."

Once she'd had a snack, Vermillion was back to her airy self. She took two more cookies from the bag on the counter.

"Cam, I was talking to these girls in the park and they said I could crash with them. They have their own commune on Kelso Street where that sock factory used to be."

He put ice in a plastic cup. "Are they living in the old sock factory?"

"It really really sounds like a cool place. Like, could we go check it out?"

"What do these girls use for money?"

"They don't use money. Everybody uses a barter system, or if they've got a lot of carrots or something, they share."

"I think you'd get tired of that really really fast."

I took the peanut butter jar from the cabinet and handed it to Kary. "Vermillion, you get so damn cranky when you're hungry. Imagine living on carrots for a week."

She got defensive. "I like carrots."

"No guarantee there'd be any food at the Sock Factory Commune."

Kary reached for the crackers. "We're still looking for a nice place for you."

Camden filled his cup with tea. "Are you that anxious to leave?"

She was a grown woman and could leave any time, but she was so spacey, I knew Camden and Kary were concerned about what might happen to her.

She munched on another cookie. "It's okay, but there's all this coming and going. I need peace and quiet to meditate. It's too busy here."

"Most of the time, it's very calm," Camden said.

The screen door slammed and Ellin's voice echoed in the foyer. "Cam! Where are you?"

Vermillion gave him a look as if to say, "See what I mean?"

Ellin stormed around the corner and flung her attaché case into the nearest chair. "You'll never believe this! Matt Graber has gone too far! He went over my head to my boss at the Psychic Service, and she loves the idea of having him on the show! They're in talks to let him have a regular program. He's commandeered an office for his own, he's designed his own set—I am beyond furious!"

I'd been joking when I thought Graber would use Sunday to stake a claim. I'd underestimated his ambition. Vermillion took the bag of cookies and backed out of the kitchen.

Camden tried to stem the flood. "Ellie, I'm sure it'll all work out."

"Are you? Are you sure about anything these days? Are you off those pills?"

"Yes, I told you."

"If you would let me create a program around you and your amazing talent I wouldn't have to put up with second-rate psychics like Graber and his snakes waltzing in like he owned the place."

"I don't think that's the answer."

"Then I'm stuck with *three* big reptiles. The PSN is my domain, and I resent his interference."

"It will always be your domain. You can work with him. He might be good for ratings."

She sat down on one of the stools at the counter and heaved an exasperated sigh. "He's just so arrogant, so—where's Rufus when I need a description?"

She had to be upset if she was calling on Rufus. "Graber's not moving in permanently, is he?" I asked. "He has his own studio."

"Oh, he calls the PSN his 'satellite.' How do you like that?" She waved away Camden's offer of tea. "There are times when I wish we had something stronger in this house."

"I can make a run to the liquor store," I said.

Kary had a suggestion. "Why not let him have his program and see what happens? It might be a flop. He might be spreading himself too thin."

Ellin was not in the mood to be comforted. "Right now, I don't know what I'm going to do."

"Let's take a walk," Camden said.

She agreed, and the two of them went out. Kary exchanged her Sixties outfit for a tee-shirt and shorts, plopped herself in the chair I have for clients, set her laptop on my desk, and went online. She found out cell phones and MP3 players could cause problems for people who had pacemakers if carried in a left-hand shirt pocket. Metal detectors and high-tension wires were a threat, and it was recommended that patients stay two feet away from industrial welders and electrical generators and avoid close and prolonged exposure to household appliances.

"So the warning about microwave ovens is true," I said.

Kary finished the article. "Batteries can last as long as fifteen years, but most are good for six or seven. Doctors check the patient's battery every three months as well as the wires to make certain none are broken or dislodged."

I sat back in my chair. "I didn't see an industrial welder in the closet, and I doubt Gallant would play with high-tension wires. Something caused his pacemaker to malfunction."

"We think," Kary reminded. She flexed her fingers. "Okay, on to the Duvalls."

After a few minutes, she said, "Ah-ha, look at this."

The black-and-white photograph captioned "Miss Isabelle Duvall in Her Parlor" showed Isabelle standing in front of a display cabinet indicating the dragonfly, which sat innocently on the top shelf. On the second shelf was a small box open to show the leafy little forks and spoons. A small round table holding the peacock vase and ashtray was positioned on one side of the cabinet with the framed poster hanging above. The only things not mentioned on Pierson's list were two unremarkable chairs and a lamp on a matching round table. Isabelle's dark hair was cut in a short bob. She wore a short fringed and beaded dress and long strings of pearls, a cigarette holder in one hand, the perfect picture of a 1920 jazz baby.

"And then there's this," Kary said.

A second newspaper article dated three months later detailed the break-in and murder of Isabelle Duvall. "Police were called to 815 Woodbine Lane at four-fifteen the afternoon of the twelfth where they discovered the body of twenty-nine-year-old Isabelle Duvall. It appeared she surprised an intruder who shot her and took several valuable Art Nouveau items from the house. The crime is believed to be related to a long-standing feud between two families concerning ownership of the artwork."

A third article was dated the following day with the headline: "Pierson Confesses to Duvall Murder." "Early this morning, police arrested Theodore Pierson of 1029 Parker Avenue, who confessed to the murder of socialite Isabelle Duvall and the theft of her Art Nouveau."

I read the rest of the article, but already knew the main point. The Piersons and the Duvalls had it in for each other. "Kary, check and see if there's been anything more about Gallant's death."

She skimmed through the *Parkland Herald*'s website. "Looks like it's the same information—oh, no, wait, here's the latest. 'According to the preliminary autopsy, Gallant's heart received a severe electrical shock, caused either by a malfunctioning pacemaker or an outside source. His body appears to have been moved a short distance. The murder investigation is still ongoing.'"

"A severe electrical shock. Doesn't sound like cell phone interference." I glanced at my calendar. "I'll be talking with

Stein tomorrow." Day five of my ten-day search. "According to Pierson, he has all kinds of electronic devices on his boat."

Kary closed her laptop. "What about the black SUV? Is that a real threat, or just an inept driver?"

"That's something else I've got to figure out."

By suppertime, Ellin's anger had settled to a dim roar, and Rufus provided her with "As sneaky as a sheep-killin' dog," which she agreed was appropriate for Graber. Angie said she'd be happy to alter one of Kary's gowns for Miss Panorama, and then Rufus and Angie rode over to River Street to check on the house they were planning to buy. Kary had promised to rehearse with one of the participants in the art song festival, so I took Camden and Vermillion to Kelso Street to check out a possible home for Vermillion. The members of the commune squatting in the abandoned sock factory were large and noisy. The smell of marijuana guaranteed the promise of a police raid. Luckily, Vermillion took one look at the drum circle, wildly gyrating dancers, and the few screaming babies and decided she'd like to return to the backyard at Grace Street. Camden was equally relieved.

When we got home, Kary was still rehearsing with the singer, a thin young woman with dark hair pulled back severely in a tight bun. Camden and I took our seats in the island and were treated to an extremely dramatic rendition of something called "O cessate di piagarmi" before they were both pleased with the results. The singer and Kary agreed on their next rehearsal, and Kary saw her out.

"What's the commune like?" she asked when she returned to the island.

"A hell hole," Camden said.

"It didn't sound like a good idea." She moved Oreo from her chair and sat down. "It's really not a problem for Vermillion to stay here, is it? Or is Ellin giving you a hard time?"

I looked around. "Yeah, where's your sweetie? She didn't go back to the studio, did she?"

"I told her to take a long relaxing bath and I would relax her further when I got home."

"I have the solution to Ellin's problem. You could always have a word with Slim and Jim. Tell them to act all floppy and unresponsive whenever Graber brings them out at the PSN. No snakes, no show." I reached for the remote and hunted through the channels. "Is *Cosmic Healing* on tonight?"

"You and Kary can enjoy another stirring adventure. I have better things to do."

We heard feet pounding down the stairs, and Kit bounded into the island. "Death coming up, Cam. Are you on Channel 14?"

I turned to Channel 14 and looked up to see Kary's quizzical expression.

"Death coming up?"

"It's like living with the Grim Reaper's cuckoo clock."

At that moment on the TV, a serious-looking fellow with hair combed way back intoned a few brief sentences about the president's latest doomed bill, a famine in Africa, a civil war in some country I'd never heard of, and then, on the local scene, prominent Parkland lawyer and financier Lawrence Stein died in an explosion on board his yacht, *Wall Street Wanderer*.

I couldn't believe it. "*What?*" I upped the volume in time to hear Mr. Combed Back say, "Details coming up after your complete weather." I sat back in my chair. "What the hell is going on?" On screen, weather statistics scrolled by, but all I could see was a cloud of black smoke and pieces of yacht and possibly pieces of dragonfly sinking to the bottom of the sea.

Kit obviously knew what had happened, and now Camden did, too, but Kary and I listened in disbelief to the rest of the report. Little was known about the accident. Stein had been out alone. His body had been recovered by the Coast Guard. A full investigation was underway by Atlantic Shores Police, but early reports cited a glitch in the ship's electrical system.

"Cam, didn't you see six deaths?" Kary asked.

"Six deaths in the past."

"Let's hope the dragonfly doesn't need six more. That's two already, and we—" she halted because the magazines on the coffee table, the remote, and all the balls of yarn from her basket rose into the air and began to circle the room. "Cam?"

"Oh, good Lord," he said as the objects sped up. Oreo ran in to see what all the excitement was about and was immediately caught up into the circle.

"Whoa!" Kit clutched his wiry hair. "This is full-on awesome, man! How do you do that?"

He watched the spinning circle in dismay. "It shouldn't be happening."

"It's because of that guy's death, isn't it? It must be the dragonfly."

I had a bigger concern. "Can you make it stop?"

He closed his eyes and put his hands to his forehead, concentrating hard. Abruptly, the objects fell, the magazines fluttering and yarn balls bouncing on the rug. I caught the remote, and Kit was close enough to catch Oreo, who struggled until he put the cat down. Oreo ran for the kitchen.

"You gotta teach me that," Kit said.

Camden kept his head down in his hands. "I am losing it."

Kary came and sat beside him, her arm around his shoulders. "It must be all these deaths associated with the dragonfly. As soon as David finds it, things should settle down."

But I'd just lost another source and possible suspect. If Richard Mason couldn't shed more light on the case, I wasn't sure I could find Pierson's artwork.

Chapter Thirteen
"*Can She Excuse My Wrongs?*"

I'd hoped to hear from Lindsey, but neither she nor Isabelle had anything to say that night. Monday, I called Lawrence Stein's office and feigned ignorance of the accident. A secretary filled me in. She agreed it was an electrical mishap on the boat, a dreadful tragedy. The office was in an upheaval, and no one was interested in hearing about curses or family feuds.

Tamara called to say she needed Camden at the store, so after giving him a ride to Tamara's Boutique in Friendly Shopping Center, I stopped off at Guardian Electric, located inside Myers, Parkland's largest department store, a building that took up one whole corner of the shopping center. I wound past racks of jewelry, scarves, and handbags, past riding mowers and air conditioners, past all kinds of power tools and automotive supplies to reach a small office between smaller offices for Premium Insurance and VisionClear Contacts. A thin bored-looking man looked up from his newspaper. If I had to place the security of my home and office in his lacka- daisical hands, I'd feel the need for Premium Insurance. His pale blue eyes blinked at me without interest. Maybe he could use some VisionClear contacts.

"Can I help you?"

I offered a hand. "John Fisher. I'm interested in buying a security system for my home."

The prospect of a sale did not perk him up. With a longing glance at the sports section, he set the newspaper aside and shook my hand. "What did you have in mind, Mr. Fisher?"

"What do you have?"

He was going to have to show me the full line, a serious dent in his reading time. With a noticeable lack of enthusiasm, he reached into his desk drawer and pulled out a large folder stamped with a bright green shield with "Guardian Electric" in gold letters. He flipped through the laminated pages.

"Basic locks, padlocks, deadbolts, cross bars, screens, electronic locks, voice- and pressure-sensitive, silent alarms, car alarms, complete home systems—"

I interrupted. "I was thinking along the lines of pressure plates, something a thief might set off and not realize it till it's too late."

"Of course. Let me show you our complete home system. It's our most popular model. We'll be glad to come to your house and give you an estimate."

"How complicated are they?"

He flipped through a few more pages and showed me a schematic. "It's really quite simple. Everything is connected to a master switch, which you can place anywhere. Most people like to have them in a bedroom. You can have lights or alarms or both. By pressing this button here, you can arm or disarm your system."

"What about a password?"

He gave a snort. "We're way past that. The system's keyed to the client's thumbprint."

"A friend of mine recommended your company—Leo Pierson."

Pierson would be hard to forget. "Oh, yeah. Big red-haired guy. Quite a job that was."

"He was robbed, did you know that?"

Nothing bothered this guy. He shrugged. "It happens."

"You don't offer any insurance on your system?"

He gave me a pitying look. "The insurance company's next door. No system's foolproof, but Guardian Electronic guarantees to keep your home or place of business safe as long as you operate the system properly. Now, obviously, the day his house was robbed, Pierson forgot to set it."

I let him show me some estimates and labor costs. I asked questions like a real customer. Meanwhile, questions of my own went round in my mind. Wouldn't Pierson have noticed it was disarmed? The lighted display on the master control panel of this alarm system clearly stated "Armed" and "Disarmed." Then I remembered Gallant's pacemaker and how the autopsy report mentioned an electrical shock.

"What about an electrical disturbance? Power outage, power surge, something like that."

"The system reboots itself."

"Does it default to 'Armed'?"

"If the client has set it up that way."

I'd have to ask Pierson about that. I thanked Mr. Personality and said I'd be in touch. On my way out, I picked up one of the brochures from a display near the door. When I glanced back, the man, who never introduced himself—a good habit, I guess, if you want to be truly secure—had folded his paper back to the sports. Another successful day at Guardian Electronic.

• ● ● ● •

A quick phone call to Marlin Enterprises in Atlantic City informed me they had their own electronics department and did not use Guardian Electric. They could not give me any more details about Stein's boat. I got the impression that Marlin Enterprises was not going to be held responsible for the explosion.

I wanted to ask Ms. Piper of the yellow leather outfit a few more questions, so I gave her a call next. She said she could spare a few minutes.

Today, she had on a purple silk suit with a very short skirt, purple hose, and red shoes. The suit jacket had a red silk flower that flopped down as if peering into that splendid cleavage. I wondered if she purposely chose outfits that admired her. She said I could call her Nancy, and she definitely had a gleam in her smoky eyes.

She settled back behind her shiny desk and gave me an impish smile. "So, what have you learned about Renoir?"

Fortunately for me, I'd done a little research on the internet. "Let's see. He was the son of a tailor. He started out painting porcelain. His work combines radical impressionistic brushwork with conventional figure painting and luminous skin tones. He often said that art should be likable, joyous, and pretty. A critic once said Renoir's work is a dream of what life could be or sometimes is for a moment." I was pleased to see that red eyebrow go up, impressed.

"Anything new on the case, or are you allowed to discuss it?"

"You heard about Lawrence Stein?"

"Yes, awful news."

"An electrical mishap, the same as Samuel Gallant."

"Really? How curious."

Something else was curious, and I realized what it was. The lamp on her desk looked a lot like the lamp I'd seen in the picture of Isabelle Duvall's parlor. The base resembled a tree trunk and the glass shade dripped with green leaves and purple grapes. "That's a beautiful lamp. I think I've seen one like it before."

Both eyebrows went up. "Are you familiar with Tiffany's work?"

"I know that kind of lamp when I see it. Where did you get this one?"

"Oh, I borrowed it from the museum's collection. I'd like to know more about you. What's your story?"

Well, she had certainly changed the subject. "Ladies first."

"I'm originally from Virginia. I majored in art history and business, worked for a while at the Riverside Museum in Temple, moved to Parkland when I got the job at the museum. Used to be married. Now there's only me and my daughter, Leslie." She opened her purple leather purse. "Of course I have a picture."

She took out her cell phone, touched the screen, and handed it to me. The sight of her child's smiling face, long brown curls, and beautiful clear eyes made my heart dip for a moment, but then I saw how Leslie Piper's nose was upturned like her mother's, and her face was pert—not as soft like Lindsey's—and with a promise of Nancy's sophistication. I returned her phone. "She's lovely. How old is she?"

"Ten." As Nancy put her phone back in her purse, I noticed the familiar green and gold logo of Guardian Electric brochure peeking up from the depths.

"Thinking of getting an alarm system?"

"Oh, this? Yes, we're checking out a few different companies for the museum. I doubt we'll go with them, though, considering Leo Pierson's experience. As for getting one for my home, I certainly couldn't afford it. It's tough being a single mother. Every time you think you're ahead, something comes up. Usually it's the car. I don't know how many times I've had to replace something on that old Camry." She smiled, really turning on the charm. "Enough about me. Your turn."

"I moved here about twelve years ago from Minnesota. Divorced but in a relationship."

Nancy Piper did not look at all fazed by this. "Congratulations. I haven't had much luck in that department, but things can always change. Plus my job keeps me busy."

We talked about Parkland and other neutral subjects until Nancy said she had a meeting. "Leslie and I like doing things together, going to craft shows, concerts, different things in town. We always check the Sunday paper and see the coming events." Her gaze behind those red-framed glasses was calm and direct. "You might like to join us sometime."

There was that look again. I'd better watch my step. "Thanks. I'll let you know."

• • ● • •

Nancy Piper had gone out of her way to distract me, but I'd fought off women before. I thought perhaps she'd been stalking me, but she said she drove an old Camry, not an SUV. I was almost certain the lamp on her desk matched Isabelle's. I scrolled through my phone and found the picture of Isabelle in her parlor. The lamp looked exactly like the one in Nancy's office, but the picture was in black and white. The leaves were probably green, but the grapes could be any color. There was no way to tell if it was the same lamp—unless Nancy had ties to the Duvall family, or Pierson's. I would find out.

A phone call from Richard Mason informed me he could meet at the Little Gallery at three o'clock tomorrow, hopefully before the dragonfly got him. Then Kary sent a text that Rainbow could meet us at Gallant's house in fifteen minutes.

• • ● • •

I've searched many houses and snooped in many more. Some are garbage heaps. Some are blindingly sterile. Samuel Gallant's décor fell somewhere in between, more hotel than home. It was the house of someone who didn't live there. If Camden had been with us, I doubt he could've felt anything other than boredom. A beige sofa and chairs sat in the living room facing a wide-screen TV. The draperies were beige. The carpet was a slightly lighter beige. The kitchen appeared to be unused. Typical toiletries lined the bathroom counter. The bedroom had a bed, dresser, nightstand, and a closet with Gallant's clothes hanging neatly, his shoes in a row on the floor.

"Not much to go on," Kary said. "No pictures, no magazines, no artwork, which is strange."

Rainbow followed us as we went from room to room. "He used to have some paintings and small sculptures. As far as I know, he sold it all."

I opened the hall closet. Beige towels. Beige sheets. "Was he in debt to someone, or just unlucky?"

"A little of both."

I shut the closet door, resigned to the fact this was another dead end. "Well, thanks for letting us have a look around."

She reached into her little fringed and beaded pocketbook. "There was one other thing." She took out a piece of paper. "It was in the envelope with his will. The lawyer said it wasn't part of the will and he didn't need it."

The paper had a few written lines that looked like poetry. I read aloud: "'Alas, that I should be so base. I beg forgiveness for my part for art that's hidden within art. The cunning means to stun my soul is now unleashed. Revenge will start.' Was your uncle a poet?"

"It's from a song his wife, my Aunt Norma used to sing, 'The Cruelest Heart.'"

"Do you have any idea what it means?"

"No."

"Did you show it to the police?"

"Yes, but I made a copy first. I don't know. That line about art hidden within art. I thought maybe it might be important."

"May we take this with us?"

Rainbow wanted us to have the paper. I thanked her and said we'd be in touch, and that if she found anything else to call me, whether or not it looked important.

Kary and I went back to Turbo. We leaned against the little car and read the lyrics again. "It reminds me of an art song," she said, "which is appropriate, since we're involved with art collectors. Do you think Gallant's trying to tell us who killed him?"

"For someone who was as scattered as everyone claims, that's a big stretch."

She was eager to find a clue, however outrageous. "But he might have been afraid, and writing in poetic code was the only way he could leave a message. 'The cunning means to stun my soul.' Did he know someone was going to zap his pacemaker? Sounds like someone threatened him."

I wasn't sure what to make of this new angle. "Then why didn't he go to the police? I think we're giving him way too much credit. Besides, I have something much more substantial for us to track down." I took out my phone and found the black-and-white picture. "Nancy Piper has a fancy glass lamp on her desk that looks exactly like the one in Isabelle Duvall's parlor. She claims she borrowed it from the museum."

Kary was immediately intrigued. "That's a Tiffany lamp. He was part of the Art Nouveau movement. It's a good connection, but—"

"But what?"

"There are lots of Tiffany lamps out there, as well as really good reproductions."

We pondered this in silence for a few moments. Nancy Piper was doing her best to distract me. Did she kill Gallant? Did she carry around a portable Taser to zap her enemies? What did he know that was so dangerous? "We need to find out if there's any family connection. Nancy's divorced. Maybe her husband was a Duvall. Or maybe that's her maiden name. There will be records somewhere. If she knows about the feud, then she knows about the money. I'll look her up while you see what you can find out about these lyrics. I've got five more days to find Pierson's artwork, so any clue is welcome."

She gave me a kiss. "I'm on it."

• • ● ● •

I took a picture of the paper so Kary could take the lyrics to the Performing Arts Center to see if anyone at the music festival knew "The Cruelest Heart," if the song had any more lyrics, and what interpretation she could find. I drove home to an unusually quiet house. I didn't see Vermillion anywhere and figured she was off on another magical mystery tour.

I got myself a Coke and some peanut butter crackers for a pre-dinner snack and took my laptop to the porch. I started to sit down in a rocking chair and noticed the squirrel was in the bird feeder again, stuffing his cheeks as if winter were staring him in the face. I snatched up the slingshot we keep on the porch rail.

"Squirrel want a cracker?" I let him have it with one of the peanut butter crackers. It smacked him in the butt and popped him off the feeder. He hit the ground running and disappeared up the nearest tree. He sat on a branch and told me what he thought of my attack. He eyed the cracker in the grass, but Cindy was quicker.

"Good girl," I told her as she climbed up the porch steps, cracker in her mouth.

I heard more rustling in the hedge and waited for the squirrel's brother to emerge demanding revenge, but it was only some sparrows. Then I'll be damned if that same black SUV came slowly down Grace Street as if looking for 302. I grabbed the slingshot and a couple of rocks from the driveway as I ran toward the car.

"Hey! Hey, you! What do you want?"

As the SUV accelerated, I fired a rock at the back window and heard the satisfying sound of a crack. My second missile bonked a dent in the back, and my third clanged off the license plate, which was covered with a shiny material that made it impossible to read. The other rocks went wild as I chased the car out of the neighborhood. Take that, Mystery Car! You have been marked.

As I jogged back to the house, Ellin's silver Lexus pulled up in the drive and she and Camden got out. They came up the walk, arguing about the psychic fair. Ellin must have picked him up at work, because he still had on his shoes. I hoped Tamara had survived the encounter.

"If you'd just come for an hour, Cam. I think that's completely reasonable. Now that Graber's decided to make himself at home at the PSN, the fair has got to be even more of a success. You could earn three times as much with the Service than at Tamara's. I don't see how you can work at that shop. Selling clothes has to be the most boring job in the world. Plus you have to dress up. I know you hate that."

He did look neater than usual in his light blue shirt and dark blue tie. He even had on dark slacks, probably his only pair. "Yes," he said, "it's boring. It's also calm and stress-free. No pressure. No floating bodies or missing children."

This did not slow her down. "If you're working part-time, you could come to the psychic fair in the evening. You're always doing things for everyone else."

"No, I'm not."

That's when Pierson drove up. Talk about bad timing.

He flung open the car door and burst forth, holding something aloft, his lion's mane of red hair billowing. "I've brought the perfect thing!" He presented the object with a flourish. "It should be the perfect link to my missing items!"

Ellin's eyes swung about like twin lasers. I'm surprised Camden's head wasn't sliced off at the neck. "Who Is This?"

Pierson stepped forward and gave her a sweeping bow. "Leo Pierson, dear lady, at your service. I'm a client of David Randall's, and Camden here has kindly agreed to help with the case."

Well, call the coroner now.

Camden opened his mouth in a vain attempt to explain, but Ellin let him have it. "I can't believe this! You said you'd never do this again! You said you hated it! You'll help Randall solve a case, but you won't spend a few measly little hours at my fair?"

"Ellie—" he tried, but it was way too late now. She had gone into overdrive.

"How could you do this? You stood right here and swore you weren't using your talents for anyone! Of all the lowdown dirty—"

"Ellie, I didn't want to. It's a piece of art with incredible energy. I couldn't avoid it."

She turned on me. "Then why did you bring this man here? You set this up!"

I held up both hands to ward off any blows. "Hold on, hold on. I didn't tell him to get involved. I can find the thing all by myself."

Pierson stood with mouth agape, probably wondering how his simple greeting had set off such a firestorm. "Children, children. My heavens! I never meant to create such strife." He spoke to Ellin. "Young lady, I came here on my own seeking psychic advice. Randall did not encourage me in any way."

I knew this wouldn't satisfy her. "But you're his client. This is Randall's case."

"Yes," Pierson said, "but I'm certainly entitled to as much help as I can get. These are my valuable treasures, my lifetime collection. I must use every means possible to find them."

Camden got another razor slice glance. "Cam didn't have to agree to help you."

"Ellie, I didn't have any choice. You know how it is."

This was the worst thing he could've said, and he realized it the minute he said it. Ellin's face went to stone.

"No." Her tone could have frozen lava in its tracks. "No, I don't."

She flounced back to her car. Camden followed, trying to make amends. They stood out by the Lexus and argued. I couldn't hear what they were saying, but from Ellin's arm waving and Camden's defensive stance, I knew it was heavy going.

Pierson rolled his goldfish eyes. "I had no idea I was going to stir up such a hornet's nest. Should I leave?"

"They're like this all the time," I said. "She'll get over it."

"I take it that's Mrs. Camden? She disapproves of her husband using his talents in this fashion?"

"She works for the Psychic Service, and she gets really pissed because she's not psychic."

"She's exactly like Florence in *Spring Takes a Fall*. A delightful farce with several mistaken identities. Do you know it?"

"We have our own delightful farces around here. Come on in. They'll thrash it out."

In my office, I told Pierson what I'd discovered so far and showed him the picture and articles about Isabelle. "You had no idea your relative Theodore Pierson killed her for these items?"

He drew back, shocked. "Good heavens, no!"

"You said six people had died because of the dragonfly. You didn't know who they were or anything about them? You knew about this feud."

He sat forward in the client chair and leaned his hands on

the top of his cane. "I assure you, the only thing my father told me was Isabelle wanted him to have the Art Nouveau. It was in her will. And as for the story about a treasure, if I believed that, I would've solved the mystery by now, wouldn't I?"

Camden entered the office, frazzled but whole. "In the interest of peace, I have agreed to attend the psychic fair. Where's your jewelry, Leo?"

Pierson stood and reached into his pocket. "Are you sure you're up to it?"

After a session with Ellin, a little psychic journey would be a springtime stroll. "Hand it over."

It was a silver peacock brooch set with smooth blue stones. I stood by in case of explosions, but this piece didn't set him off.

"It's beautiful." He rubbed the stones. "And user-friendly." In a few minutes, he shook his head. "Nothing. Sorry. No impressions at all."

Pierson looked taken aback. "It's genuine, I trust?"

"Oh, yes, it's real. Some objects don't have any resonance, that's all."

The big man sagged in his chair. "So we're at another dead end."

Camden continued to smooth the blue stones, his expression puzzled. "I really should be getting something. Usually the older objects have a lot to say."

He should've been relieved the jewelry hadn't affected him. "Either too much or too little."

Pierson's attention was all on Camden. "Perhaps if you came to my home, to the scene of the crime? Would you come? Would that help you zero in on the missing objects?"

Camden looked up. He seemed dazed. "What?"

Pierson repeated his question. "Would you come to my house? I think it would help in the search."

He looked back at the brooch in his hand. "Yes. Yes, I think I will."

I didn't like the way this was headed. "Wait a minute. Pierson, you want Camden to come drift in your house, in case of leftover vibes? This brooch is a dud. What makes you think anything else will work?"

Pierson looked at me with his standard bulging eyeballs. "Could you come around ten tomorrow morning?"

I didn't think it would do any good, but Pierson was a paying customer. "Sure, why not? What's one more wild dragonfly chase?"

Pierson was delighted. "Excellent! Thank you very much! I'll see you at ten tomorrow." He hurried out, his cape billowing behind.

Camden's eyes were clouded. There was something else in the deep blue depths, something that looked like doubt. Doubt? What was he doubting? He was always right. The bigger question was how many pills had he taken today?

He correctly interpreted my skeptical expression. "I should have picked up something."

"Maybe you'll pick up something tomorrow. Maybe you'll be foaming at the mouth, okay? Have you been into the Tranquillon?"

"I only took two." He held up a hand. "And before you start, that was this morning at work, and I had Tamara stand by in case anything happened, which it didn't. That peacock brooch must not have belonged to Isabelle. Not everything has to have a curse on it."

"Well, have a seat because I've got a lot to catch you up on."

I told him about the possibility of a matching Tiffany lamp in Nancy Piper's office and the outside chance she might be related to the Duvalls. "So she'd be angry about Isabelle's decision to leave her belongings to a Pierson. Even more interesting, the same black SUV we saw in the park, the one Kary and I had a close encounter with in Baxter's parking lot, was cruising down Grace Street this afternoon."

Camden sat up. Any threat to his neighborhood set him on high alert. "Did you see who was driving? Get the license number?"

"No, but I used the squirrel slingshot to make an impression."

He went to the window and looked out as if to assure himself no one was spying on the house. "What could they want?"

"Pierson may believe all this about the artwork holding clues to treasure is a story, but someone thinks it's real, and maybe they think we have the answer."

While I hunted for Duvalls on the internet, Camden sat out on the porch to watch for intruders. To my disappointment, I couldn't find any connection to Nancy Piper. Piper was her maiden name. Her ex-husband was a Henley. In the vast lists of Duvalls available on genealogy sites, there were no Nancys.

The mystery SUV didn't make a return appearance, but Rufus' bigfoot truck roared up and parked in the driveway. Rufus came in carrying three large boxes. "Brought pizza for supper."

"Thanks," Camden said. "I really didn't feel like cooking tonight."

We followed him to the kitchen, and he set the boxes on the counter. "What's the problem? You look like you been runnin' over hell's half acre."

"Leo Pierson was just here with one of the surviving pieces from his collection," I said. "Camden's bummed because it didn't electrocute him."

"Was it s'pose to?"

"Not necessarily."

"Maybe it wasn't special enough. What's new on the case?"

"Another person of interest is dead."

Rufus scratched his scraggly beard. "So somebody's goin' around knockin' off people, and it all may be connected to this glass dragonfly trinket what's got a curse on it? Business as usual for you, ain't it, Randall?"

"Yes, and now we have a few obscure lines from an art song Gallant left behind." I showed him the lyrics on my phone.

He read them and shook his head. "Don't make no sense to me."

I turned my phone so Camden could read the lyrics. "'Revenge will start' sounds ominous," he said.

"If we had the original copy, you might get something off of it—or not, the way you're operating these days."

Rufus parked himself at the counter. "Well, good luck with that." He indicated the boxes. "If you two want some of this, come on. Once these boxes are open, pizza's gonna be gone real quick."

I had to ask. "How quick?"

He gave me a wink. "Quick as a hiccup."

Chapter Fourteen
"I Do Not Feel More in My Heart"

There was still some pizza left when Kary came home. She was brimming with excitement. She plopped down at the dining room table where we had gathered to eat and pulled a piece of paper from her pocketbook.

"Not only did the festival organizers know 'The Cruelest Heart,' they knew Norma Gallant. They said she used to sing with the Parkland Oratorio Society and was always in demand for solos at the Renaissance and Madrigal fairs in Asheville. Here's the rest of the song, but I didn't see anything pertinent to our case."

She read the paper aloud. "'O loving hands that once caressed my face, I would expire for one embrace, but your sweet words do not erase the cruelness of your heart. Can you but find some kindness to impart? My love for you lives on despite your cruel heart.'"

I agreed there wasn't much to go on. "Sad, but not useful."

"One of the older organizers who knew Norma said she loved to sing and sang right up until the last few weeks before she died of cancer. He said Gallant always came to her concerts."

"Sounds like Gallant did not have a cruel heart."

Kary took a paper plate from the stack on the table and peeled a piece of pizza from the open box. "About the lyrics he left behind—have you had any flashes of brilliance?"

"Not a one."

"Cam, hold this paper and see if you get anything."

He held it for a few minutes. "Nope."

"He's got a hole in his screen door today," Rufus said.

Kary gave Camden a keen glance. "You stopped taking those pills, right?"

"Just a couple this morning."

She set her pizza down. "Cam."

He pushed his plate aside. "Kit had some concerns about a vision he had, and after we worked it out, I took two pills to hold off a headache. That's it. Tamara can tell you I was okay. That doesn't mean I can't get something from these lyrics the old-fashioned way. 'Art that's hidden within art.' Has anybody looked through the museum? Leo's poster might be hidden behind another poster, or his ashtray with other ashtrays."

"Not a bad idea," I said. "There's your assignment for tomorrow, Kary. Camden and I will go touch Pierson's remaining Art Nouveau while you check under all the paintings and sculptures in the museum."

"I'm up for it," Kary said. "Coming with me, Rufe? You can lift the heavy stuff."

He took a swig of his Mountain Dew. "Pump the brakes, girl. I've got real work to do. You want this last piece?"

"Yes, thanks."

He tossed it onto her plate. "You go hunt for dragonflies. I'll be paving another section of I-40."

Kary caught the chunk of sausage that fell off the pizza slice before it hit the floor. "How did your search go, David?"

"Sorry to report that Nancy Piper has no ties to the Duvall family."

"None at all? Shoot."

"But the mystery car came by."

Her reaction was very much like Cam's. "Oh, my God, are you serious? On Grace Street? Did you see the driver? Did you get the license number?"

"No, but I put a few holes in it, thanks to the slingshot."

"So these sightings are not random."

"What's this?" Rufus asked.

"A black SUV has been very interested in us," I said. "Somebody thinks we know something."

His brow lowered. "I'll be on a lookout for 'em. They try anything, I'll see 'em deep in hell as a pigeon can fly in a week."

I couldn't help but laugh. "Damn, that's deep."

"Better believe it, Yankee boy."

Tuesday morning we set out on our missions—Kary to the museum, Camden and me to Pierson's house. I thought Amber Street was in town, but Pierson's directions lead us out to Old Route 60. On a Tuesday morning, the traffic was light. I had a suspicion traffic didn't get much lighter on Old Route 60, which doubled as Main Street for Windale and Far Corners, Fairmont, and Dixley—little rundown towns sitting amid fields of corn, soybeans, and tobacco, with only a deserted train station or stop light to boast about. These little towns remind me of Pond, Minnesota, of Florence and Potter and Evan Fields, except the Southern towns seem to be sinking back into the land, pulled down by kudzu and warm wet rot. The Minnesota towns dry up, rust, and blow away.

Camden and I passed shops dead and alive, gas stations barely breathing, old farms with sagging barns, cows, horses, and a few sheep, all suspended in the thick haze of July, like pollen dust in the heavy air. Weeds grew high around the unused railroad tracks that ran alongside the road. Homemade signs fluttered from telephone poles, signs for yard sales, gospel sings, car races, and auctions. Between the tired little towns, we could see green fields and woods and glimpses of rounded dark blue mountains.

Camden had been quiet during the ride, his gaze far beyond the scene outside the windows.

"Okay," I said. "I'm over it. I'll admit I was annoyed that Pierson insisted on this little road trip, but I'll go along for now."

"That brooch. I should have gotten something from it."

Was he still concerned about that? "So it didn't have anything to say, so what?"

"It's puzzling, that's all."

I slowed down to let a wild granny in a huge old Ford pull out in front of me. After her mad dash, she predictably drove twenty miles an hour. "You're always telling me what a curse clairvoyance is. You should be happy you're not reeling back from some evil vibrations—and since we're talking vibrations, if Pierson's house starts acting up, I'm taking you home."

He turned a worried blue gaze my way. "What if it doesn't?"

"Then consider yourself cured."

We drove on for a few more poky miles until Grandma decided without signaling that she'd swerve onto a dirt road and leave us. "Aw, please don't go," I said. "Look, Camden, we can go forty now."

I didn't really want him to look, because he now had that power stare going, the stare that could bore holes into mighty oaks.

"About Nancy Piper."

"Is she actually a secret Duvall?"

"There's some sort of connection, but I can't see it."

The answer to this seemed obvious to me. "Have you considered the fact that Tranquillon is blocking your visions?"

"Yes, and you'll be happy to know I didn't take any this morning."

We finally got to Amber Street. Pierson's house didn't surprise me. Somehow a big gray stone English-style farmhouse, all flat in the front with little square windows was exactly his style. The door was a treat. It looked like a squid had been plastered overhead, its arms curving down to squeeze you as you walked through.

The squid door was only the beginning. Inside, there wasn't a straight line anywhere. Everything curved—the chairs, the mirrors, the staircase, the clock. Somebody needed to control the horizontal and the vertical. I felt like that guy in the painting who's screaming because wiggly lines are all around him.

I stared at a bureau that looked as if it had been pulled out of taffy and left to harden. "What is all this?"

Camden gave the bureau a careful touch. "I would guess this is Art Nouveau."

"Calm quiet Art Nouveau, or screaming with past horror Art Nouveau?"

"This bureau has nothing to say."

Pierson came forward to greet us. "Come in, come in! I've prepared a brunch in the sunroom. This way."

Weaving our way around the squiggly furniture, we followed Pierson to a large dining room that was practically all windows. The chairs were curlicues and carved flowers, but the table looked solid enough. We had flowery plates and leafy spoons and glassware with vines for stems. The food was good—biscuits with plenty of butter and jam, cinnamon buns, and fruit piled in flowery glass bowls.

Camden put more sugar in his tea and complimented Pierson on the decorations and the snack. "You have some amazing things here, Leo. You really should have a better security system."

"I'm having one installed today," he said. "I thought the other one was sufficient, but, alas, I learned a hard lesson."

Yes, he really did say "alas," the old ham. I was more interested in the robbery. "Where was the break-in? I want to see the master switch for your alarm."

"I'll show you everything after we've eaten." He watched Camden eagerly. "Although, perhaps you've picked up on something?"

"Not yet."

When we finished our brunch, Pierson led us into the front parlor, another large cool gray room. "This is where I had the objects arranged exactly as they were in Isabelle's parlor." Pierson looked at the empty table sadly. "I haven't had the heart to touch it. As far as the police and I can determine, the thief, whom I assume was Gallant, broke this window here, and when he came in, he knocked over this table. Then he took my silverware, green box and all. He tore the poster off this wall, grabbed the ashtray and the dragonfly, and went back out the window."

Camden carefully touched the window and the small three-legged table which had been set upright. He touched the wall where the poster had been. By now, he should have been tuning way out, but he stayed with us.

"I'm not getting anything."

Pierson looked disappointed. I had mixed feelings. On one hand, I was glad Camden wasn't lying on the floor, twitching uncontrollably. On the other hand, why wasn't he getting any signals? If taking too many pills set him off like a wild man, why would only two shut him down?

"Try again," I said.

He touched everything. "I see someone, but I can't tell who it is. I can't see any features. Broken glass. He's very happy he's found what he's been sent to steal."

"Can you tell if it's Gallant?"

Camden shook his head. "I can't tell. Policemen—" He stopped. "Now I'm getting all the policemen's lives. Wait a minute." He put his hand over his eyes as if to clear the picture. Then he touched the windowsill. "He went out here." He looked up at Pierson. "I'm sorry, Leo. I'm not being very helpful."

"No, no, don't apologize," Pierson said. "This is fascinating."

Camden sat down in one of the swirly chairs. He had that puzzled look again, and he rubbed his forehead as if it hurt. "Could I have some more tea?"

"Yes, of course." Pierson rushed off to get it.

"Level with me," I said to Camden. "Are you really not getting anything?"

He leaned back in the chair. "I don't understand this. I'm in a room that should be full of psychic reverberations, complete visions of past events, plus the lives and fortunes of all this stuff, and all I'm getting is a slight murmur."

"I'm telling you it's those pills."

When Pierson returned with the tea, Camden apologized again for being useless. Pierson insisted that he was not disappointed and gave us a tour of his house, which was all as wiggly and screwy. The only items with straight lines were several framed theater reviews from Raleigh and Greensboro newspapers. Some were about Pierson's performances, but others were reviews he had written.

Pierson pointed to one review. "This was my first published piece. I'm very proud of it."

The review of *The Odd Couple* was well-written and full of humor. "This is very good."

"I'd love to do more, but I really prefer acting." He smiled at the review. "Still, it would be a nice little occupation. Oh, look at this one about my performance in *King Lear*."

I don't know a lot about Shakespeare, but I'd heard *King Lear* was one of the more demanding roles. The review was glowing. "Pierson reinvents the role with vigor," was one comment. Another said, "Masterful control of the material." So, maybe old Leo could act, after all. I wondered for a moment if all this about a theft was an act. No, he seemed genuinely upset—or was his emotional state merely "masterful control of the material"?

We went upstairs to have a look at the main alarm switch, located on a swirly little table next to a huge bed shaped like a sleigh with mermaid heads. Like the switch at the Guardian Electronic office, it had clearly marked "arm" and "disarm" panels.

"Pierson, was there any kind of electrical disturbance the night of the robbery? A thunderstorm? Power outage?"

"No, nothing like that."

"You're sure? Think about it. You said Gallant, Nancy Piper, and Richard Mason came to have lunch. Did you show them your alarm system? After they left, did you notice if your system was armed or disarmed?"

"I don't remember. But if one of them turned it off that day, I'm sure I would've noticed and turned it back on. The luncheon was a week ago. Now Cam can't see anything. It's too late."

"Don't give up. I'm going to figure this out."

"I appreciate that, Randall." He lowered his voice about two octaves. "Please don't see this as having lost faith in your abilities. After that remarkable reaction the other day, I had to try Camden out."

"I understand."

"When I heard about Lawrence Stein, it gave me quite a shock. Is it possible the dragonfly is at work?"

"That's what I'm trying to find out."

Pierson's eyes bulged again, and for a scary moment, I thought they'd float loose in tears and leave his sockets. "If you can find the other objects, that's all well and good, but the dragonfly—" He gulped down some emotion. "Do you have any idea what it's like to lose the most precious object in your life?"

Her image formed immediately: white lace dress, long brown curls, the world's sweetest smile. "Yes," I said, "that's why I'm still on this case."

Chapter Fifteen

"On the Day When Death Will Knock at Thy Door"

If I thought Camden had been quiet on the trip to Amber Street, on the trip back, he was nonexistent, lost in some psychic zone, and uncharacteristically irritable. He said his headache was gone, but he still looked confused. I thought maybe we'd better swing by the doctor's on our way home, but he said no. When we stopped for gas, I asked him if he wanted a Coke, and he shook his head.

"Anything? They have ice cream."

"No."

Definitely a bad sign. I got my drink, paid for the gas, and we were on the road again.

"Quit blaming yourself for not being Superman this time out," I said. "I've said all along I could find this stuff."

"I've said you shouldn't take this case."

"Only because you saw too much death."

He pushed his hair out of his eyes. "That was a particularly strong power surge. I don't know how to explain it other than to say it was the curse."

"When did you first notice these surges?"

"A couple of weeks ago." He hesitated. "I can think of only one reason."

I didn't have to have a link with him to know what he was thinking. Since no one can really explain his psychic talent, Camden's decided it must come from an alien source, aka his missing father. I've offered to find the man, but Camden's all, "I don't want to know," pretty much the way I am about my future with Kary. "Tell Dad you don't want to ride around in those UFOs anymore."

The dark look he sent my way was intense. "Don't joke about this, Randall."

"The Evil Seed of Doom."

"Shut up."

"That would be you. I guess we call Dad Doom. Mr. Doom, perhaps. No wait. Camden's a Scottish name, isn't it? Mr. McDoom. I like the sound of that."

"We could call him a heartless bastard."

"Don't hold back."

"He appears out of nowhere, gets my mother pregnant, and then disappears. He might as well have beamed back to his spaceship."

"I believe you might have an issue with this."

He sighed and rubbed his forehead. "No. It's just stupid."

"If Tranquillon makes you crazy and you're still having headaches, you ought to see a doctor."

"Just shut up."

I dropped him off at Tamara's. He could be in a foul mood if he liked. I had an appointment with Richard Mason at the Little Gallery.

I went to the Little Gallery for my appointment with Richard Mason. The Little Gallery lived up—or maybe I should say down—to its name. It was about a tenth of the size of the Parkland Museum, a square brick building covered in ivy across the street from a small Parkland Bank and Trust. But what interested me more was the black SUV parked in the parking lot. Not only did it have a crack in the back windshield, it had a fat rock-sized dent above the right rear tire.

Mason met me by the natural history exhibit. He was a skinny, well-dressed man, nervous and eager to please, with a voice that went up at the end of every sentence. He reminded me of Barney Fife, if Barney had gone to Harvard—thin hair, nose, neck, and elbows, not much chin.

"Mr. Randall? Hello. I'm Richard Mason. I don't mind telling you up front this whole business with Gallant stealing Leo Pierson's artwork and then found dead, possibly murdered, and Stein's boat exploding—it's all very unnerving. How can I help your investigation?"

"I'm checking with everyone who was at Pierson's luncheon a week ago."

"Oh, I was there. Wouldn't have missed it. I wanted to see Leo's collection. Absolutely super. He's really upset. I know I would be."

We paused before a display of North Carolina wildlife. A stuffed beaver peered out over a log at a stuffed gray squirrel holding a nut. Fake turtles poked their heads out of plastic water, and a fake copperhead coiled near the shore. A stuffed blue heron gazed out at us, head cocked very much like Mason's, eyes curious and glassy.

"Do you have a collection of your own, Mr. Mason?"

He looked modestly at the floor. "I'm an artist, myself. In fact, I'm talking with Nancy Piper about mounting an exhibit at the Parkland Museum."

"That's great. Congratulations."

Up came his head. I almost expected the stuffed heron to fly off, startled. "Oh, I have a long way to go, but I'm encouraged by my dear friends who feel I have talent. Leo's one of them. I'm horrified by the theft of his work. Are you any closer to solving the crime?"

"I have a few leads. You have a security system in your home from Guardian Electronic...is this right?"

"Not anymore." Mason looked at the animal display, lips pursed as if deciding how to rearrange the critters. "After what happened to Leo's, I don't trust mine. I'm getting something else." His little eyes tried to bulge. "You think Guardian Electronic is involved?"

"Possibly. Then again, it could've been faulty wiring, like Lawrence Stein's boat."

"Wasn't that awful? You'd think a large boat like that would be safe. Or do the police think someone meant to blow it up?"

"Right now, they're calling it an accident."

"Well, Lawrence wasn't all that easy to get along with." He cocked his head again, maybe to shake loose some memories. "He could be quite cold. But I was invited to parties on his boat several times, so he wasn't completely indifferent to me or the other board members. He did enjoy showing off that boat."

"Can you think of anyone who'd want him dead?"

"No, and I can't think who'd kill Gallant, either. Such horrible news. I still can't believe he stole Leo's art."

"When's the last time you saw him?"

"At Leo's for lunch."

We walked past the beaver and his lakeside friends to a second display, this one featuring a family of stuffed deer, heads up as if sighting a family of hunters. Mason's large forehead wrinkled in thought.

"Mr. Randall, who do you think is responsible for the murders?"

"I think it has something to do with twenty-five million dollars."

He looked as stunned as the deer. "What? Is the artwork worth that much?"

"There's a possibility the stolen items hold clues to the location of the money. It has to do with a feud between Pierson's family and the Duvall family. Had you heard anything about that?"

"A feud? Isn't that sort of old-fashioned these days?" We reached the end of the hallway where a huge stuffed hawk hung over the doorway. Mason gazed at the hawk and shook his head. "Of course, there will always be people who can't get along." He motioned to the right. "Would you care to see one of my pieces? It's in the next hallway."

I expected a nerdy little landscape, or a still life with apples, but Mason pointed with pride to a pile of scrap metal and springs set on a block of shiny black stone.

"I call it *The Last Gasp of Freedom in a Material Society*. It's my favorite piece."

I walked around the mini-junkyard. "I've never seen anything like it."

"Oh, you have to get the full effect. Allow me." He took what looked like a remote control from his pocket, aimed it at the pile, and the piece screeched to life, rotating slowly, the springs going up and down as if trying to escape from such a hideous collection. "All my pieces move. I feel that art should be alive, not static. You can truly sense the angst of a society caught within the grasp of materialistic *ennui*."

"You certainly can."

"There's also a button on each one for a more interactive experience." He pressed a button on the stone and *Last Gasp* halted in mid-screech. I couldn't decide if it was uglier moving or at rest. "I used to paint, but I feel I've truly found myself in the world of movable art. I'm hoping to mount a full exhibition of my work."

Junkyard of the Damned. I took a closer look at the sculpture. I couldn't be exactly sure, but when I was first searching for Samuel Gallant, hadn't Camden picked up a piece of that same twisty copper wire to repair the screen door? Come to think of it, hadn't Andrew Winston mentioned the top of a mobile left behind? "Did you have a piece of artwork at the Princeton Gallery?"

"Yes, one of my earlier mobiles, *Motion Carried*. Unfortunately, I had to retrieve it when the museum closed and some clumsy person had broken the top. People are always calling it modern art, which is not the point at all. Modern art doesn't appeal to me."

If there was a piece of art more unappealing than *Last Gasp*, I wanted to see it.

"Where do you find the materials for your work?"

"Everywhere. Whatever calls to me."

Hmm. Did something call and say, *Meet me at the Princeton where we can plot a burglary and murder?* I thanked him for the tour. "Good luck with your exhibition. I'll keep in touch. Oh, by the way, whose black SUV is that, the one with the broken window?"

Mason leaned over his sculpture to adjust one of the gears so I couldn't see his expression. "That must belong to someone at the bank. They use my parking lot all the time, even though I've asked them not to park there." He straightened. "Was there anything else, Mr. Randall?"

"No, thanks."

I saw myself out and took another good look at the SUV and made note of the license number. The back window was tinted, as well, but thanks to my peep hole, I caught a glimpse of the interior. I wasn't surprised to see pieces of wire, screws, and odd hunks of metal. Richard Mason had been prowling around. What did he hope to achieve?

Then there was my client. When I called, his answering machine boomed with another obscure quotation. "Who calls? The cry goes out from far and wide, and yet there is no reply. Vouchsafe thy message unto me, and I will respond anon."

"Vouchsafe." Now there was a twenty-five-dollar word. "Pierson, this is David Randall. Respond anon. Farewell."

I had to consider the fact that Pierson might have killed Samuel Gallant. Wouldn't Camden have picked up something from the handshake? No, the dragonfly vibes had been too strong. Or did those vibes include his murderous activity? Did Pierson know Gallant was the thief, track him down, stuff his cell phone in his shirt pocket, and wait until it zapped the pacemaker's battery? That seemed unlikely. For one thing, if Pierson killed Gallant, he'd never recover the rest of his Art Nouveau. But maybe he still had his treasures and the robbery was a cover for a larger crime. Was Pierson that good an actor?

I called Jordan and asked him to check on the license number. Then a text from Kary alerted me she was on her way home with news.

Chapter Sixteen

"I Do Not Have To Die For Love"

I got home first and found Wally's van parked in the drive. Wally wasn't hunkered down under a sink or unhinging a shower. He was sitting in a porch rocking chair, drinking a Mountain Dew. I hadn't seen him dry, but he looked pretty much the same.

"How's it going, Wally?"

"Taking a break," he said. "I been at it all day. Tell Cam he'd better take a look into the future and see some winning lottery numbers."

"Not a bad idea." I stood where I could see down Grace Street.

"You expecting someone?"

"I'm waiting on Kary."

Wally took a swig. "You sweet on her?"

"Yes, I am, Wally."

"She's a taking little thing, but I suppose you've noticed Cam's house is full of good-looking women." Wally crossed his fingers over his tubby belly. "I don't mind telling you there's one lady here I especially admire."

"Yeah, Ellin's not too bad when she's calm."

He looked at me as if I were crazy. "Ellin? No, I'm talking about Miss Evans."

"Miss Evans? We have a Miss Evans living here?"

"Vermillion Evans."

I tried to rearrange my features into polite interest. I'm not sure how well I succeeded. "I didn't know her last name was Evans. So you and she—you've been—you have something in common?"

"Hell, yes," Wally said. "Woodstock!"

I would never have figured Wally for a flower child. "How about that?"

"We got to talking, and when she found out I'd been there, she was so tickled. Started asking me all kinds of questions. It's really cosmic, if you think about it."

Cosmic is certainly one of the terms I'd use. "It's nice you two have a love of the Sixties in common."

Wally gave me a wink. "We're hoping to build on that. She's agreed to go with me to the Plumbers Ball next month."

"You'll have to buy a new plunger."

Wally roared with laughter and slapped his knee. "My old one works just fine, son."

I saw a possible solution to the problem of Vermillion. "In your line of business you must go into a lot of apartments and condos."

"Sure do."

"As much as Camden would like Vermillion to stay here, he's concerned about looking after her. He and Kary have been trying to find a place that can take her in, a quiet place where she can meditate."

Wally gave me a serious look. "Really?" He took another big swig of his drink. "Besides the Ball, I was considering asking if she'd like to have dinner with me sometime. Think she'd go for it?"

"Wouldn't hurt to ask."

"You say she needs a place to stay?"

"Yeah, we're not always here, so she spends a lot of time at the park to be with other people."

"Sure do hate to think of Millie being lonely."

"Millie" for Vermillion. Millie and Wally tiptoeing through the tulips, sharing hits from a bong, putting flowers behind each other's ears—my mind wouldn't go any further with that scenario, tempting though it was.

The Mountain Dew had given Wally courage. He finished his drink and set the can down with a firm clank. "I'll do it. Thanks, Randall."

"Good luck." Hopefully, two flower children would not have an issue with free love, and Millie could move into Wally's swinging bachelor pad.

Finally, Kary's Turbo came down the street. She parked and got out, adjusting a large bag onto her shoulder. I met her in the driveway.

"Any luck looking for art in art?"

"No, and I got through less than half of the exhibits. The museum is much bigger than I thought."

She was wearing a white sundress and sandals. "Unless you're undercover as the most beautiful girl in a summer outfit, you're not wearing a disguise. How did you manage to peek under things?"

She reached into her pocketbook and brought out a sketchbook. "Ta da! You always see people and art students sketching the paintings to practice technique. That gave me an excuse to peer closely at everything."

"Let's see your work."

She kept the sketchbook from my grasp. "Oh, no. I have no talent at all. You'll laugh."

"Come on, I need a good laugh."

After a brief giggling skirmish, I won a look inside, and I did laugh at the odd stick figures and indefinable shapes. "Well, it works as modern art. I hope no one was looking over your shoulder."

"No one would be so crass."

I flipped through the pages. "Can we put one on the fridge? Art should be for everyone."

"Of course. Oh, there's Wally. I hope we haven't had another emergency."

She waved and Wally waved back.

"You're going to love this," I said. "To Vermillion's delight, Wally was at Woodstock. He seems smitten, so I'm attempting to unload her."

"That would work. He's a nice guy. Oh, but I haven't told you my big news! I was leaving the Renaissance Gallery when Richard Mason charged in all a-quiver and took the stairs two at a time. Naturally, I followed him, and he went straight to Nancy Piper's office."

"He must have run over to the museum right after I left. Please tell me you overheard their conversation."

"I did until he slammed the door shut. He was all riled up. I heard him say, 'Why didn't you call me?' and she said, 'What are you talking about?' He said, 'They know about the feud.' She said, 'It's not a secret.' He said, 'The money is, isn't it? Plus I'm pretty certain he knows that's my car.' That's when he slammed the door. I couldn't hear what they were saying after that, but they argued like crazy until he stormed out. I pretended I was admiring a landscape down the hallway, and he didn't even notice me."

"Anything further from Nancy?"

"All was quiet. What do you think it means?"

I didn't have time to tell her I wasn't sure what it meant. My phone beeped with a message from Camden. "Camden needs a ride to the Ramada," I told Kary. "It's psychic fair time. Want to go?"

"I'd love to, but preliminary pageant interviews are tonight and I must prepare for all those tricky questions, like 'If you were in charge of the world, how would you address climate change?' You can tell me all about the fair later, and we'll hash out all the details of this case."

We kissed, and she ran up the porch steps to greet Wally. I picked up Camden at the shopping center where we got takeout Chunky Chicken and fries and ate in the car.

Camden spread his fries out on a napkin. "There's enough room in your car for a seven-course meal."

"Another reason to choose the '67 Fury." I passed him one of the ketchup packets. "I met Richard Mason at the Little Gallery this afternoon. He creates pretty horrible metal sculptures and is hoping for an exhibit at the Parkland Gallery. He also seems to know something about electronics. All his gadgets are remote-controlled. Plus he knows about the feud, drives a black SUV with a couple of rock holes in it, and Kary overheard him talking with Nancy at the museum about how we were on to him."

"Case closed?"

"I don't have any evidence that he or Nancy had anything to do with the break-in or the murders. It sounds like they're after the big money, though. They know about the feud and the reward."

Camden ate a few bites of Chick Snacks and returned to the fries. "Maybe Gallant agreed to steal the artwork for a cut of the profits, and they cut him out."

"Nancy Piper had a Guardian Electric brochure in her purse, which she must have picked up from the highly enthusiastic salesman I talked with. She could've told Gallant how to disarm Pierson's system, or Mason could've shown him." I finished eating, wiped my hands on one of the many napkins Chunky Chicken had provided, and started the car. "The thing is, if they stole the artwork, then they have the keys to this twenty-five-million-dollar puzzle. Why haven't they found the money? Oh, Wally the plumber might take Vermillion off our hands. She has been charmed by the unmistakable lure of Woodstock. I hinted strongly that she needs a good home."

"Nice job, Cupid. It might work."

When we got to the Ramada, I parked the car and turned off the engine.

Camden looked surprised. "You're coming in?"

"Wouldn't miss this for the world."

The psychic fair was located in ballrooms A and B. As we went down the hallway, I heard wind chimes and rustling leaves. People gathered about long tables, picking up brightly colored brochures. Ballroom A had many small tables set up for Tarot cards, palmistry, and other readings. Ballroom B had long tables set up for dealers, who were selling crystals, herbs, candles, feathers, jewels, and lots of dragons, unicorns, stars, and moons. I inspected a few of the brochures. As well as the more familiar palmistry, astrology, and numerology, there were brochures advertising Angel Readings, Get to Know Your Guardian Angel, Vibrational Adjustment, Chakra Alignment, Personalized Talismans, and Gemstone Elixirs.

Ellin approached us looking very professional in her gold suit and white blouse. Small crescent moon earrings and a large crescent moon pin sparkled as she moved. "Cam, I have a place all set up for you."

"Ellie, I told you I don't want to take anyone's money."

"We are trying to raise money for the service." She was practically grinding her back teeth she wanted him there so badly. "With Graber breathing down my neck, this fair has got to be a success."

Camden quickly glanced around, but the area was snakeless. "Is he here?"

"No, this is my deal. Now, you promised. Come talk to a few people and tell them some nice things. Nothing drastic." Her smile was tight. "We have people waiting." She hardly spared me a glance. I guess my aura needed adjusting.

I followed as she pulled him past the different booths, easily resisting the advanced energy healing, the out-of-body travel agency, the live antioxidant enzymes, rebirthing, and transmission meditation. A hell of a lot of ways to find meaning in your life, each and every one guaranteed to give you happiness and success.

Ellin led Camden along a row of round tables where people leaned forward anxiously, ready for the words of wisdom from the wispy so-called psychics, the swarthy palm readers, the ascetic-looking shamans, the earnest Tarot card readers. No wonder Camden didn't want to have anything to do with this circus.

His table was covered with a blue cloth patterned with gold stars. There was a blue chair for him and a white one placed opposite. A line of people stood waiting patiently. Before he sat down, he said to Ellin, "One hour, Ellie."

"Yes, thank you."

Camden sat, took a minute, and then smiled at the first person in line. "How can I help you?"

I stood off to one side and prepared for whatever shocks and explosions that might occur. The questions were routine. Is my mother happy in heaven? Where is my grandfather's Civil War rifle? Can you see any ghosts around me? Did my father see me graduate? Apparently, no one had a deadly secret or a violent wish.

I've heard Camden give psychic advice for some time now, and his answers were also routine, maybe a little too routine.

"Yes, your mother is very happy and is watching over you," he told the first woman in line. "Look for the rifle in your uncle's barn," he said to the second woman. "It's underneath a fake drawer in the old chest." He didn't see any ghosts around the man who was concerned he might be haunted, and he assured the young man that his departed father had attended his college graduation. He was calm and understanding, but he sounded exactly like someone giving cold readings the next table over.

At the end of an hour, he'd talked to everyone in line. Ellin came back, thanked him, and gave him a kiss. "Now that wasn't so bad, was it? I'll see you at home. I've got to make sure the panel on Crystal Healing starts on time."

"Sure you don't want to hang around a little longer?" I asked Camden. "Get your soul realigned or your life regressed?"

"No, thanks. I'd better leave while I can. This really wasn't as bad as I thought it would be. I expected a major headache."

And I expected him to be more in tune with the universe. Must be some lingering aftereffects of Tranquillon.

Chapter Seventeen
"The Death of Loves"

Wednesday morning there was still no word from Pierson, and I had a day filled with tasks, the main one being another chat with Chance Baseford. Baseford was in his office at the *Herald*, chewing out a cringing assistant. Something about his coffee being too cool. The assistant was a scrawny young fellow with slicked-back hair and an unfortunate bow tie. In his agitation, a lock of Baseford's white hair stood up over one ear, and his broad face bloomed with angry color.

"I specifically asked for nondairy creamer. Can't you even handle the smallest request? Get out. I have work to do."

The assistant scurried past me, head down. Baseford smoothed back his hair. He looked at me as if I had slithered up from the primordial ooze. "What do you want?"

"A little information. Mind if I sit down?" I didn't wait for his answer. I slid into the empty chair in front of his cluttered desk. "Thanks. It's about the mystery surrounding the specific Art Nouveau items belonging to Leo Pierson. You of all people should know the answer to that riddle."

"If I did, do you think I would be sitting here, dealing with fools and the daily nonsense that is the *Parkland Herald*?"

"Come on, you love being ruler of your empire, and you know it. Two Ls, an H, an M, whoever made the ashtray's initial, and words off a poster. What initial and what words are we talking about?"

I knew Baseford couldn't resist showing off his vast knowledge. He pursed his lips a moment. "The poster by Mucha, I believe is the one titled *Chansons D'Aieules*. That's 'Song of Grandmothers.' But you could also take into account the first initial as well as the last. So you'd have 'R.L.' for Rene Lalique, 'A.M.' for Alphonse Mucha, 'J. H.' for Josef Hoffmann, and so on. Plenty of letters to choose from."

"But someone wouldn't have to have the items if they knew all this."

"I agree." He leaned forward. "Why on earth are you pursuing this, Randall? It's bound to be a hoax. Why, I've tried solving the puzzle and if I can't solve it, I don't see how anyone else can."

I thought of Mason's black SUV circling like a shark and the anxious words Kary had overheard between Mason and Nancy Piper. "Somebody's serious about it."

As I left Baseford's office, I almost bumped into his assistant. The man had another cup of coffee. I hoped for his sake it was the proper temperature.

"I'm all done," I said. "You can go in now, if you dare."

He gave me a sickly smile. "Baseford's a jerk. He's hell to work for."

"I would imagine so. What's his problem?"

"He wants to be God. But that job's taken, so the next closest thing is to judge everyone's artistic efforts. Only 'judge' is far too nice a word. He shreds them, annihilates them."

"Are you speaking from personal experience?"

He took the spoon and stirred the coffee violently, as if enough stirring hard enough could turn the coffee into poison. He lowered his voice. "He's a heartless bastard. A friend of mine had a perfectly respectable opening at the Little Gallery. Just starting out, a fresh vision, nice technique. Old Yahweh in there decided to call the paintings infantile and clumsy. He ruined the exhibit. My friend was crushed. I don't know if he'll ever paint again."

"But that's only one man's opinion."

The assistant gave me a pitying look. "You're not an artist, are you? You wouldn't understand."

"You shouldn't let him bully you. I hear he got his start in the tabloids."

"Hah! To hear him tell it, there wouldn't be any tabloids without his first important efforts in the world of exploitive journalism. Even being editor isn't good enough for Baseford. He has to be the reviewer, the features editor—hell, he'd be sports editor if he knew anything about sports. We thought he'd like someone to take over some of the work. And write some of the reviews. Boy, were we wrong."

I knew someone who wrote very good reviews. "Was Leo Pierson considered for the reviewer's position?"

"Oh, yeah. What a blow up that was! Here we thought we were doing the boss a favor, and he accused us of mutiny. I say Pierson's lucky he didn't get the job and have to deal with all the jealousy. But that's okay. One of these days, Baseford will burn out. Now that'll be front page news." He gave Baseford's closed door a worried glance as if he expected the man to burst forth. "I'd better get this coffee to the Lord before he smites me in his rage."

I went back to my car, my mind full of new ideas. Did Baseford know more about my case than he was telling? Was something going on between him and Pierson? I still had trouble imagining my flamboyant client as a criminal master-mind. Could he have sabotaged Stein's boat? Killed Samuel Gallant and stashed the body? Was he on some angry warpath of revenge for his lost items? He'd joked about the wrath of the dragonfly, and I'd envisioned a clunky superhero. Maybe this was a lot closer to the truth than I thought. Pierson could easily take on another persona. Not a complete chump, either, if the review of *King Lear* was to be believed.

This time when I called, Pierson answered on the first ring. "I was about to call you."

"Pierson, where have you been?"

"Where have I been? What does that matter? If you have to know, I was visiting a friend."

"So this friend can verify that?"

He made some snorts and insulted noises. "Yes, of course! I'm not wandering about picking off members of the museum, Randall."

"Where were you when Lawrence Stein's boat blew up?"

"Here in town, of course!"

"With this same friend?"

Pierson continued in his injured tone. "You don't have to believe me if you don't want to, but yes, with the same friend." He went off on one of his tangents. "I don't mind telling you I find this very disturbing. I feel as if I am responsible. I never should have let anyone know I had such a thing as the drag-onfly. Then it wouldn't have been stolen, and this awful curse wouldn't have been unleashed onto an unsuspecting world. It's exactly like *The Eye of Death*, you know, when the explorers come across the rare pearl, and bodies start appearing all over the stage! 'To your left! I say, isn't that Sir Nigel? And across his chest there blooms the rose of bloody death!'"

I was not in the mood for dramatics. "Who is this friend you were with? I'd like to talk to him."

"Francine and I were at a Dramatists League meeting discussing my future theater. You can check."

"Were you with Francine the night your artwork was stolen?"

"Yes. We've been seeing each other for some time now." He heaved a theatrical sigh, and I could imagine him rolling his large eyes in dismay. "I wouldn't kill anyone, Randall. What's my motive?"

"You're heartbroken over your treasures."

"Heartbroken and psychotic are worlds apart."

Sometimes I wondered about that. "Give me Francine's number."

Francine sounded like a Southern Dame Edna.

"Oh, Leo is one of my dearest friends. Whatever can I do to help?"

"I need to know if he was with you the night his artwork was stolen and this past Sunday and yesterday."

"Yes, we've spent many hours together. He is distraught over the loss of his art treasures. This past Sunday, we dined in Asheboro, at Delman's, a perfectly divine new place. They had the most wonderful spinach soufflé. Have you been there? I can already tell it will be one of our favorite places to dine. Yesterday, we were at my house, and my maid was in attendance, if you need an eyewitness."

I started to ask her another question, but she plunged ahead.

"Leo has told me you're helping him solve this mystery and find his Art Nouveau so he can finally purchase his own theater. I'm so glad he has assistance. He hasn't been the same since the theft of his artwork. I can't imagine anyone hating him enough to steal it. He's a wonderful man. If you don't find anything else, you must find the dragonfly. Even though it's cursed, it means the world to Leo."

She finally took a breath and I jumped in with my question. "Where were you the night the thief broke in?"

"We attended the monthly meeting of the Dramatists League. Have you heard of it? A simply wonderful organization for those of us who love the theater. Leo is one of the leading lights. Now, I haven't done as much acting as he has, but I don't mind telling you I was a hit as Lady Macbeth during our summer season of reader's theater at the Angels of Grace Chapel in Merryville. 'Out, damned spot!' Oh, it even gave *me* chills!"

These two were certainly well suited. I imagined Francine as a large imposing woman with prominent eyes dressed in one of those tent-like dresses covered in big sequined flowers.

"Now, when I move in with Leo, nothing as horrible as a burglary will ever happen again."

"You're planning to move in?"

"Yes, of course. If I had been there that night, you'd better believe I would've stopped that thief. The nerve some people have!"

She proceeded to tell me exactly what she would have done. Twenty minutes later, I managed to thank Francine for her time and hang up. I wondered if Pierson knew about her plans for his future. Sounded to me like the Curse of the Dragonfly was out in full force.

● ● ● ● ●

I got back to the house around lunchtime. Vermillion was poking around in the 'fridge.

"Hey, Randall, what's happenin', man? You want some of this macaroni?"

Macaroni and cheese had turned out to be one of Kary's culinary successes. "Yeah, that sounds good."

"I'll heat some up for you."

Camden's aspirin bottle was on the kitchen counter. I shook out a handful and looked at them. They looked like ordinary aspirin.

"Did Camden take some of these today?"

She pulled the baking dish out of the 'fridge and set it on the counter. "Took some with those Pop-Tarts he likes."

"Did you happen to notice how many he took?"

"No. I reckon he has to be careful and not take too many like he did the other day."

"Did you see what happened?"

She took one of the wooden spoons from the holder on the stove and scooped a heap of macaroni onto a plate. "Kary and me had started to the park, and we were almost there when that little green car of hers whizzed by. She didn't think it was hers at first, but when it went around the corner, she saw Cam was driving. She'd left her phone at home, so we had to run back and get it so she could call you. She told me later he'd taken too many pills. Gotta be careful with any kind of pill, you know. You can overdose on anything. I told him that's what happened to me."

I realized I'd never had a real conversation with Vermillion. I sat down at the counter. "Can you talk about it?"

"Oh, sure. It was about a year ago. I was hanging loose with some friends and we decided to take something called Light Fantastic. It was new stuff and made real pretty pictures in your head. Seemed harmless, but then we took too many and got way strung out. Some other people called 911. I was lucky. Some of my friends weren't." She put the plate in the microwave and turned it on. "I still have flashbacks, but it's better than being dead."

"Have you told Camden this?"

"Yeah, he knows. He says whenever I have a flashback, he can see those pictures in my head, too. But he hasn't seen them lately." The microwave dinged, and she took out the plate. "Here you go. See if it's hot enough."

"Thanks. I have an idea Tranquillon is shutting off Camden's visions as well as his headaches. What do you think?"

She handed me a fork. "I think you oughta take that bottle and throw it away."

After lunch, I took the bottle right to the Drug Palace and let Ted O'Neal, head pharmacist, have a look. Ted's a big cheerful man with a fringe of black hair around an ever-growing bald spot. I've done some store detective work for him in the past, and he's always willing to help me on a case.

He examined the pills. "Yep. It's Tranquillon. I told Cam they were safe as long as he didn't take too many. Has he had a reaction to them?"

"Of course he has. He says he's stopped taking them, but could there be some aftereffects?"

"Best thing would be for him to see a doctor, have some blood work done, check everything out."

Given Camden's intense concerns about doctors. hospitals, and anything resembling a needle, this was not likely to happen. Hopefully, the Tranquillon would run its course.

Speaking of motive, I had something to say to Camden. I went by Tamara's Boutique. It was a small shop, all chrome and silk flowers, with lots of black and silver mannequins in the windows dressed in pieces of silky stuff that looks like oil in water and probably costs as much. Tamara Eldridge was talking with a customer by the dresses, her own dress a slinky gold creation, her long dark hair braided with a gold ribbon. She looked like a Greek goddess. Tamara, Goddess of Good Times. Camden stood at the cash register, ringing up a suede jacket for a bored woman and her equally bored teenage daughter. I had a moment to observe him. He looked remarkably neat in his shirt and tie, and most of his hair was cooperating. He smiled at the woman as he returned her credit card. There was no way on earth he could convince me he was enjoying this.

When the woman and her daughter left, I took their place at the counter. "Any messages for me?"

He shook his head. He rearranged the money in the drawer. "Nothing. Sorry."

"Then lay off the pills."

This earned me a dark look. "I finally feel normal—if this is what normal feels like."

"Nobody knows what normal feels like." I glanced around the store. The few pieces of clothing on display were artfully arranged in subdued lighting, as if this were the Expensive Dress Museum. "I don't believe in the Curse of the Dragonfly, but I need to find it and all the other pieces so you need to be back online."

His gaze was steady. "I told you not to take this case. I told you there was too much death involved."

"Yeah, back when you were surfing the psychic tidal waves. You also said, 'This is not the life you want.' Who were you talking about then?" I knew he couldn't possibly want what was passing for his life these days. "I think you were talking about yourself. Look, get rid of those pills. Whatever they're doing, it can't be good for you."

Behind him, several dresses had been hung back askew. He paused in the act of straightening them. "I know at first

I was concerned about what was going on, but now—" He sighed and pushed his hair out of his eyes. "Randall, you don't know what it's like to have this silence after years of being bombarded by thoughts and pictures. It's eerie. It's like being at the bottom of a calm blue lake."

"That's because you're drowning, you idiot. Give them up. You can't stay on them forever. I took the bottle out of my pocket. "Vermillion saw you take some this morning. How many? Six? Fifteen? Thirty-three?"

"Two, if it's any of your business." He gave up on the dresses and faced me. "The visions were going away. That's why I didn't see the pipes breaking or get anything off Leo's peacock brooch or the things in his house. That's why I didn't see Stein's death or hear from Isabelle or Lindsey. No more visions, no more telekinesis. I can't get anything to move now, not even a pencil or a penny. For once in my life, everything is quiet and maybe I like it that way. As long as I don't take more than two, I don't freak out and run to the PSN."

Just as I had suspected. "But you don't know the long-term effects. You don't know what it's doing to your brain."

"Right now, I don't care."

I slammed my hand on the counter. "Damn it, listen to me! Get rid of them. I know you think you want to be normal, but believe me, this isn't the way to do it."

Tamara and her customer gave me curious looks. Tamara started over to see what the yelling was about. Camden had that steely look that meant he wasn't going to listen to anything I had to say. I had to find another way to get through. "Fine. Go to hell any old way you like."

He turned back to the dresses. "See you there."

Oh, this wasn't over. I knew exactly who he'd listen to.

I went back home and hauled Kit out of bed. "Emergency," I said. "I need a translator."

He stared at me groggily. "Huh?"

"How are you with snakes?"

He rubbed his eyes. "They're okay, I guess. What's this about?"

"An intervention." I punched in Ellin's number. "Is Graber at the studio?" I asked when she answered. "How about his snakes?"

Her voice was terse. "The gang's all here."

"Kit and I want to talk to them."

"If you can get them to leave, have at it."

Since Kit slept in his clothes, he didn't need to get dressed. He dozed in the car all the way to the TV studio, then yawned and stretched and said he was awake. We went inside where Graber was having a discussion with one of the cameramen. Slim and Jim rested in a pile in the corner of their cage.

Kit stopped. "Whoa. You didn't tell me how big they were."

"They're friendly. Can you tune in?"

He approached the cage cautiously. Slim opened one golden eye. "What do you want me to tell them?"

"Tell them Camden is taking too many pills and they need to make him stop."

Kit looked at me askance. "Are you sure? I thought he was afraid of snakes."

"Yes, he is, and he needs to be scared straight."

"Well, okay. If you say so."

Now Slim had both eyes open and raised his head. Jim shifted and opened his eyes, too. Both snakes stared at Kit. He stared back. I watched Graber, but he was still talking to the cameraman. After a few minutes, Kit chuckled.

"These guys are hilarious."

"What did they say?"

"They'll do it, but it'll cost you three rats apiece. Slim wants his sautéed, and Jim will take his au gratin." He grinned. "Not really. Snake humor." He communicated a few minutes more.

I saw Graber glance our way. "Better finish up."

"I got it."

Graber left the cameraman and strode over, his tight smile in place. "Mr. Randall. I see you've brought someone to admire my pets."

"This is Kit Huntington, one of Camden's tenants. He'd heard about your snakes from Ellin. I hope you don't mind. They seem to like him."

Slim and Jim obligingly stretched their bodies up as if wanting a pat on the head.

"Can I touch them?" Kit asked.

Graber stepped forward and covered the cage with the star-patterned cloth. "I'd rather no one touch them except myself."

"They're really neat. Wouldn't mind having them in my act."

Graber gave Kit's grubby black jeans full of holes and slits and his many piercings a disdainful look. "I would imagine you are a musician."

"Yeah, Runaway Truck Ramp. These snakes would be killer."

"I'm sure they would, but you need to get your own."

There was no sign of Bonnie or Teresa, and Reg seethed from a distance. The audience hadn't arrived, but one young woman sat in the front row, checking her makeup and fluffing her hair. Must be Reg's Honey here to support her man in this time of crisis.

"How are things here at the PSN?" I asked Graber.

"We had somewhat of a rocky start, but we're working on it. A special edition of *Cosmic Healing* is in the works for next week—if I can get the camera people here to understand what I want," he added with a pointed look in the cameraman's direction. "I imagine I'll have things running smoothly in a few days."

"Everything okay with Ms. Belton?"

"Of course. I would expect resistance. After all, I'm intruding into her territory. But once she sees how ratings improve, that should ameliorate our relationship."

Ameliorate. A Graberesque word, if I ever heard one. In my opinion, the only thing that would ameliorate their relationship would be for Graber to fall into a black hole. "Good luck with that."

"Two people don't have to like each other to work together toward a common goal, Mr. Randall. We both want the PSN to succeed. That's all that should matter."

Kit slouched back to the car, but I stopped by Ellin's office. She looked up from her computer. "Are they gone?"

"Not yet, but I may have the answer to Camden's pill problem. Kit and Graber's snakes."

She shook her head in disbelief. "Honestly, Randall, I don't want to know."

● ● ● ● ●

I expected Kit to be asleep in the car, but his chat with Slim and Jim had energized him.

"Man, I never tried communicating with snakes. They are way more interesting than cats."

"Did they say when they might stop by?"

"They want it to be a surprise." He tugged at an earring.

"Why don't you just throw those pills away?"

"They aren't illegal. Camden can buy more at the drugstore. Can't you tell what's going on?"

He shrugged. "Got a little insight for you, though."

"Let's hear it."

"I had a go at that paper with the song lyrics on it. Great lyrics, by the way. It wasn't Gallant's idea to steal those things, but he needed money for his niece."

"Yeah, kinda figured that. Could you tell who hired him?"

Kit fiddled with a row of safety pins. "Lots of people."

"What, the Art Nouveau Gang?"

"Two or three. I couldn't see anything else, except Gallant had a feeling they'd double-cross him, so he tried to make a run for it. The lyrics aren't much of a clue. I mean, if you're gonna leave a note for the police, you write down the names of the people you're afraid are gonna kill you."

"So the song's a dead end?"

His brows drew together as he thought this over. "Maybe not. He really loved his wife, and that was her favorite song. I don't know, man. It's like one last love letter. You could ask Norma."

For a moment, I didn't know who he was talking about. Then I remembered. "Gallant's wife?"

"Yeah, ask Lindsey about her."

"Not a bad idea."

He grinned and then yawned. "Anything else I can help you with? Better ask me now. I'm fading fast."

"I don't know how Gallant disarmed Pierson's security system. According to the man at Guardian Electric, it was keyed to Pierson's fingerprint."

"Oh, my bass player knows how to dismantle all kinds of stuff like that. Saw it on YouTube."

"You're kidding."

"All you need is something to disrupt the signal." He sat forward in his seat. "You know in the olden days when all you needed was a magnet to erase a VHS tape? It's kind of like that. When we get back to the house, I'll show you."

At home, Kit wandered into my office and sat down at my laptop. In a few minutes, we had an array of videos to choose from, including an interesting one on building your own EMP jammer, using a plastic box, a lithium ion battery, a high-voltage converter, and some enamel copper wire. The little box buzzed as it turned off cell phones and video games. I imagined a similar little box, if modified, could turn off a security alarm.

Something very much like the remote Richard Mason had used to turn on his art.

Chapter Eighteen

"Consoled and Hoped"

Later that day, I escorted Kary to the church covered-dish supper and softball game. We'd invited Vermillion, but as we were getting ready to leave, Wally showed up in a tie-dyed tee-shirt and his best khakis to ask Vermillion out to dinner. When she learned the tee-shirt was an original from the Sixties, she was thrilled. Wally apologized about the pants.

"I still fit in the tee-shirt, but my cords are long gone. Corduroy pants, you know. Used to wear 'em tight."

Vermillion didn't mind about the khakis. "You look so fab, Wally."

He beamed at her. "And you look neat-o."

"You two have a blast," I said.

They got into Wally's van and we waved good-bye. "This looks promising," Kary said. "Wally's a good man."

"There's a bit of an age gap."

Her grin was full of mischief. "That doesn't hamper *our* relationship."

"Six years, not sixty."

"Oh, he's probably only twenty-five or thirty years older. Age doesn't matter."

"I'm so glad to hear you say that. Where's your covered dish? What exciting food have you prepared for this evening?"

"I'm trying a new recipe called Ham and Cheese Rollups."

"Is it ham and cheese rolled up together?"

"How did you guess?"

As a child, I always hated covered-dish suppers, being dragged away from play or my favorite TV show to sit in a dismal fellowship hall on a cold folding chair and eat weird noodly casseroles, lukewarm green beans, and those pink and orange gelatin desserts with cream on top and nuts floating around inside like shipwrecked roaches. Covered-dish suppers at Victory Holiness are feasts of delight. Fried chicken, potato salad, macaroni and cheese, barbecue, ham biscuits, big chocolate cakes with gooey frosting, fresh coconut cakes, pecan pies, and all the iced tea you could drink. The men haul out the folding tables, and the ladies cover the tables with real cloths, not that paper stuff that rips if you look at it. Folks bring their own chairs or blankets to sit on out under the trees. If it's too cold or it rains, we eat in the fellowship hall, a big cheerful room with lots of pictures the kids had drawn and photos of other successful suppers, not one of those industrial gray cinder-block rooms with a cement floor.

The evening was perfect, still warm, but clear with a breeze, and Kary looked amazing in her white shorts and lace top. Camden was warming up with the church team. Kary and I fixed our plates and sat down on the faded patchwork quilt we'd brought from home.

Before we came to the supper, I made a list of all the letters from Pierson's artwork, and Kary and I put together as many words as we could. While we discovered "ruins," "chains," "solar," and even "feud," we couldn't come up with any phrases that made sense. I told her Pierson had been highly insulted that I would accuse him of any wrongdoing, quoted from one of his obscure plays, and said the curse was on the move.

Kary handed me a napkin. "You don't really believe it's a curse, do you?"

"I think somebody might be trying to make the deaths look like the curse at work, and more and more I'm convinced that the somebody is Richard Mason and or Nancy Piper."

"So now we need proof."

There was a crack as a bat hit the ball. We watched the ball soar over the heads of the other team as our player dashed for first base. Whoops and cheers echoed around the field. I saw Camden sitting with his teammates on a bench behind the backstop. He clapped and cheered with the others. I'd tossed the bottle of pills I found in the kitchen, but I was pretty sure he had another stash.

"Kary, what did Camden say when you talked to him about those headache pills?"

"He said he'd thrown them away."

"Well, he may have thrown them away and then retrieved them from the trash. He's found a sneaky way to avoid outright lying."

That's when Nancy Piper and Leslie arrived.

It took me a moment to process seeing them here. Had I mentioned the church picnic to her? She saw me, smiled and waved, and then came over. I got to my feet.

"Well, this is a nice surprise. Kary, this is Nancy Piper from the museum and her daughter, Leslie. Nancy, this is Kary Ingram."

The women shook hands. "Nice to meet you," Nancy said. "Leslie goes to school with Audrey Garcia, and she invited us."

Leslie pointed toward a group of children by the swing set. "There's Audrey! I'll be right back, Mom."

Nancy had on a red sundress, red sandals, and a necklace made of oddly shaped beads. Leslie was in red, too—red shorts and a cute little red and denim blouse. She joined the kids on the swings, and soon they were chattering like little birds as they sailed up and down. Leslie was tall for her age and suntanned, her hair cut in a short bob that emphasized her resemblance to her mother.

Audrey's mother and father spread their blanket next to ours. I introduced Nancy to everyone and she sat down with the Garcias. The rival team, Gethsemane Baptist, set up camp on the other side of the ball field. The game began. The feasting began.

I couldn't pay much attention to the game. Nancy had angled so she was sitting on one side of me, her leg almost touching mine. It was so obvious she was flirting, even with Kary sitting on the other side of me. Kary put her hand on my leg.

"So, Nancy, did David tell you we're engaged?"

She moved back a fraction. "Congratulations."

This was a surprise to me, too, but I recognized a lifeline when I saw one. "We're planning a big wedding next spring," I said. "We're pulling out all the stops, right, honey?"

Kary kept her smile, a tiny glint in her eyes warning me not to take things too far. "We'll be sure to invite you, if you're available. Do you plan to stay at the museum?"

Nancy waved some tiny sweat bees away from the biscuits. "Yes, I enjoy my job, and Leslie loves her school."

Sweat bees are a nuisance, but they don't bite. It would take twenty of them to make a Minnesota mosquito. I swatted them off, glad we were onto a neutral subject. "You said you and Leslie liked to do things together."

"Leslie needs a lot of things to do these days. She still misses her father, but I don't. He was very careless with money and left me with a lot of debt." She waved her hand again, dismissing the sweat bees and her ex. "But I don't want to talk about him."

Yelps and cries from the ball field were a timely distraction. Somebody had been hit by a foul ball. Somebody else tried to slide into third and jammed his knee. The game halted while everyone's injuries were tended. Camden took advantage of the lull in the action to come over and introduce himself to Nancy.

She motioned to the playground. "That's my daughter, Leslie, on the swings."

"She's having a good time, I see." Cam noticed how Kary had entwined herself around me and raised his eyebrows.

"We're okay here," I said. "How's the game going?" I meant something else entirely and he knew it.

"I'm not much help today."

He wasn't reading anyone, wasn't picking up any thoughts. Damn it, I wanted to say, it's those pills.

Nancy, of course, took his statement at face value. "You're not doing too bad. I thought I saw you hit a double."

"Thanks. That was my one good hit."

Yeah, you've taken one too many good hits. Glad to see you're worried. "Still planning to take in the fair tonight?" I asked him.

Nancy looked interested. "The fair?"

"The psychic fair at the Ramada Inn."

"Oh, yes, Leslie's scout troop is going there on Saturday. Sounds like fun. Are either of you psychic?"

A nicely loaded question. I gave Camden a significant look. "Not today."

He was called back to the field before he could answer, and what could he have said to me, anyway—"*I've decided being an addict is better than being psychic*"?

Kary handed me her plastic cup. "David, would you get me some more tea?"

This gave me a polite excuse to wander up to the buffet tables. Some of the older church ladies were sitting around the dessert table, snacking and gossiping. A round little Hispanic woman named Sara eyed me.

"You get enough to eat, Mr. Randall?"

"Way too much, thank you. It's wonderful, all of it. Kary and I need some refills on our tea, please."

Mimosa, the little black woman who played the piano in church, poured more tea into our paper cups. I used to think she was named after a mixed drink until she explained that her parents had been fond of the pink milkweed-like blossoms that grew on mimosa trees. "Now, who is that red-haired woman sitting beside you, David?"

"Nancy Piper. She works at the art museum."

"Who are her folks?"

This was a question of primary importance. In the South, family is All. Knowing the elaborate family trees and connections was a favorite pastime, especially among the older people. I never understood how they could sit for hours, discussing who was related to whom and why.

"Her family's from Virginia." I knew this would put a plug in the conversation.

They exchanged significant looks. If the family wasn't from North Carolina, that didn't count. The fact that I was from Minnesota had stymied them for a while, until Camden made up some stuff about my Aunt Maude from the eastern part of the state.

Mimosa decided to console me. "Anyway, she's a pretty girl. I believe that's her little girl with Audrey Garcia? No papa in the picture?"

"Not that I know of."

"Thought you was sweet on Kary."

"I am. Ms. Piper's a friend of the Garcias."

They gave each other another look, and I could hear the wheels turning. They'd have me down the aisle with someone before Christmas.

"Want some of this cake? It's Luella's special brown sugar pound cake."

Carefully juggling a plate and the cups, I returned to find Kary had positioned herself on the other end of the quilt, away from Nancy, who was inundated by Garcias.

At my look of inquiry, Kary took her cup and grinned. "I told the Garcias that Nancy was on the lookout for a husband. They have five eligible sons in the family."

"You are a wicked woman."

She corrected me. "A possessive woman."

"Have you set the date?"

She punched my shoulder. "You know that was just for show."

"Can I help it if all women want me?"

"Get real. She wants you on her side if and when things go south."

Out on the ball field, Camden caught a fly ball, bringing the sixth inning to a close. This reminded me of my plot. "Don't panic if you see Graber's pythons in the backyard again. They're planning a surprise visit to reboot Camden's system."

She shivered, which gave me an excuse to pull her closer. "I will not stand in their way. Is Graber going to stay at the PSN?"

"Looks like it."

"If we put our brains together, we can think of a way to oust him."

"First of all, ten points for 'oust.' Second, we've got bigger problems."

I thought of my suspects and victims. I was running low on both. I had to find proof that Richard Mason had killed Samuel Gallant and Lawrence Stein and stolen Pierson's art-work, possibly aided by Nancy Piper, in the hopes of scoring the big money. I still couldn't believe Pierson had anything to do with the crimes. I couldn't believe Camden was taking drugs. I couldn't believe I was sitting here, no further along on the case than before with only three days left.

● ● ● ● ●

That night, I dreamed of Lindsey. She'd been skipping rope with some other little girls and left them to come to me.

Are you looking for someone else, Daddy?

"Yes, a woman named Norma Gallant."

Delores usually talks to the grownups. I'll ask her.

"Ask her if there are any other people who owned the dragonfly car mascot and if they'd be willing to talk to me."

I thought I'd have to wait until another night for her reply, but she shimmered, disappeared, and then reappeared all in the space of a few seconds.

Norma is singing. She's very happy because her husband is here, too.

I felt like slapping myself. I hadn't even considered I might be able to contact Gallant.

"Lindsey, can you get them to talk to me?"

I'll try.

"What about Isabelle? Is she still there?"

I'll look. But Cam isn't singing. You have to help him.

"He's not being very cooperative."

You can do it, Daddy. I know you can.

Words that kept me going.

Chapter Nineteen

"Blow, Blow, Thou Winter Wind"

No one else came through that night. Thursday morning we were all up around nine, except Ellin, who left at God-knows-when to defend her territory. At breakfast, Camden apologized for his bad mood. After the church supper, he'd put in his time at the psychic fair and hadn't experienced any problems, so he felt fine.

I looked closely in his eyes for the lights that indicated he was lying. "No more Tranquillon?"

"No more Tranquillon."

All clear. Still, he seemed a bit off. I wasn't going to cancel Slim and Jim just yet.

Vermillion talked cheerfully of her fun night with Wally. "We're going out to lunch today," she said through a mouth full of crunchy cereal. "Wally says he knows a funky place where we can hang loose."

Not a picture I wanted in my mind this morning. "Sounds like a cool scene."

She turned to Camden. "Think it'd be okay for me to crash at his place, Cam? I'm sure it's way better than the commune."

"You could see if you like it, and if not, you can always come back here."

"Thanks." She poured more cereal into her bowl. "I told Wally to meet me in the park this morning. I want everyone to meet him. It'll be a blast from the past."

Kary wandered in wearing her white bathrobe.

"Everything working in the shower?" Camden asked.

"No problem."

"Wally's the best," Vermillion said proudly. "I'll bet every one of his pipes is in good working order."

There was no straight answer for this, so I kept quiet.

Kary gave me a smile that said 'good choice,' and sat down next to Camden at the counter. "What's the plan for the day?"

I typed a search on my phone. "The Riverside Museum in Torrance, Virginia. It's where Nancy Piper used to work. I'd like to know more about her and why she left."

The Riverside Museum was located at 1026 Riverside Drive, and, according to its website, housed a splendid collection of Civil War art and letters. The current director was Joyce Maxwell. I called and asked to speak to Ms. Maxwell.

Ms. Maxwell sounded calm and efficient, with the slightest hint of a lisp.

"Joyce Maxwell. How can I help you?"

"My name is David Randall, and I'm curator for the Baxter Museum here in Parkland. You may not have heard of the Baxter. We're new and small, and we specialize in Civil War artifacts." And barbecue. "I was told you're an expert in this area."

"I know something about it, yes."

"I understand you have a Nancy Piper on staff who is also an expert?"

Ms. Maxwell's tone changed. "Nancy Piper is no longer with Riverside. You can reach her at the Parkland Museum. However, she doesn't know anything about Civil War collections. She's a business manager. When she was here, she handled our accounts and donations."

"So she's director at the Parkland Museum?" I asked to see what Ms. Maxwell would say.

There was an edge to the efficient voice now, the lisp more pronounced.

"No. Nancy Piper does not have the skills or qualifications to be any sort of director. In fact, I'm a little surprised they hired her to do anything more than manage the books."

"Was there some problem?"

"She was quite vocal when she wasn't chosen to head up acquisitions for our new department. I hope she's happier at Parkland and receiving the attention she thinks she deserves. We had strong words, I'm afraid, so when the offer came from Parkland, our board of directors encouraged her to take it."

"Ms. Maxwell, I also have a particular interest in Art Nouveau. Do you have any?"

"We have some beautiful posters and glassware, as well as a stunning brooch of a butterfly woman. You should come have a look."

"You don't by any chance have any of Lalique's car mascots, such as a glass dragonfly?"

"No, no dragonfly."

"I'd like to see your collection."

"Please come visit. We're open until five today."

I thanked her and hung up. "According to Ms. Maxwell, she and Nancy had a difference of opinion, and Ms. Piper was encouraged to take the job in Parkland. Ms. Maxwell says she's only qualified to do museum finances. If I can get ahold of Pierson, I'll take him to Riverside to make sure none of the items there are his. Who's up for a road trip?"

"I have to work," Camden said.

"And I have Music Festival this morning and preliminary swim suit tonight," Kary said

"Well, you two are useless. I'll have to detect on my own."

"Not necessarily," she said. "While you're gone, I'll keep working on the word puzzle."

We kissed to seal the deal, and I called Pierson. For once, my prodigal client was home and agreed to be ready in thirty minutes for a journey to the Riverside Museum.

Torrance, Virginia, was only a few miles over the state line. I had plenty of time to get there as soon as I swung past Amber Street.

Pierson arranged himself in the passenger seat of the Fury. "I certainly don't feel comfortable being alone in my house today."

"I thought you had a new alarm system installed."

"Yes, and I've been staring at my empty parlor long enough. It's time for some action."

I didn't want to get his hopes up. "There's no guarantee any of the stuff at Riverside is yours."

"I know. Still, an excellent idea. How is Cam today? Couldn't he join us?"

"He's at work."

"He reminds me a great deal of my friend, the one I was talking about."

"The one who was haunted?" That was a pretty good description of Camden these days.

"An overactive imagination, I fear. We actors are highly strung."

When I didn't reel back in amazement, he felt compelled to explain. "I am an actor, you know."

"You've made that perfectly clear. Okay, so who do you think is murdering people?"

"Perhaps Lawrence Stein faked his own death in order to pick them off." At my skeptical glance, he added, "You're supposed to choose the least likely suspect."

"That would be you."

"But I don't want anyone dead! I want my treasures back. I also have a perfectly good alibi. I know you've talked with Francine. She told you I was with her, didn't she?"

"She could be lying to protect you."

"That's preposterous! How can you be so suspicious?"

"It's my job to think like that."

Pierson was offended, and a sudden thunderstorm kept my attention on driving, so we didn't say anything else. My job. It was a great job, wasn't it? Here I was, driving to Virginia with a bug-eyed actor looking for a glass dragonfly.

Pierson felt the need to quote again. "'Heavens, drop your patience down! You see me here, ye gods, a poor old man, as full of grief as age, wretched in both.'" When I gave him the eye, he clarified. "*King Lear*, Act Two, scene four."

"Thanks."

He wasn't finished. "But perhaps more appropriate, from Act Three, scene one: 'I am a man more sinned against than sinning.'"

More sinned against than sinning. I hoped he was right.

• ● ● ● •

The storm had blown itself out by the time we reached Torrance. At the Riverside Museum I parked the car, and we got out. The first thing we heard was a discordant clanging sound like a wind chime badly out of tune. A strange rusty looking sculpture with several sections about three feet long dangled from a hook set in a block of concrete. There was something familiar about it.

As Pierson and I stood looking at it, a small trim woman all in black came out of the museum and met us on the lawn. She noticed us regarding the sculpture.

"Not a particularly attractive piece, is it?"

I recognized her lisp. "Are you Joyce Maxwell? I'm David Randall from the Baxter Museum. We spoke earlier."

"Oh, yes. So glad you could come over."

I gestured to the spastic wind chime. "The artist's name wouldn't happen to be Mason, would it?"

"My heavens, don't tell me he's that well known."

"I've seen some of his later work."

"Yes, this is by Richard Mason. He's supposed to come pick it up, but I guess he's been too busy at his new job at the Little Gallery in Parkland. This is *Anguished Fortitude*."

Anguished Fortitude grated in the breeze. Joyce Maxwell winced. "I try to be open-minded, but I can't see any artistic merit in this piece. I'll be glad when it's gone."

"We'll be glad to take it to him."

She pointed to the top of the building. "I don't suppose you'd care to climb on the roof and take that one, too?" A strange spiky object jutted up, a metal ball on the tip. "Although I have to admit it makes a decent lightning rod."

I introduced Pierson. "We wanted to see your Art Nouveau."

"Right this way."

Like Joyce Maxwell, the Riverside Museum was trim and neat. Everything was clearly marked with white cards in black frames. While Pierson drooled over the bright glass vases and flowing, wiggly chairs, I asked Ms. Maxwell about Richard Mason and found out he had also worked at the museum.

"For a short while," she said, "we displayed his work, but the response was so negative, we felt it best not to have any permanent collection. He wasn't happy about that, so we tried to appease him by having *Anguished Fortitude* on the lawn. When the position at the Little Gallery opened, we were relieved when he applied for that position and was accepted. It saved everyone a lot of grief."

"So the split was amicable?"

"Oh, yes, Richard was always civil, but his vision and our vision didn't match."

As if Mason's vision would match with anyone's. "What was his relationship with Nancy Piper, if you don't mind me asking?"

"They're related in some way."

This was news. "Related?"

"Cousins, I believe, although the way they fussed at each other, you'd think they were brother and sister. They had very different ideas about art."

But maybe the same idea about theft and murder. "Do you know if Mason had any family members named Duvall?" At her curious frown, I added, "We may be related, too."

"I couldn't tell you. Ours was a purely business relationship. He never talked about his family."

"Randall," Pierson said. "Come look at this pin. It is exquisite."

"Is it yours?"

"No. Would that it were!"

"I'll look at it in a minute."

"Randall, these lamps! I'm in heaven!"

Ms. Maxwell smiled at his enthusiasm. "Perhaps you'd like to see our Civil War collection now, Mr. Randall."

Not really. The only war I ever found interesting was *War of the Worlds*. I was anxious to return to Parkland and see how this new information fit into what I already knew. Still, I followed Ms. Maxwell from exhibit to exhibit and listened as she explained where this cannonball had been found and how this poor soldier had died and why these fragments were so important, when they all looked like dirt.

"This is an excellent collection, Ms. Maxwell. First rate. You'll have to come to the Baxter some day and help us with our dioramas."

"I'd be happy to."

"We'll haul *Anguished Fortitude* back to Mr. Mason, if you'd like. And should I take your greetings to Ms. Piper?"

She gave me a look. "That won't be necessary."

Climbing up onto the roof wasn't in my plans for today. We left the spiky lightning rod. Pierson helped me unhook *Anguished Fortitude* and fold it into the trunk. It made a lot of noise. All anguish and no fortitude.

Chapter Twenty
"No Longer Mourn For Me"

Kary sent a text to let me know she was still at the Music Festival, so after taking Pierson home, I drove downtown to the Performing Arts Center, a shiny glass-and-metal building with a faceted dome that covered the inside performance space. The sound of someone over-emoting in song led me to Younger Hall, a vast circular room filled with rows of seats facing a gleaming white stage, where rehearsals were in full swing.

Kary sat with the same severe woman who'd come to the house. "David, over here." She introduced me to the woman, whose name was Anya. "Would you excuse us for a moment, Anya?"

Anya gave us a gracious nod. Kary led me up the aisle.

"How are you managing this and the pageant?" I asked. "I know you're a superhero, but don't you have to bend time to fit everything in?"

"I've got it all figured out. The festival rehearsals are during the day, while all pageant rehearsals are at night. The pageant is Saturday night, and the festival is all day Sunday."

"But as the newly crowned Miss Panorama, won't your duties interfere?"

She laughed. "I'm not Miss Panorama yet, and all she does is wave and smile at ball games and supermarket openings." She pushed open the glass door. "We have to keep our phones off inside. Any progress on the case?"

"According to Joyce Maxwell at the Riverside Museum, everyone was glad to see Richard Mason and Nancy Piper move on to other museums. She also told me they are related, cousins, she thinks. We need to find out if Mason's family includes any Duvalls."

We stayed in the shade of the center's ornamental trees as Kary clicked on phone.

"This might take a while." She glanced at the time. "I'd better get back to Anya, but I'll keep looking."

"I'm heading back to the Parkland Museum to see what Nancy has to say."

She smiled a teasing smile. "You sure you don't want to come back in and listen for a while?"

"No, thanks. One serving of 'O cessate,' or whatever that was, is enough."

"'O cessate di piagarmi.'"

"Which means?"

"'Please stop bothering me.' It sounds better in Italian."

• ● ● ● •

Please stop bothering me is probably what Nancy Piper was thinking. As I approached her office, I could hear her quarreling with someone. Slowing my steps, I recognized Richard Mason's angry voice.

"I don't care what you think, I'm going to do it."

"We've been through this," Nancy said. "What you want to do is stupid and selfish. It isn't part of the plan."

"To hell with the plan! They don't have any of the artwork, and even if they did, they'll never figure out the puzzle."

"In case you hadn't noticed, Richard, we haven't figured out the puzzle, either."

"Because of that dragonfly! I keep telling you, it's the key."

"Well, I don't know where it is."

"You'd better not be lying to me!"

Mason came charging out of the office and down the hallway. He was so angry he didn't see me. I followed him. He ran down the stairs and smacked the glass door open. He paused on the sidewalk, taking deep breaths, his fists clenched.

"Mr. Mason," I called cheerfully, "glad I caught you." As he whirled around, I said, "I brought *Anguished Fortitude* from the Riverside Museum."

He took a moment to get control of his emotions. "Oh, thank you! I've been meaning to pick it up, since it obviously isn't wanted," he added darkly. "Where is it?"

"It's in the trunk of my car. I can bring it by the museum, or we can transfer it to your car."

He paused. "If you'd be so kind as to bring it by the museum. Not just now, though. You'll have to excuse me. I've just had an extremely frustrating meeting with Ms. Piper. You've been to the Little Gallery. You've seen the lack of visitors. How is my work ever going to be noticed by people if there aren't any people to notice it? I keep trying to convince Nancy to get my work into the Parkland Museum, but she refuses to help me. This on top of Baseford's horrid criticisms—it's a wonder I can create at all."

So Baseford had gotten to him, too. "Ms. Maxwell said you and Nancy worked together at the Riverside Museum."

"Yes, worked together back when we wanted only the best for each other." His voice was bitter. "I was there for her all during her divorce, and she encouraged me through some very rough artistic patches. I am very disappointed our relationship has become so strained."

"You're cousins, right?"

"Distant cousins." He didn't say, why the hell would you want to know that? But he was thinking it. If somewhere along the line he was a Duvall, he had to be adding things up. "Thank you so much for bringing *Anguished Fortitude* home. If you'll excuse me."

I started to go inside the museum, glancing back in time to see him take out his phone, jab in a number, and start a terse conversation.

"It's time," I heard him say. "Do it now."

Oh, I'd set something in motion and it wasn't a rusty piece of metal.

I went up to Nancy's office and knocked on the door. Nancy was composed, arranging papers on her desk into a neat stack.

"Oh, hello, David."

"The Mason rocket just launched past me. What was that all about?"

She stacked the papers again and set them aside. "We've had this discussion a thousand times. Richard wants his work displayed here, and right now there's nowhere to put it. He thinks we should move something out to make room for his sculptures. I think his sculptures are fine where they are."

So this was their cover story. Mason's outrage about his art had been genuine, though.

Nancy picked up her tablet. "I'm going to check on some things. Care to come with me?"

We walked down to the statue gallery, a long pale-blue hallway filled with marble and bronze figures. Nancy touched in notes on the tablet. Today's admiring outfit was a tight jade-green suit over a tight gold bodysuit. Her glasses had green frames that matched her suit.

"I didn't realize you and Mason were related," I said.

Her expression gave nothing away. "Oh, some distant cousin."

I followed her past two more marble fauns and a javelin thrower. We paused for Nancy to check an odd sculpture that looked like a bird, but when I approached it from the other side, it looked more like a fish. "What's this?"

"That's a piece by a contemporary artist, Jon Vass. He calls it *Fulfillment.*"

"Looks like a bird on one side and a fish on the other."

"Keep looking."

"Now I see an insect of some kind and maybe a girl's face?"

"Vass says people see what they want to see, like finding familiar shapes in the clouds. He has a painting with a similar theme in one of the other galleries. It's a whole shelf of books, but the closer you look, the more objects you see, until it's no longer books. The kids enjoy it. It's like one of those hidden objects puzzles."

Art that's hidden within art.

We moved to a large display case where a light flickered. Nancy frowned. "I thought I fixed that."

The case was full of tiny Japanese sculptures, owls, turtles, and fat little fishermen. One of the lights was having an epileptic fit. Nancy dug into her pocket and brought out a key. She set her tablet down and unlocked the case. In a few minutes, she had twisted some wires and wiggled the bulb and the light remained steady.

Did everyone on the museum board have a degree in electronics? "You're pretty good with that."

She locked the case and retrieved her tablet. "You have to know a little of everything to keep a place like this running." She brushed her hand on her skirt. "This whole case needs rewiring."

"Would you be able to do that?"

"I think so. It's fairly simple."

Nothing about this case was fairly simple.

•●●●•

I picked up Kary for lunch and took her to How Soon's House of Food where we sat down in one of the red leather booths in the dim little restaurant and enjoyed chicken lo mein, fried rice, and sweet and sour pork. I told her about the argument I'd overheard and how Mason had called someone to "Do it now."

"Sounds like something's getting ready to happen," she said.

"It also sounds like they don't have the artwork and can't solve the puzzle, just like us. But Nancy was angry Mason wasn't following the plan, so they have a plan. If only this plan would lead to proof against them."

She wound the last long lo mein noodle around her chopstick. "I hate to be the bearer of bad news, but I didn't find any Duvalls in Mason's background, either."

"How about the puzzle letters?"

"Oh, I've made dozens of words, but still no combination makes sense." The waiter brought a little tray of fortune cookies, and she thanked him. "Maybe the answer's in here." She broke open a cookie and pulled out the little paper. "Okay, mine says, 'There will be great changes in your life.' An excellent fortune. It goes right along with my career plans."

I chose a cookie, broke it, and unfolded the paper. "Mine says, 'You will get your wish.'"

"That sounds nice. What do you wish for—besides an answer to this case?"

What did I wish for? Well, Kary, of course, but here she was, thank goodness. To solve the case? I was getting closer to an answer. To find the dragonfly and end the curse? Hopefully that was part of the answer. But on a more personal note, like Camden, didn't I want a family? But I had a family, didn't I? I had an almost wife, a somewhat brother, a couple of large redneck cousins, and a daughter on The Other Side.

Kary waited expectantly, so I said, "I don't know about a wish, but things are pretty good right now."

How had that article about Renoir put it? "A dream of what life could be—or sometimes is for a moment."

I could deal with that.

"Camden said Ellin wanted him for another hour at the fair. I haven't had a chance to see the fair," she said. "How is it?"

"We can stop by right now," I said. "Prepare to be amazed."

The fair was surprisingly crowded for early afternoon. We wandered around, checking things out when Ellin came over. I never thought pink was her color, because when I think of pink, I think of things that are sweet and soft and nice, but she looked very good in a pink suit and white blouse. Even her shoes and stockings were pink. She looked like some very sexy cotton candy.

"Things are going really well, Ellin."

Any snide remarks she had planned for me died in the light of this compliment. "Thank you. Over three hundred people, so far."

"Is Camden here?"

"Yes, he's at his table. Kit just stopped by, too."

"I see you have a glassblower," Kary said. "I didn't expect that at a psychic fair."

"He's a psychic glassblower. Angels, UFOs, and unicorns."

"I'll have to check this out, David. Be right back."

Ellin watched her go. Then, abruptly, she said, "You and I both know Cam is a terrible liar. He's still taking those pills. Maybe it's Tranquillon, maybe it's not. He's getting something from somewhere!"

"Okay, calm down and tell me what's going on."

There was an announcement that a demonstration of Celtic

music was about to begin. The crowd shifted. Ellin and I moved out of the way behind a table full of brochures trumpeting the merits of channeling your own past selves.

Ellin straightened the already-straight stacks of brochures. "He's way too calm. It's like he's sleepwalking. Tamara said he'd been like that all morning."

"Tranquillon's taking its time getting out of his system."

"I don't think so." She set down the next stack of brochures with more than enough force. "I will never understand why he considers his gift such a burden, why he feels he has to go to such lengths to suppress it. He's helped so many people, seen so many good things. I can't imagine anyone not wanting to be psychic."

Since this was what she wanted more than anything, her statement was not surprising. "I'll talk to him. What's the latest on Graber? Has he been causing any more trouble at the station?"

"I don't want to talk about Matt Graber."

One of her assistants ran up. "Ms. Belton, you need to come right away. Cam is—you need to see this!"

Ellin hurried off with me close behind. Ballroom A was filled with amazed fairgoers gaping at the little tables that flew about, their starry tablecloths flapping like wings. Joining the tables were flocks of Tarot cards, colors flashing as they wheeled and swirled above. Kit was grinning, but the other psychics, the palm readers, and the shamans stood a cautious distance back from Camden, who stood in the middle of this whirlwind, fireworks blazing in his eyes.

"And now, this!" He waved a hand and the tables dipped and swerved and then landed. The tablecloths billowed like parachutes and settled back onto the tables. "And this!" The cards sailed down to form little houses that then collapsed into neat stacks. There was a huge round of applause. Camden bowed and so did the chairs.

Ellin, torn between concern and delight, waited until the applause died down. "Thank you, Camden. Everyone, I'm glad you enjoyed this special demonstration."

"Oh, I'm not finished," he said. "Let me see how many of you folks I can lift."

A few members of the crowd stepped forward eagerly, but Ellin caught his arm. "We don't have flying insurance, Cam. That was enough for now."

He gave her a big kiss and spun her around. "I feel terrific. What else would you like me to do? Want to dance? I feel like dancing."

Ellin gave me a frantic glance. After the rush came the crash. Might as well get ready. "Camden," I said, "why don't you come with me and sit down for a while? Kit can take over for you here."

Kit was all admiration. "You have got to teach me how to do that, Cam."

"Maybe later," I told him. "Just give these people regular psychic advice, will you?"

Kit sat down at one of the little tables where a line formed immediately. Ellin and I took Camden to the hallway. A few Tarot cards fluttered behind him like sparrows hoping for a handout, but he was already deflating. By the time we sat him down in one of the chairs, the fireworks faded and the cards spiraled to the carpet.

"I don't understand," Ellin said. "He was calm earlier. I told you, too calm."

"He must have had another power surge," I said. This one hadn't been as intense. "That's what happened, isn't it, Camden?"

"Whew! What a rush." He sat forward and put his head in his hands. "I felt it coming, and it took over before I could stop it."

"You're back a lot sooner," I said. "Maybe the surges are decreasing."

"Maybe." He didn't sound convinced.

Ellin gave him a hug. "Kit can fill in for you until you feel better."

I wasn't surprised by her insistence he stay. I offered to take him home, but he said he was okay. When Kary returned from the glassblower's booth, I filled her in on the latest telekinetic spectacle. She gave Camden one last worried look as we walked away. "What are we going to do?"

"Why don't you and I see if we can find his stash?"

At home, we searched all the drawers and closets, all the kitchen cabinets, and behind all the books in the bookcase. I even felt down behind the sofa cushions, and Kary looked in the piano bench.

She let the lid fall with a bang. "What is he taking and where did he get it? That's what I want to know."

"Leave him to Ellin."

After about an hour, we gave up our search. Kary had to get to her pageant rehearsal. Camden and Ellin came in much later and climbed the stairs without a word. I figured they'd hammered things out in the car. I'd have to wait until tomorrow to see who'd won the drug war. My money was on Ellin.

Chapter Twenty-one

"Sorrow, Stay"

I would've lost my money.

Ellin was in full-blown tornado mode the next morning. I was waiting for my toast to pop up when she stormed into the kitchen. "I can't believe he doesn't see what's happening!"

"I take it you couldn't convince him?"

She managed to get most of her coffee in her cup. "He insists nothing's wrong and refuses to go see a doctor." She stirred the coffee with enough force to create a whirlpool. "I can't deal with this right now. I have to make certain the fair is a success or we will all be out of house and home, and Graber will have won."

I took a seat at the counter to avoid any explosions. "Can you calm down for a minute? I know you're the primary breadwinner here, but we're not approaching financial ruin."

"Have you seen the household expenses for this month?"

"I've still got a little money from my last case. We're not in any danger of going under—well, Camden might be, but we'll get him out."

Usually, Camden is the recipient of her sudden emotional turnarounds, but this time, I got the full benefit. She burst into tears.

"Whoa, hold on!" I grabbed a tissue from the box on the counter. "Ellin, it's okay. He'll be all right."

She snatched the tissue and wiped her eyes. "He won't listen to me. Last night, he didn't say anything. He went to bed, and he's still asleep, or pretending to be."

"When does he ever listen to you?"

I was trying to lighten the mood, but her glare told me I was pushing it. "I know you think I care more about my job than I do about Cam, but if he's shut me off, I can't do any good staying at home, moping around and waiting for him to snap out of it." She gulped back a few more tears. "He hasn't been singing, either."

Lindsey had said the same thing. I couldn't remember the last time I'd heard him burst into song. Usually, I have to tell him to give it a rest.

"What can we do, Randall?"

"You're going to go to work and take care of the fair. I'm going to continue my investigations and see if Camden's trying out some new drug, and where he's getting it. Once we cut off his supply, he'll have no choice but to quit." I didn't tell her I still hoped Graber's snakes would put in an appearance.

Her voice was wobbly. "That's a pretty good plan." She tossed the tissue into the garbage can and took a drink of coffee. "I guess I've been a little stressed lately."

"A little."

"You'll keep me posted."

"Sure thing."

"Thanks." She took another drink and set the cup down. She gathered her purse and her attaché case from one of the dining room chairs. Before she left, she paused as if she'd like to express a little more gratitude, but one thank you was all I was going to get.

As Ellin hurried out, Vermillion drifted in, beads jingling, her red hair tied back with a paisley scarf.

"Hey," she said, "Wally says you encouraged him to ask me out. That was real nice of you."

"I thought you two might be able to make a rainbow connection."

"Yeah, well, we did, thanks." She settled onto a stool at the counter.

"Vermillion, do you know what Camden is taking now?"

She shook her head causing her giant hoop earrings to clunk against the sides of her head. "Told you, I'm clean."

"Has anyone been by the house, anyone you might not have seen before?"

"I've been in the park, so I don't know."

"When you're here, will you be on the lookout?"

"You want me to tune in to what's happening?"

"Yes, for real." My phone rang. The caller ID said, *Parkland Herald.* I didn't recognize the caller's voice.

"I found something you might be looking for."

Could this possibly be a breakthrough? "Who is this?"

"Baseford's office. A green box on the bookshelf behind his desk."

I started to ask another question, but the man hung up. "That was about the case, Vermillion. I'd better get bookin'."

I'd gotten into my car when my phone beeped again. It was Pierson.

"Randall, I've had the most amazing phone call. Someone said I should look in a green box in Chance Baseford's office. What could it mean?"

"I had a similar call. I'll meet you there."

"Is it possible Baseford has my Art Nouveau? But what could he possibly hope to gain? Everyone knows those things are mine. I don't understand any of this!"

Neither did I. "This could be a prank, Pierson. Don't get your hopes up."

•●●●•

Chance Baseford was not happy to see either of us. "What is it now?"

I looked at his bookshelves. Like the optical illusion of *Fulfillment*, a small green box sat on the second shelf, innocently masquerading as one of Baseford's many books. Without explaining or asking, I walked over to the shelf, took the box down, and opened it. Inside lay the set of little leafy Art Nouveau silverware.

Pierson gave a choked cry and snatched the box from my hands. He cradled the box in his arms. "Thief! How dare you take my priceless treasures?"

Baseford looked stunned but not as guilty as I'd hoped. "I—I don't know how that got there, I swear! I've never seen that box before!"

"You'll probably want to make up a better story for the police."

"Wait! I'm telling you I did not take anything!"

Pierson tore around the office in a frenzy. "Where is my poster? My ashtray? My dragonfly?"

"I didn't take them! I didn't take anything!" Baseford's face was gray. "I swear I didn't know that box was there. Someone must have put it there."

For the first time, Chance Baseford wasn't sneering or preening. He looked genuinely upset.

Pierson shook with indignation. "Liar! You've hated me for years, and this was your feeble attempt to get back at me for some imagined slight. Well, it won't work. Call the police, Randall."

Baseford attacked. "How did you know that box was in my office? You're in on this together. It's a setup. You won't get away with it. I'll call the police myself."

"Thief! Dastardly villain!"

"It's your word against mine, Pierson. If you accuse me of theft, I'll say you planned all this to discredit me. I know you wanted my job. The *Herald* will do a full investigation. They'll prove I had nothing to do with this."

I kept myself between the two men. "Who would plant these things in your office? Who has access?"

"Anyone could come in here. As for planting evidence, you need look no further than this man right here." He pointed a trembling finger at Pierson. "I did not steal those stupid spoons, and I did not steal anything else. That box was planted here. I am innocent of any crime. Get out."

"Randall, have this cad arrested!"

"Both of you, calm down," I said. "There's no real proof Baseford took your spoons, Pierson. When the person called you, what did he say?"

"He said, 'I found something you might be looking for. It's in a green box in Chance Baseford's office.'"

Exactly what the mystery source had told me. "Baseford, have you discussed the robbery with anyone? Who else besides you knows about Pierson's missing artwork?"

"Everyone who reads the paper, you dolt. Take your idiot client and get out of my office."

Pierson clutched the box. "This isn't over. I'll find some way to prove you took them."

"And I'll prove you set this up. Get out!"

Pierson kept a tight hold on the box all the way back to the parking lot. "How can we expose Baseford as the thief he is? We must force him to return my dragonfly."

"I'm not sure he has the dragonfly."

"You think he's telling the truth?"

"It's as you said. He has nothing to gain by stealing your artwork. He wouldn't jeopardize his cozy job at the *Herald*. I think he was set up."

"Then who has the rest of my treasures?"

"Are you sure you don't know anything about this?"

He stopped in his tracks and reacted with theatrical astonishment. "*Me?*" I'm surprised he didn't say, "*Moi?*" "We've been through all this, Randall. You know full well this is the dragonfly at work."

"No, I don't. I don't believe in curses. Someone planted your silverware in Baseford's office to throw blame his way. No curse. Just some clever thieves who are trying to find the money."

The expression in his huge eyes was mournful. "I can't imagine anyone hating me that much. I feel exactly like the fisherman in *The Wake of the Storm.* 'My nets lie empty, and all have now deserted me, even those I considered friends and companions. How unkind is fate, as unpredictable as the ever-rolling sea.'" He looked down at the box of spoons, and his large hands caressed the lid. "At least my silverware has come back to me."

"We'll find the other things." I wished I could be more certain.

• ● ● ● •

Pierson took his silverware home where he no doubt spent the rest of the day staring at his spoons. I found Jordan's squad car parked in the driveway of 302 Grace, and Jordan parked in one of the rocking chairs on the porch, his short black hair at attention and his small blue eyes narrowed.

"You're racking up the points today. Chance Baseford called with a complaint. You been roughing up the old curmudgeon?"

"'Curmudgeon.' Good one."

"You and Cam are not the only ones with a vocabulary. What's going on, Randall? How many people have to die before you get the message?"

I sat down in another rocker. "I have the right to remain silent, unless you'll share some information. I think Baseford's telling the truth. Someone planted the missing spoons in his office."

"So, does this someone also have the rest of the stolen articles, and if so, would he or she be obliging and plant them, too?"

"Wishful thinking. Whoever it was, called me and Leo Pierson with the tip. He said, 'I found something you might be looking for. It's in a green box in Chance Baseford's office.'"

Jordan rubbed his chin. "Baseford has so many enemies in town, I imagine there are hundreds of people who wouldn't mind seeing him in trouble. What's the connection to Pierson?"

"Professional jealousy. At one time, Pierson was considered for Baseford's job."

"When did you get your tip about Baseford?"

"About an hour ago."

"No caller ID?"

"The person called from the *Herald*. Could be any one of a hundred employees." All of whom hated Baseford and wished him ill. It would be a daunting task to interview that crowd.

Jordan's eyes narrowed further as if daring me to lie. "And you don't have a clue where the rest of Pierson's stuff is."

"Not at the moment. Now it's your turn. Anything new on the Stein case?"

"They found more pieces of the boat, including something that looks like a television remote. But since Stein had not one but four televisions on board, a TV remote is not surprising."

"What does it look like?"

"It's nothing special. A small silver box about five inches long."

Richard Mason's remote control for his artwork had been a small silver box about that size. Hadn't he said something about being invited to parties on Stein's boat? A good opportunity to snoop around to see what he could zap. Or he could've rewired the remote so the next time Stein turned on one of his TVs, everything exploded.

"That's all the sharing I'm up for today." Jordan's chair creaked as he adjusted position. "How're things with Cam?"

"He's off Tranquillon, but there may be something else, and I don't know where he's getting it."

"Well, say the word, and I'll help with the intervention." His phone beeped, and he answered it. "Be right there." He wedged himself out of the chair. "Have you ruled out that weird hippie woman he's got living here?"

"Yes."

Jordan shook his head as if he couldn't understand why Camden felt the compulsion to take people in off the streets. "Someday I need to have a word with him about who he lets move in here." He pointed at me. "That includes you."

Chapter Twenty-two
"*Let Me Die*"

I was wondering what to do next when Turbo came up Grace Street and turned into the driveway. Kary got out and came up the walk, her arms full of music books.

"I am through with the festival for the day," she said. "Everyone is as ready as they're going to be."

I took the stack of books. "You must have left the house at dawn."

"I had to be there by seven-thirty. Did I see Jordan's squad car heading out?"

"He stopped by for an exchange of information."

"Anything useful?"

"Not really, but I found Pierson's silverware in Chance Baseford's office. Looked like he'd been set up. Pierson and I got the same anonymous tip." I held the screen door for her, and we went inside to put the books on the piano bench.

"In Baseford's office?"

"Hidden in plain sight." I thought of Pierson's little silverware and how the green box had been right on the bookshelf. Was the ashtray at a flea market on a table with other ashtrays? Was the dragonfly sitting around a pond with other dragonflies?

"Why would someone do that?"

"Baseford's got plenty of enemies."

Kary hung her pocketbook on the hall tree. "Well, this complicates things, doesn't it? Have you seen Cam today?"

"I guess he's still in bed."

I started toward the island when footsteps pounded down the stairs, and Camden ran into the kitchen, wild-eyed.

"Snakes! In my bedroom! They came down the chimney! Get them out!"

At that moment, Slim and Jim Python came slithering down the stairs.

"Oh, Lord." Kary retreated to the island. Camden made a dash for the front door, but the larger snake blocked his way.

"They're harmless, remember?" I said. "Calm down and listen to them."

"They scared the hell out of me!"

Way to go, guys, I thought, as the smaller snake passed me and reared up in front of Camden. "Relax and listen. It's probably tree time."

The smaller snake, Slim, cocked his head and peered into Camden's eyes. Camden was breathing hard, but slowly his expression changed. "They say I'm going to die."

"What, now? We haven't had the official death report from Kit."

"I'm going to die if I keep taking pills."

A bit harsh, but if it worked, okay. "Sounds like good advice."

Camden spoke to the snake. "How did you know? You came all this way back to Grace Street to warn me?" Jim, the larger snake, moved closer and stared up at him. "What? Wait, no. You're going to keep coming back until I quit?" Slim nodded and must have said something else. "You're going to follow me around—you're going to sleep in the *bed* with me?" He shuddered. "You don't have to do that. I quit. I promise." He got a double-barreled stare from both snakes that made him hold out his hands as if keeping them away. "I promise. I haven't taken any today."

"Where are they?" I asked.

"In my room in one of my sneakers."

I went upstairs and found a small plastic bag with three red pills. When I returned, Kary was still watching from a safe distance in the island, and Camden was gingerly patting Slim on the head.

"Yes, okay, I promise," he said again. "Now you need to get back to Graber before he misses you." He edged past Jim to open the screen door. "There you go."

The snakes paused for one more hard look before rippling out and down the porch steps. Camden braced himself on the hall tree, one hand to his heart. "Oh, my God."

Kary put her arm around his shoulders, led him to the sofa, and sat him down. "You're okay. You just need to do what Slim and Jim said, and you'll be fine."

He took a deep breath in and out. "I was asleep and heard a noise. I turned over and there they were, right at eye level, grinning."

Surprise! If that didn't do the trick, nothing would. "What were their parting words?" I asked.

"'We'll be watching you.'"

Way to go, snakes.

Camden winced. "Something's coming in."

"I'm impressed you can see anything," I said as the sound of more footsteps on the stairs heralded Kit and his inevitable announcement.

"Almost death this time, Cam!"

Camden stared at me. "Baseford. In his office. Go now. Hurry!"

Kary and I didn't pause to question either of them. We jumped up and ran out to the Fury. I drove as fast as I could to the *Herald* office. We hurried past the main desk and up the short flight of stairs to Baseford's office. At first I thought he'd fallen asleep at his desk. Closer and careful inspection revealed an empty bottle of pills, an empty vodka bottle, and a message on his computer monitor:

I can no longer live with myself. I stole Leo Pierson's artwork and destroyed it. I was jealous and angry. Forgive me.

Exactly the kind of melodramatic high-flown suicide note the man would write. But was it suicide? Was it real?

As I called 911, Baseford's assistant and a group of people came dashing into the office. They ignored me, all talking and exclaiming at once.

"Did you call 911?"

"It's too late for that! He's dead, can't you see?"

"But what's this about somebody's artwork?"

"Somebody needs to call the police!"

The office was soon crowded with paramedics, reporters, and gawkers. Kary and I moved back and listened. Baseford's assistant stood to one side, white-faced, wringing his hands. By all accounts, he should have been doing the dance of joy. Instead, he looked like his best friend had been snuffed. I watched his face as the paramedics worked, and when one said, "He's stable," the relief on the assistant's face was palpable.

The paramedics hauled Baseford out of his chair and onto a stretcher. People jostled each other to take cell phone pictures, and one reporter asked if there was room on the front page of tomorrow's edition for the story.

Baseford was carried out to the waiting ambulance. The rest of the crowd followed for a better view of the action. Kary gave me a little nod and followed them. I hung back. The assistant had stayed in Baseford's office. He steadied himself on a desk and took several deep breaths.

"Pretty scary, huh?" I said. He turned, startled. "Did somebody's practical joke backfire?"

"Joke?" The word caught in his throat. "It was a suicide attempt. Didn't you see the note?"

"Anybody could've typed that. You really think Baseford's the kind of guy who'd commit suicide?"

The assistant's face was gray. "But he'd stolen some artwork."

"How did you know about that?"

He stammered. "Y-you were here before with that actor, Pierson. We heard a commotion. All of us, not just me."

"Some stolen artwork was found in Baseford's office. Someone called me, and I found it, but anybody could have put it there. What do you know about it?"

He edged away from me. "I don't know anything. Don't be ridiculous."

"Pierson won't press charges. He's happy to have his spoons back. But somebody with a big grudge against Baseford might have thought to make major trouble for him by planting them in his office."

"Why wouldn't Baseford have taken them himself? He and Pierson have never gotten along."

"Yeah, I heard about that." That same day I almost ran over the assistant as I came out of Baseford's office. "I think you might have heard some things, too." I imagined this guy's ear was always pressed against the door.

The assistant closed up. He looked away, and his throat worked as if he were trying to swallow something impossibly large.

I figured I had his number—literally. "You called me, didn't you? I don't recall discussing Pierson's missing artwork with you. How did you know his silverware was in a green box?"

He gave up. "The other day, when Pierson was in here bellowing about his stuff, I couldn't help but overhear. I happened to find that box, that's all. I looked inside and knew those things didn't belong to Baseford."

"So you called me, hoping to get your boss in trouble?"

"He shouldn't have taken it! I was trying to do the right thing."

"The police are going to question everybody on the paper about this, and as Baseford's unhappy and underpaid assistant, you're suspect number one. I happen to know somebody on the force. I can help you out."

He gripped the edge of the desk. "I don't need any help because I haven't done anything wrong. Baseford took those things. Leave me alone."

I would—for now. "If you change your mind, give me a call. I think you already know my number."

Kary and I met at the Fury. I told her my suspicions about Baseford's assistant, and she reported that Baseford was going to pull through.

"We'd better get home and see what's left of Camden," I said.

Kary and I expected a complete meltdown on the sofa, but Kit was sitting with Camden and from their seriously concentrated expressions, they were shutting psychic doors like crazy.

Camden came back for a moment to ask if we'd been too late.

"No, Baseford's alive. Looks like attempted suicide, though. You all right?"

"Everything came crashing back in. It's worse than before."

"It only seems that way," I said, as if I knew what I was talking about. "You've been in a vacuum for days. It'll readjust."

"Yeah, that's what I told him," Kit said.

Kary got out her cell phone. "I'll call Ellin."

I went into the kitchen and fixed some tea with plenty of sugar. I brought it to him, and he took a big drink. He was trembling and his eyes were huge, as if he were seeing the universe.

"It's like ten days' worth of visions all at once."

"Okay, it's rough, but you can handle it."

He tried to set the glass on the table and almost missed. I caught the glass and set it down.

"Sorry, Randall."

I knew he wasn't apologizing for slopping tea on the rug. "No big deal."

"You told Slim and Jim, didn't you?"

"I might have mentioned if they were in the neighborhood they could stop by. Transfer some of that glare to Kit. He's the one who talked to them."

"It was really cool," Kit said. "Why didn't you tell me they were here? I would've liked to see them again. Maybe I could've convinced them to join the band for a couple of nights, maybe even do a dance or something. The crowd would go ballistic." Camden's narrow-eyed glance shut him up. "Or not."

Camden shook his head. "If I hadn't been so zoned out, maybe I could've prevented all of this murder and attempted murder and theft—"

Kit interrupted. "Man, this is just what we've been talking about. It's like my drummer's sister. Sometimes you see things you can't keep from happening. But you need to be able to see things."

"Kit's right," I said. "We're up against a curse, remember?"

"That's what started this whole thing. When I shook Leo's hand—" He shuddered. "I couldn't take it."

Kary hadn't been able to reach Ellin. "She must be in a meeting. I left a message."

"Did you see Pierson committing any of these crimes?" I asked Camden.

"No, Leo couldn't hurt a fly."

"Did you see anybody?"

Another shudder. "The dragonfly's six deaths." He slowly recited six names. "Frederick, Alston, Bernice, Ira, Joshua, Isabelle. . ." his voice trailed off. "Isabelle. She tried to reach me, and I couldn't hear her." He put his head in his hands. "I couldn't help her."

"That's okay," I said. "I'll take care of it. Did you see the dragonfly?"

He straightened and wiped his eyes. "Yes, it's surrounded by other artwork."

I handed him the tea glass. "Drink some more." He had a few more spasms left in him, but the worst seemed to be over. "You have any idea where it is? Let's find the damned thing and put it out of its misery."

What little color he had left in his face drained away. "I can't. Not yet. Kit?"

"I can't see it. It must have something to do with you guys."

"Maybe once the dragonfly is back with Leo, it'll settle down." I sat down in the blue armchair. "Anyway, without the benefit of psychic powers, I found Pierson's leafy little silverware. The box was sitting in plain view on a bookshelf in Baseford's office. Baseford swore he was the victim of a setup. We may never know now."

"Any suspects?" Camden asked.

"The entire staff of the *Herald*."

"If Baseford didn't steal the spoons, how did they get into his office? If someone planted them to make him look like the thief, why would he try to kill himself?"

"That's what I'd like to know."

Kit looked interested. "Okay, what's the deal here? Is Baseford the bad guy?"

"He's *a* bad guy, but he's not the bad guy. I've got two suspects. Nancy Piper, who works at the museum in the finance department, and Richard Mason, director of the Little Gallery and a frustrated artist. Both of them knew about Pierson's artwork and had been to his house to see it. Both of them have some expertise with electronics and are familiar with Guardian Electric, so either of them could've tinkered with Pierson's alarm system, allowing Samuel Gallant to break in and steal some of Pierson's collection, including the deadly dragonfly."

"So how does Baseford fit in?"

"I'm not sure. Maybe to throw us off the trail? Everyone hates him, so he's an easy target."

"We still don't know who killed Gallant and Stein," Kary said. "I can't see Nancy Piper blowing up Stein's boat or murdering Gallant and hauling his body into a closet. I can't see her running over to the *Herald* to kill Baseford and running back to the museum without anyone seeing her."

"She could've sent someone," I said. "More and more I'm thinking that someone is Richard Mason and his Magic Remote."

Chapter Twenty-three

"*She Never Told Her Love*"

Since Kit had to get back to bed, Kary said she'd stay with Camden until Ellin arrived. I headed for the hospital and asked to see Chance Baseford. He was as superior and pompous as ever, bossing the nurse around and demanding more pillows. The nurse left, rolling her eyes. When Baseford saw me, he pointed a finger and ordered me out.

"This is all your fault! If you and Pierson hadn't had the utter gall to suggest that I would steal his ridiculous silverware."

I stepped in and closed the door behind me. "I haven't come about that. I want to know who tried to kill you."

For once in his life, he was speechless, if only for a few seconds. "Kill me?"

"Didn't the police tell you? The whole thing was set up to look like suicide: pills, vodka, a note."

He gaped at me. "But that's utterly preposterous! I'd never kill myself."

"I didn't think so." I pulled up a chair and sat. "Level with me. Did you take those spoons?"

"I've never stolen anything in my life."

I guess we won't count all those artists and poets and dancers who never realized their dreams because of a few unkind words from your bloody pen. "All right. Let's say I believe you. Now, who wants you dead besides half the city?"

He smirked. "Only half? You insult me."

"Who was in your office yesterday? What's the last thing you remember?"

"I have an excellent memory."

"So prove it."

He leaned back against the pillows and gazed at the ceiling. "My assistant, of course, being his usual useless self. Reporters checking in with news for me. Some hysterical woman, claiming I'd ruined her life. I believe I told her she flattered herself to think I'd bother with such a second-rate talent."

"What's the last thing you remember?"

He frowned at the ceiling as if he disagreed with the arrangement of the tiles. "I was at my computer, typing my column. Someone came to the door, but I was busy. I didn't look up to see who it was. I assumed it was my assistant. When no one said anything, I assumed—no, wait." His brow furrowed. "I believe he had a cigarette."

"You smelled cigarette smoke?"

"No, I caught a glimpse of something that looked like a lighter, which, if this person planned to smoke, is completely against the rules. The *Herald* offices are smoke-free." He rubbed his eyes. "There was a loud buzzing sound and things got very fuzzy after that. Someone was in my doorway, and then, I don't remember a thing until I woke up here."

"You can't remember who that person was? Male or female? Short? Tall? Dark hair?"

He looked baffled. "You know, I can't recall a single detail. This is highly unusual. I have an excellent memory."

"Maybe it'll come back to you. You've had a bad shock. Oh, one other thing. Do you have a pacemaker?" I didn't believe the old grinch had a heart much less a pacemaker, and it would have been an amazing coincidence if he had either one.

"No, of course not. My heart is as sound as can be."

"Any metal anywhere?"

He stared. "What on earth are you getting at?"

"When you go through the metal detector at the airport, do you set off any alarms?"

For a moment I didn't think he was going to answer me. Then he lowered his voice. "If you tell a living soul about this, I will ruin you. I wear hearing aids."

"Lots of people do. Why does that have to be a secret?"

He reared back. "Are you being purposefully dense? How do you think the artistic world would react if they knew Parkland's premiere critic turns off his hearing aids whenever a performance is especially excruciating?"

"Baseford, I don't think they'd be surprised. Your secret is safe with me. What does it have to do with your fake suicide attempt?"

"That loud buzzing sound. It made my hearing aids squeal like demons in torment."

"That's why you passed out."

"Yes, the doctors agree that if the sound had gone on any longer, it could've done much worse damage to my brain."

Again, someone used a zap of electrical current to get rid of an enemy. I got up. "I'm going to look into this. If you think of anything else, give me a call."

"I will." I must have looked surprised at his cooperation, because he added, "You're the only one who's bothered to come by."

I didn't want him to think I was his pal. "I needed information."

"I thought at least one person would call."

"I wouldn't count on it."

Usually a close brush with death makes people a little mellow. Not this guy. "Well, then," he said, "I certainly don't need anyone's support."

My daughter on The Other Side came in bright and clear that night, pleased I had helped Camden.

That was smart to use the snakes, Daddy. I knew you'd think of something.

"Now that everyone can hear everybody, does Isabelle have anything else she needs to tell me? How about Norma or Samuel Gallant?"

Delores will find out. There are lots of people here, you know. Delores doesn't come to the playground very often. Don't worry. I won't forget.

There were so many things I wanted to ask Lindsey. Was she happy there? Did she see me all day, or just in these dreams? Did she communicate with her mother? How long was she going to be able to help me? I hated the thought of losing her again.

Be grateful for what you have, I reminded myself. Don't try to explain it or analyze it. Say "Thank you" and keep going.

"Thank you, baby," I said. "See you later."

I certainly hoped I would.

Camden staggered down to breakfast Saturday morning with a warning for me. "Don't think of anything."

"Stuff still pouring in?"

"Like Niagara Falls." His hand shook as he opened the box of Pop-Tarts.

"Can't you shut it off?"

"I spent years learning how to control it. I take a couple of days off, and I'm back to the beginning."

"You can do it, though, right? Do I need to call Psychics Anonymous?"

"Pass the sugar."

He sat down at the counter and stirred sugar into his tea. I brought my coffee and toast over and perched on another stool. "Speaking of sugar, did you get any from your sweetie last night?"

"I was too addled to fully enjoy her company."

"'Addled.' Haven't heard that one in a while. It's short, but I'll give you five points. Did she lecture you about drug abuse?"

"She was really concerned. She also made it clear I needed to be at the fair today."

Good God, the woman never lets up. I must have been thinking a lot harder than I realized because Camden winced. So our link was back online. That was a good thing.

"Did you tell her about the snakes?"

"The fact they came down the chimney into the bedroom? No."

He decided he needed one more nap before facing the fair. I took my breakfast to the porch. It was hot, but maybe the heat would be able to bake some answers into my head. I'd settled in one of the rocking chairs to think over the facts of my case when the hedge rustled and Lily Wilkes came through. She wore a shapeless green sweater with huge rhinestone buttons, a long brown skirt with a pink ruffle on the bottom, three pearl necklaces, and a green Girl Scout beret.

She held her skirt and came up the steps. "Hello, David. You're looking very serious this morning."

"I'm trying to get inspired. There are things about this case I don't think I want to know."

Lily sat down in the chair next to mine and looked at me

intently, as only someone who has been repeatedly probed can look. I took a drink of coffee and tried out my theories on her.

"I started out with a long list of people, and it looks like they're being picked off one by one. If I wait, the only suspect left standing is going to be the murderer, but I don't want anyone else to die, especially not over a glass dragonfly."

"A glass dragonfly? That sounds wonderful. According to the Chinese, the dragonfly is a symbol of longevity."

"Lily, Janice told me everything in China is a symbol of longevity. The pine tree, the bat, the doughnut. This dragonfly may be many things, but it's no guarantee of long life."

"Get Cam to hold it for you."

"It's already blown his head off."

She gave a little gasp. "Don't say things like that."

"Sorry. He's been having some headaches lately, and the pills he was taking are making things worse."

She stopped rocking. "Pills?"

The way she said "pills" made me set my coffee cup down to give her my full attention. "Do you know anything about that?"

I didn't think she was going to answer, but finally she gulped. "Um, I may have given him some of mine."

"Are they called Tranquillon?"

She cringed. "No. A few days ago when he came over, he had a headache, and I offered him some Rest-All. He said that worked really well, so I gave him some more. Did it make him sick? I never meant for that to happen."

I was surprised and relieved that little Lily was the supplier and not some crime boss I would have to take down. "It's okay. He's not going to take any more. But you really shouldn't share medications, especially with Camden. He can flip out over cough syrup."

"I am so sorry."

"You were only trying to help. I'll explain things to him." Her face lit up like...well, a UFO. "Will you, David?"

"Yes, of course. You know he won't be angry with you."

"That's true. He never loses his temper. He doesn't realize how much he helps people. The ASG would be lost without him. He's always so kind, and he never makes fun of anyone, even though—and I hate to say this—we have a few odd people in our group."

A few. "What does he tell them?"

"He listens mostly and everyone calms down." Puffs of her cottony hair tried to escape the beret. "You see, nobody believes their stories. It's frustrating not to be believed, and they're laughed at, too. They really hate that. It goes on for years and years until finally some people do go crazy. It's so sad. They just want someone to listen and say it's okay."

"Camden will be okay, too, Lily."

"You know he isn't human."

"I keep forgetting."

"Anyone with that much psychic ability has to be from another more advanced civilization."

Not the kind of crap he needs to hear right now. "You're right. Stupid of me."

"I'm surprised he married Ellin. Inter-species mating isn't always successful."

I don't know when I've ever been so glad to hear my phone ring. "Please excuse me."

She hopped out of the chair and down the steps. "Oh, I've got to go. See you!"

I answered the phone. It was Pierson.

"Checking in, as ordered, Randall. I went to visit Baseford. I know we've had our differences, but I never wanted anything to happen to him. If he had killed himself over my spoons, I'd feel responsible."

Not exactly the words of a cold-blooded murderer. "You don't think he was mad enough to steal your artwork?"

"I thought so at first, but it's really not his style, and now, after this attempt on his life, I'm even more certain he had nothing to do with the theft. Are you any closer to solving this? The buyer will need an answer tomorrow. If you have any possible way to find my treasures, you must do it now."

Do it now. That's what Mason had said into his phone, setting his plan into action. I had a good idea his plan was to plant the spoons, zap Baseford, and frame him for the robbery and murder—and I had an even better idea of who helped him.

Chapter Twenty-four

"I Rage, I Melt, I Burn"

The *Herald* office bustled as if nothing had happened. The police had finished in Baseford's office, and his assistant was stacking books on the desk. He swung anxious eyes my way. "Oh, it's you again. What do you want now?"

"Need to ask you something."

He kept working. "The police have already asked a thousand questions. You can't pin anything on me. I know I wanted him dead, but I didn't do it. We all wanted him dead, and he was obliging enough to try to kill himself."

I moved a stack of books and sat on one corner of the desk. "This friend of yours you say Baseford ruined. Wouldn't be Richard Mason, would it?"

His eyes flickered to me and away. "What if it is?"

"I'm a private investigator, and I'm trying to solve a couple of murders. You can help by clearing up a few things."

He stopped stacking. "Ricky hasn't said anything about being in danger."

Oh, Ricky, was it? "He probably didn't want to worry you."

"Yeah, I have to get after him for this macho thing he has going sometimes. He'll do the wildest things."

"Like taking Art Nouveau spoons and planting them in Baseford's office? I don't think you happened to find that box. I think you put it there."

"Why would I do that?"

"Two reasons. You hate Baseford and want to get him in trouble. You also wanted to help your old pal Ricky get revenge for his art show. Did Ricky tell you those spoons were part of a collection stolen from Leo Pierson?"

"Stolen?"

The assistant looked as if he might bolt any minute. I got up, closed the office door, and leaned against it. "Take it easy. I'm not accusing you of anything. What's your name?"

"Flynn Hardison."

Flynn? Hold on. Wasn't that the name of Patricia Ashworthy's houseboy? "Mr. Hardison, do you work for Patricia Ashworthy?"

He eyed me warily. "What if I do?"

"Richard got you the job there, right?"

"What does that have to do with anything?"

Patricia Ashworthy hated Baseford, too, and was determined to blame all the crimes in Parkland on him. Was it possible she was the mastermind behind all this?

Hardison backed away, hands out. "All I know is, Ricky brought me this green box and told me to hang onto it and one day he'd have me hide it in Baseford's office because it would cause Baseford a lot of trouble, so naturally, I did it. I heard all the fuss the other day, and believe me, I enjoyed every minute."

"Did he call you Thursday around noon? Did he tell you it was time and to 'Do it now'?"

"Yes." His face tightened. "If you could have seen the way Baseford shredded Ricky's exhibit, you'd understand. Baseford deserves all the grief he can get."

"But you didn't want him to die. That scared you."

"Yeah, it scared me. I thought we'd gone too far."

"Did you know he wore hearing aids?"

"Only because I had to get batteries for him all the time. No one's supposed to know."

"You might have mentioned it to Mason, right?"

"Maybe. I don't know what difference that makes."

"Do you smoke?"

The question threw him. "Smoke? What's that got to do—no, I don't. It's a filthy habit. Nobody smokes in here." He pointed to the No Smoking sign posted on the wall. "This is a smoke-free office."

"Does Ricky smoke?"

"No, he does not. What the hell kind of question is that?"

"Baseford remembers seeing someone with a cigarette or a lighter in his doorway before he passed out."

All of a sudden Hardison decided that he, too, could be macho. "I don't have to answer any more of your questions. If you'll excuse me. I have work to do."

He made a feeble attempt to leave. I blocked his way. "Yes, you do have to answer my questions." But did I really have any more questions for this guy? I'd learned all I really needed to know for now.

Hardison's plaintive voice brought me out of my thoughts. "Are you done? Can I go now?"

I stood aside. "Thanks for your help."

He put his nose in the air and stalked out. No doubt he'd call Mason to warn him. But I was going to get to Mason first.

• • ● • •

Before I left for the Little Gallery, I looked up Patricia Ashworthy. Husband number three was Reginald Thomas Duvall. So not only did she know about the feud and the mysterious treasure, she probably knew about the last little clue the dragonfly might provide. Richard would've told her about Pierson's parlor set up and how he could easily disarm the alarm system with one of his gadgets. Looking for someone who'd do anything for money, they found the perfect sap in Samuel Gallant. Looking for another sap willing to hide the silverware in their mutual enemy Baseford's office, well, here was faithful Flynn, who no doubt thought he'd get a cut. Stein had been at Pierson's that day. He had to go. Nancy had been there, too, and might be next.

But where was Pierson's artwork? If Ashworthy and Mason had it, wouldn't they have solved the puzzle, found the twenty-five million, and skipped town?

The main hallway of the Little Gallery was empty of people but crammed full of art with little regard to spacing, type, or theme. It was as if Mason had decided, hey, I'll put art here, and shoveled it in. I passed old dark landscapes, red triangles, marble cupids, and bronze horses. The effect was dizzying.

I paused by a still life of dead ducks and rabbits, their heads hanging over the edge of a rough wooden table, their eyes staring in disbelief, as if to say, I got killed for a lousy painting? The still life was incongruously placed beside a picture of nearly clothed maidens frolicking in a swing. I went past this jumble to the ugly little metal sculptures I'd seen earlier. They were still ugly.

I pressed one button, and the first sculpture cranked up like a rusty scarecrow waving its arms. I pressed button number two, and the second sculpture shuffled its coat hanger feet. I kept pressing buttons until all the artwork screeched and rustled and clanked.

"Mr. Randall, I didn't hear you come in." Mason stood in the doorway. His pale eyes darted from one gadget to another.

"What are you doing?"

"Playing around."

"These are not toys." He hurried around to each sculpture, switching them off. "You're meant to experience them one by one."

"Maybe I wanted to experience the full range of your art. You're a damn good electrician, Ricky."

He stiffened at the sound of his nickname. "Did you stop by to return *Anguished Fortitude*?"

"No, I stopped by to clear up a few things. You can correct me as we go along."

He folded his arms and gave me a narrow-eyed stare. "What's this all about?"

"It's about Samuel Gallant's pacemaker giving out and Lawrence Stein's boat exploding. It's about Leo Pierson's stolen Art Nouveau. Oh, and Chance Baseford's hearing aids. I guess your trusty assistant Flynn told you about that. He did what you said and planted the silverware in Baseford's office. He wasn't real happy to hear the silverware was stolen, but he seems loyal. Not like Nancy Piper. What does she have on you, Ricky?"

His voice got very calm. "When we worked together at Riverside, I thought she was my friend. I thought we had the same goals in life."

"To kill everyone who gets in your way?"

"To be in charge of our own museum where we could display whatever we liked."

"You're not satisfied with the Little Gallery? Perhaps the huge crowds here annoy you."

He ignored my insult. "I was a fool to trust her. You want to know why her husband left her? Oh, she'll tell you it was because he couldn't handle money. No, it was because she *spent* all his money, the greedy bitch. It takes money to buy all those fancy outfits she wears. It takes money to send her little girl to that private school. It was never enough."

"So the two of you hatched this plan to get the Art Nouveau for yourselves."

"She has it! We were supposed to keep all the pieces together, but she refused to do that. I had the silverware, but she's got the rest hidden away in the museum basement where she can keep moving it around so no one finds it. But I intend to get it away from her."

"If she's the mastermind behind this plot, why didn't you go to the police?" I knew the answer. Nancy may have been the brains, but Mason had done the dirty work. Even now, he reached into his pocket for his Device of Death.

"I'm sure you're too young to have heart problems, Randall, but a nice zap of electricity can take care of that. Then I'll see what I can do for Cousin Nancy—oh, and Patricia Ashworthy, too."

I took a few steps back. "She's the one who told you about the money, isn't she?"

"Double-crossing old baggage! All that talk about millions of dollars if you solve a puzzle. What a load of crap. She was only after the dragonfly."

I'd hoped to keep him talking, but he clicked on the remote and lunged forward. I fell back over one of the sculptures and landed with a crash on the hard stone floor, my arm entangled in coat hanger. He pounced, the remote buzzing like a live wire. I grabbed his wrist and tried to keep the gadget away from my face while his other fist pounded into my chest. For a skinny guy, Mason was stronger than I expected, plus he was mad as hell. We rolled over and crashed into another sculpture. Gears and tinfoil flew. I imagined the current zapping through a vital part of me. I tried to shake the coat hanger loose, but the rusty wire had bonded with my arm. I shook

Mason's wrist, but couldn't dislodge him. He panted like a wild animal, his eyes blazing.

"Damn you! Stop it! My sculptures!"

If I was going down, I was taking those ugly things with me. I rolled into another, satisfied to hear the *boing* and clang of scrap metal as pieces hit the floor, a discordant jangle that set my teeth on edge.

"Stop it! Stop it!" Mason was distracted by the destruction of his precious artwork long enough for me to swing around with the coat hanger and let him have it across the face. With a shriek, he fell back, and the deadly little remote skittered across the museum floor like an ice cube. As I ran for it, Mason snagged my trouser cuff with a coil of wire from the litter of broken parts. I tripped and landed on my stomach, narrowly missing a sharp-edged piece of metal.

Mason staggered to his feet and ran for the remote. I grabbed the nearest object, a tarnished hubcap, and slung it like a Frisbee. It clipped him at the knee. When he fell, his fingers brushed the remote and sent it spinning further down the hallway.

On my feet now, I raced for the remote but tripped on another piece of that damned artwork, bounced off another of Mason's sculptures, and fell again. By the time I got up, Mason had retrieved his gadget and stood, gasping in triumph.

I backed up and brushed off the gears and wires that had attached themselves to me. The hallway looked like blow-out day at the junkyard. Where was something I could use? Pieces of pipe, coils of wire, screws, and rusty tools, a chunk of metal with paper clips stuck all over a large curved magnet—wait a minute. Where was Mason's favorite piece? Where was *Last Gasp of Freedom in a Material Society*?

There it was, at the end of the hall, still intact, still hideous. I made a run for it, grabbed it, and swung around, holding it out like a shield.

Mason gave a strangled cry. "You wouldn't dare!"

"Put that gadget down, or *Last Gasp* will be doing exactly that."

"It's my finest piece!"

"It's scrap if you don't turn that thing off."

He hesitated a moment, and I flung *Last Gasp* at him. As I'd hoped, his treasure meant more to him than his homemade taser. He dropped the remote, made a desperate lunge for the sculpture, and managed to become one with his art, falling with a crash. I kicked the remote away.

Mason tried to untangle himself. He was furious. "Do you realize what you've done? I'll never be able to recreate it, never!"

I hauled him up, pieces of wire and tinfoil clinging to his clothes. "Oh, I think you'll have plenty of time to do that." I twisted one skinny arm behind his back and marched him to the nearest closet. I shoved him inside, used a few more pieces of coat hanger to fasten the door shut, and called Jordan to come and get him.

Next up, Nancy Piper.

Chapter Twenty-five

"*Turn Not, O Queen, Thy Face Away*"

The Parkland Art Museum hallway was longer than I remembered. Nancy Piper was in her office and looked up, smiling. "Hello, David. To what do I owe the pleasure?"

Oh, that wasn't going to work on me. "I think I'm on to something. Does this place have a basement?"

"There are some storage rooms downstairs."

"Would you show me?"

"Sure." She got up, her expression puzzled. Her outfit of choice was a silky black blouse and a tight gold skirt. Her shoes were leopard-print high heels. I hadn't thought about it before my encounter with Mason, but all her clothes did look as if they'd come from an expensive shop like Tamara's Boutique. "Do you have a clue?"

"More than a clue, I hope."

She led me back down the long hallway to an elevator. We got in and she pressed a button marked "B." We rode the short distance down.

"David, do you think Pierson's artwork is in the basement?"

I wasn't going to let on that her partner in crime had given me the info I needed. "I didn't pay too much attention in school," I said, "but there was this one story about a stolen letter. The police looked everywhere for it, and it was right there in plain sight with other letters. Seeing that sculpture by Jon Vass started me thinking. At first, you see what the artist wants you to see, and then your eyes readjust. What better place to hide artwork than in a museum?"

"That seems awfully risky. Why would the thief hide things so close to home?"

"A little farewell clue from Samuel Gallant. 'Art that's hidden within art.'"

The elevator stopped. The doors slid open and we got off. We walked down a short hall. Nancy unlocked a large door and pushed it open. We entered a cluttered room full of packing crates, wrapped canvases, and statues covered with cloth. Some ancient-looking spears leaned in a corner next to some Romanesque helmets. Victorian furniture and dressmaker's dummies in old beaded gowns, feathered hats, and what looked like an old canoe crowded another corner.

I didn't know where to start. It could take days, weeks, to find Pierson's art. I walked up and down the aisles, going farther and farther back into history. Then back in a corner in a box labeled "Pre-Columbian," I found Pierson's mermaid ashtray, the blue peacock vase, a rolled-up poster.

And the dragonfly.

It was a beautiful piece of glass, shining in the dim light. The white wings had delicate tracings of green veins. The realistic head sported two large Pierson-like eyes. The segmented body in transparent green and white looked like a long fancy Christmas ornament. I cautiously picked it up. No vibrations tingled in the palm of my hand, no visions of death popped into my head.

Nancy looked over my shoulder. "My God. It was here all the time. Why didn't I see it?"

I carefully set the dragonfly back in the box with the ashtray, the vase, and the poster. Now I knew why the stolen items were conveniently stored together and sitting here in plain sight. After their argument, Nancy must have realized Mason would come hunting for them. She had the artwork packaged up and ready for a quick getaway.

I picked up the box. "That was pretty daring of you."

She took a step back. "What are you talking about? If I were responsible, this is the last place I'd bring you."

"Oh, I don't know. You've got plenty of nerve. Plenty of charm, too, and it worked on Richard Mason and on Samuel Gallant. You got the guys to rob Pierson and then I imagine it wasn't hard to convince Mason to get rid of Gallant—I mean, you weren't really going to share any profits with him, were you? How did Lawrence Stein find out?"

"This is crazy. *You're* crazy."

"Maybe you tried to cozy up to him, too, and he rejected you. As for Baseford, well, I think Mason let his hatred of the man get the best of him. Here were some handy little spoons he could get his buddy Flynn at the *Herald* to put in Baseford's office. Then he could stop by later and use his disrupter to zap Baseford and frame him for the crime. Or was that your idea, too?"

"I had nothing to do with any of that. This is ridiculous. Let's go."

She marched to the door, her high heels clicking, and waited for me, arms folded tightly across her chest in a classic Ellin Belton gesture. Severely pissed. Her eyes flickered to me as if summing me up, deciding whether or not to confide.

"Not a word of your wild story is true, David."

"Tell me your version." I shifted my grip on the box and got out my phone. "Or maybe you'd like to tell it to the police."

"Oh, I have a better idea. Why don't you let me call the

police? You're so sure I'm this heartless villain. That ought to prove to you I'm not."

I wanted to see how she got out of this one. I handed her my phone. But she didn't call the police. She did something I didn't expect. She reached into the box, scooped up the dragonfly, and kicked me in the shin with those spiky leopard heels. I almost dropped Pierson's box of treasures. While I was hopping around swearing, Nancy ran out, slamming the storage room door behind her. I heard the click of the lock. I put down the box and pounded on the door.

"Nancy!"

Great. I had Mason locked up in a storage room, and now I was locked in one, too. By the time I got out, Nancy would be halfway across the country with the one object Pierson wanted most. I looked around. Time to see how strong those ancient spears are.

They were pretty ancient, bending and breaking off in the door. The beaded dresses were no help. I unpacked a few crates, finding only old bones and skulls.

That's you, if you don't find a way out, I told myself. Nancy sure as hell won't tell anyone you're down here. You better be glad Mason didn't arm her with one of his remotes.

I made my way to the back where a small window gleamed high in the wall. It looked canoe and Victorian sofa high. I dragged over the sofa, put the canoe on top, and balanced myself on my makeshift ladder. Using someone or something's leg bone, I broke the window. It was nice to know all this art was good for something.

First, I climbed down and put Pierson's ashtray in my pocket. I had to leave the poster and the vase, but didn't figure he'd mind. I made it back up my historic escape route, crawled out into the dirt and bushes at the back of the museum, and ran around to the front steps.

Nancy was gone. Where would she go? Would she leave without Leslie?

I was standing there, frozen with indecision, when Pierson's Mercedes screeched up to the curb, and Camden called, "Randall!"

I hopped into the car.

"He insisted I bring him here," Pierson said. "He said you needed help."

"Nancy locked me in the basement." I pulled the mermaid head ashtray out of my pocket. "The vase is in the storage room with the poster. They're safe. But Nancy got away with the dragonfly."

He grabbed the ashtray. "Oh, my God! I can't believe this! Nancy Piper?"

"Any idea where she would go?"

"She'd have to find a safe place to hide the dragonfly," Pierson said. Or," he added with a tremor in his voice, "the curse will destroy her and we'll never find it."

"Forget the curse. She and Richard Mason have been behind this whole thing, and so has Patricia Ashworthy. We have to figure where she would go now. Camden?"

He rubbed his forehead. "I saw you needed help, but things are still fuzzy."

I tried to think where Nancy would go. She wouldn't leave Leslie. If she was planning to run, she'd have to get her daughter. Someone in the museum had to know.

Then it hit me. Not a vision or some psychic blast. A real solid memory. Nancy had said Leslie's scout troop was going to the psychic fair on Saturday.

"I know where she is." I leaned over the seat. "Camden, call Jordan. Pierson, the Ramada Inn, as fast as you can."

His bulging eyes gleamed with superhero fervor "At once!"

There must have been a two-for-one special on past lives today, because the fair was packed. Loads of kids and teenagers, plus a senior citizens group and dozens of psychic salesmen crowded the convention rooms. We got to the doorway and Camden's knees gave way.

"It's here," he gasped as we hauled him up.

I dumped him in the nearest chair. "You stay out here." I turned to Pierson. "Let's split up. No questions. If you see Nancy, grab her."

Pierson set forth like a clipper ship parting the waves of people.

I plunged into the crowd. People were standing in long lines to have their fortunes told and to buy the crystals, feathers, and other psychic stuff. "Excuse me. Excuse me, please." I pushed through, looking for short spiky red hair. She had to be with a group of scouts, trying to get Leslie. Then what? Would they hop a plane and fly off to Mexico?

I didn't want to think about it. I kept inching my way past the tables and booths. Maybe she was in the other ballroom. I squeezed past a group of gypsies and another group of Moonie clones to get to the hallway, which was just as crowded. I saw kids bunched up by the angel display, but I didn't see any in scout uniforms. Maybe we were too late. Maybe she and her mom had already made their getaway.

No, Camden had said the dragonfly was here, and I knew, after his reaction, it was here.

The other ballroom was as hot and crowded as the first one. I looked all around, and there she was, pulling Leslie along with her. The little girl's face was puzzled. Nancy's was set in stone. I couldn't reach her by running down the aisle. I couldn't push past so many people. There was only one other way—up and over.

I'd been wondering where Ellin was. I found out when I

jumped up on the nearest table, a table containing magical herbs and spices, and ran along the top, sending little jars and bottles bouncing everywhere and crunching bundles of aromatic weeds underfoot.

"Randall! What the hell are you doing?"

Nancy heard Ellin scream my name. She whirled around, saw me charging down the display tables, scattering crystals, amulets, and books to the anger and dismay of the sellers. She turned and pushed her way frantically through the crowd.

"Pierson! She's coming your way!"

People screamed and yelled and began to panic in all directions. Pierson made a grab for Nancy, but missed. He landed with a huge crash onto a display of crystal balls that went careening everywhere like giant marbles. There was another banshee cry from Ellin.

"What the hell is going on? Stop it! Stop it!"

Pierson managed to grab Nancy's foot, but she shook him off, leaving him holding a high heel. She stopped for a second to kick off the other shoe and ran right into the gypsies, who were coming to see what all the screaming was about. In the mass confusion, I ran along the rest of the tables, skidded on a starry tablecloth, and slid off the end, taking out a whole family of ceramic dragons and landing with a thud.

By now, half the crowd was up against the walls, watching with wide eyes and probably thinking it was some sort of psychic show. The other half fled out the fire exits. Teachers rounded up their kids, who were clapping and cheering. Nancy pushed past the gypsies. I scrambled to my feet and ran after her. This time, everyone gave me plenty of room. She was halfway down the hall when I tackled her. We hit hard and rolled on the carpet.

She pounded me with her fists. "Damn you! Let me go!"

"You stole the dragonfly. You locked me in the storage room. When you saw me, you ran. What am I supposed to think?"

She didn't answer because two security men grabbed us and pulled us upright. They didn't look like they would believe anything I had to say. Pierson came huffing up.

"This young woman has stolen my property!"

Nancy straightened her clothes. "I don't have anything that belongs to you. Your artwork is in the museum, safe and sound."

"But my dragonfly—"

She raised her hands, revealing her skin-tight blouse and skirt. "Does it look like I have a dragonfly on me?"

What had she done with it? "Why did you run?" I asked. "Why lock the door?"

She glared. "You were talking crazy. I was afraid."

I could see the security guards measuring her petite height against mine. She took Leslie's hand. Throughout the whole chase, the little girl hadn't made a sound. She stood beside her mother, eyes wide. "If there are no further questions, I'd like to take Leslie and go home now."

I spoke to the security guards. "Jordan Finley of the Parkland Police Department should be arriving any minute. Tell him that besides a murder suspect locked up at the Little Gallery, there's another suspect right here." They eyed each other, not wanting to believe me. "Don't let this woman get away. She's an accessory to murder."

Ellin arrived, white-lipped and furious. She pointed a quivering finger at me. "Arrest this man and his accomplice. Randall, I am going to sue your ass into the next century."

Nancy gave me a long hard stare. "I had nothing to do with this."

A distant wailing of sirens helped the security guards come to a decision. "Let the police straighten it out," one said. "I'll go meet them. You watch these two."

Ellin turned on me. "What is going on here? What is all this about?"

"I'll explain everything later. Right now, we need to find Pierson's dragonfly."

"You disrupt the fair, knock down an innocent woman, terrorize my customers—you are out of here."

"We just want to find the dragonfly." I started to tell her Camden knew the dragonfly was here. I got as far as his name when she broke in.

"Cam is here? You dragged him into this? I should have known!"

"A few minutes, that's all we need."

She took several deep breaths, closed her eyes as if silently counting to ten, then opened her eyes. They were arctic blue. "You and Pierson stay right here. I have some damage to control. When I've taken care of everything, you can look for your stupid dragonfly."

With a curt nod of her head, she gestured a third security guard to follow her into what was left of the fair. Pierson paced anxiously while she dealt with curious customers, angry dealers, a crystal ball-smashed toe, and a crystal necklace puncture. Meanwhile, Nancy tried to convince Leslie everything would be all right.

In a short while, Jordan arrived with two other officers.

"If you'll come with us, ma'am?"

She gave him her frostiest stare. "This is complete nonsense. This man attacked me."

"We'd appreciate your cooperation."

Nancy gave me a murderous look and went with one of the other officers. She held her head high and pulled Leslie along. "Don't worry, Leslie. This is nothing."

Jordan grinned. "We found Mr. Mason. He sang like a little bird. Accused her of everything. Claims he's an innocent bystander."

"That'll be her story, too, I'm afraid."

"We'll sort it out."

Pierson wrung his hands. "Now what do we do, Randall?"

"We go get Camden."

Chapter Twenty-six

"*My Thoughts Are Winged With Hope*"

Camden was where we'd left him, still shaking.

"Great," I said. "It's still here. Where is it? Ellin's going to give me about two seconds."

His teeth were chattering. "I can't see anything through this headache. Find the damned thing and get it away from me."

"Okay. Hang on."

Back in the ballroom, the last of the fairgoers filed out, followed by a tightly smiling Ellin, who thanked them for coming and apologized for the disturbance. Her flame-thrower gaze swung to me. "Find the damned thing." She unconsciously echoed Camden's sentiment, "And get out."

Pierson and I entered the ballroom, which was now deserted except for a few dealers trying to make repairs. I tried not to let my jaw drop. The room was a shambles. It would be a miracle to find anything in the mess, much less a small dragonfly. I wouldn't be surprised if it were in a thousand rainbow pieces by now. No, Camden would have sensed that. The dragonfly was here, and we were going to find it.

Pierson and I waded through the scattered herbs and broken candles, the brochures like large confetti on the carpet, tables, and chairs, the crunch of wind chimes and talismans under our feet.

Pierson was in awe. "It's amazing the amount of damage one can do in such a short time. Are all your cases this messy?"

"Only the important ones."

"Any luck?"

"Not a thing." A sparkle of green caught my eye and I hurried toward a collapsed table and bent chairs. I reached down, thinking, this is it! It was only a piece of broken crystal. "Damn."

Pierson glanced my way, his bulging eyes full of hope. "It has to be here, Randall. Cam wouldn't have reacted the way he did."

"Yeah, and it could be more withdrawal pangs." I surveyed my masterpiece of destruction. "If only I hadn't been so dead-set on catching Nancy."

"But you did catch her, my boy. That was an impressive tackle."

Pierson gathered up some silk scarves, anxiously peering under each one. After at least thirty minutes of wandering through the psychic debris, we slumped down, dejected, into two chairs that had somehow managed to stay upright. No wonder Camden was half crazy all the time, seeing things that weren't there, trying to make sense out of visions and premonitions. The answer was probably staring me in the face.

Like the spoons on the bookcase. Hidden in plain sight. Art that's hidden within art.

Wait.

We'd managed to trash only one ballroom. There was another.

Kary's favorite display, in the other room, was thankfully away from the carnage. The glassblower.

"Randall?" Pierson said as I slowly got to my feet. "What is it?"

I motioned for him to come with me. I didn't say anything until we were in front of the glassblower's booth. There on the glass shelf with the unicorns, angels, wishing wells, and little flying saucers, sat the dragonfly, almost completely and successfully camouflaged within the glass and mirrors. Its big staring eyes and delicately veined wings caught the light.

"Oh." Pierson gently picked it up. I thought for a moment he was going to kiss it. He held it in his hands, tears rolling down from his big eyes. "Oh, thank God. It's all right. It's all right."

The happy reunion was punctuated by Ellin's angry theme of complaints on her cell phone to the Psychic Service.

"I don't know what happened. They burst in here like mad men and destroyed the fair. We had a huge crowd, our biggest yet. Yes, I intend to get to the bottom of things."

She put the phone away and marched up to us. When she saw the dragonfly, she wrinkled her nose in disgust. "Is this what all the uproar was about?"

"Yes," Pierson said. "This, my dear, is my finest treasure, and I am grateful to you for allowing me to find it."

"Out," she said.

We stopped by the door to retrieve Camden. He looked a lot better. "You okay?"

"Yes, thank goodness. Once Pierson had it back, everything settled down."

I eyed Ellin, who was coming up fast. "Can you not be okay for a few minutes?"

He saw her, too. "Sure." He closed his eyes.

"Ellin," I said when she was upon us, "Camden's still not back."

She changed in midstride from righteous indignation to concern. "Oh, dear." She knelt beside his chair. "I knew this would be too much."

And while she was holding his hand, Pierson, the dragonfly, and I made our escape.

• • ● • •

After stopping by the Parkland Museum to retrieve the rest of Pierson's artwork, he rushed home to contact his buyer. I went back to 302 Grace Street where the relentless beat of Kit's guitar sounded from upstairs as he wailed his latest song, "Hit Me Like a Lightning Bolt." Kary was at the pageant all day, so I left a message on her phone saying the dragonfly had been found and all guilty persons arrested. Then Jordan called to tell me what he'd learned from Mason and to hear my part in all the adventure. Everything Mason had told me was true. He was responsible for the deaths, but Nancy Piper had been in on the scheme from the beginning.

"We'll also be having a little chat with Patricia Ashworthy," Jordan said.

"I think she set the whole thing up as a way of getting back at Baseford. Any idea why?"

"They've been at odds for years."

"Perhaps he spurned her advances." Jordan's snort made me hold the phone away from my ear. "Well, she came onto me pretty hot and heavy."

"Because you're so irresistible. Oh, I have your cell phone. Some Good Samaritan found it in a trash can outside the Ramada Inn. That was a dumb move, Randall."

"I know. Sometimes I'm too trusting."

He chuckled. "Well, it made my day."

"Since you're in such a good mood, how about a little credit?"

"'Thanks to an unnamed source'?"

"You'll have to do better than that."

Another chuckle. "I'll see that Baseford mentions your name. He owes you."

Leo Pierson felt he owed me, too. Not long after Jordan's call, his pearl-gray Mercedes rolled up behind the Fury, and he made a dramatic entrance into my office to hand me a large envelope with a flourish. "There isn't enough money in the world to repay you for finding the dragonfly, but I hope you will accept this."

"You don't owe me anything else, Pierson."

"Nonsense. This is exactly like the end of *Eternal Treasure*, when the robber baron realizes what he truly loves." He took his dramatic stance, hand to heart. "'My heart once wrapped in gold and silver breaks the bonds of callous wealth and reaches for the only true thing that gives my life purpose— my heritage, my blood, my name. No one can take that from me.' Well, perhaps not exactly that, but you understand the emotion involved. You worked hard, you didn't give up on what I know at times you felt was a foolish quest, and now I am reunited with the one true thing that gives my life purpose. Plus we made it on time, and soon, I shall have my very own theater! I can't thank you enough."

"You're welcome. Come back and visit sometime. And bring Francine. I'd like to meet her."

"I shall certainly do that."

He gave a sweeping bow and went out. I started to open the envelope when Vermillion came in, waving a piece of paper.

"Solved that puzzle."

I couldn't believe it. "What?"

"The word puzzle. The one worth millions of dollars." She sat down in the client chair and pushed the piece of paper across my desk to me. "I'm real good at that kind of thing."

The paper was filled with long lists of words, names, and phrases she had created out of the letters found on the Art Nouveau. "This is impressive, Vermillion. What did you come up with?"

She leaned forward to point to the paper. "Well, first I thought the answer was 'Rich Man,' but you wouldn't be a rich man unless you found the money. Then I thought 'Also Ruins' would work, but there aren't any ruins around here. Then I came up with 'Under Lamp,' which was exciting because of the Tiffany lamp, but Kary and I went to that woman's office in the museum to look, and there wasn't anything under the lamp. So, I think the very best answer is this."

I looked where she pointed. "'No Cash'?"

"Uh huh."

"I suppose that's possible." Pierson hadn't heard of the money, and he was directly related to the Pierson/Duvall feud. Was it something Patricia Ashworthy made up to convince Nancy and Mason to go along with her scheme? Baseford had said it was a hoax. I hated to admit the old buzzard might be right.

Vermillion took the paper. "I can keep trying."

"If you want to, but Pierson has his dragonfly back, and that's all that matters." At least, I hoped that was all his letter was about. I slit open the envelope and took out the cream-colored letter. Curly gold letters trumpeted:

Dear Randall!
Mere words cannot express my joy at having my dearest treasures returned to me. So for once I have put mere words aside. I know we settled on your fee, but I felt you earned a bonus. Enclosed you will find a check for ten thousand dollars. I hope it will help your agency.
Best regards,
Leo L. Pierson

I shared this good news with Camden and Ellin when she brought him home. She stayed long enough to congratulate me before returning to the studio. Camden went to the kitchen for a Coke and a Pop-Tart. I followed, declined a Pop-Tart, and made some peanut butter crackers.

"If you were hoping for twenty-five million dollars, Vermillion and I decided the puzzle was a hoax."

"Really? A hoax that cost a lot of people their lives."

"You're not channeling any more of them, are you?"

He took a drink. "Things are thankfully quiet. All I have to do now is get myself back on track."

I started thinking about the incidents of the past week. Finding Samuel Gallant dead in the museum closet. Pierson's dragonfly creating psychic havoc. Stein's boat exploding. Camden's power surges and sudden bursts of telekinesis. When Ellin had assured Camden he could handle the changes, he'd said, "I like to think so, and then lightning strikes."

I thought of Mason's weird sculptures, especially the spiky post on top of the Riverside Museum. I thought of Kit's latest song. Hit me with a lightning bolt. "Camden, I know what's going on. The surges started a couple of weeks ago, didn't they? When did Kit move in?"

"A couple of weeks ago."

I counted off the incidents. "You had a big surge just before Kit called about Gallant. Kit was there when you shook Pierson's hand and when we found out about Stein's accident and you sent the island into a tailspin. He also stopped by the fair the same time you had your latest telekinetic show. *Kit's* the reason your power's off the charts. He's a not an early-warning system. He's a lightning rod."

Camden didn't say anything, but stared at me, taking it all in.

"Makes sense, doesn't it? Have you ever been around another

real psychic?" He shook his head. "You've been working with him, helping him sort through and shut off the visions. You've been getting a double dose."

He looked relieved. "That's. . .entirely possible."

"It sure as hell isn't your alien DNA."

His relief changed to worry. "But, Randall, if that's true, can he go on living here? He's part of the family now."

"Now that you know he's the cause, you might be able to find a solution. We're not the Piersons and the Duvalls, you know. We can work things out."

To take our minds off weighty psychic matters and to be our favorite contestant's cheering section, Camden, Rufus, Angie, Vermillion, Kit, and even Ellin went to the Miss Panorama Pageant that evening. We sat through the cheesy opening number, which featured a panorama—get it?—of the city and all the women dressed in black and gold. We whistled at Kary's bathing suit and oooed and ahhed at her evening gown, which, thanks to Angie's alterations, looked brand new.

Rufus gave Angie's arm a squeeze. "Nice work on the dress, honeybun."

For the talent portion of the program, Kary played a Chopin prelude. For her Important Question, she was asked about climate change, and assured the audience it was supported by science and our planet's future was everyone's responsibility. She was the best by far, so it was no surprise when she was crowned Miss Panorama and received a big gold trophy, a bouquet of red roses, and five thousand dollars. Not a lot by Miss America standards, but enough to make everyone at 302 Grace happy.

"Now we're both rich," Kary said as she hopped into bed that night. "My pageant money will pay for several classes with some left over for the adoption fund."

"You'll be Miss Guidance Counselor in no time."

"I'm excited about it. A new direction. And you've got a nice chunk of cash to keep the Randall Detective Agency open a little longer."

I put my arm around her and tucked a strand of her silky hair behind her ear. "As long as you save some time to help me solve crimes. I hear you and Vermillion went on a secret mission to the museum."

"We were so sure that 'Under Lamp' was the right clue. But we can keep trying. There might be a real solution to that puzzle. Wouldn't Baseford be annoyed if we solved it?"

"It would be worth it to see the look on his face."

She leaned against my shoulder. "I hope the return of the dragonfly to Pierson helped Isabelle find peace. Did Leo say what he plans to do with it?"

"Carry it with him wherever he goes, I would imagine." I turned off the lamp on the nightstand. "Now I plan to sleep with royalty, Miss Panorama."

"What's that line from *The Cruelest Heart*? 'I would expire for one embrace.'"

"Only one?" I pulled her closer. "There will be a lot more than that."

Chapter Twenty-seven

"O Deare, That I With Thee Might Live"

Sunday afternoon, Wally made good on his promise to look after Vermillion and stopped by to help carry her things out to his van. They laughed and carried on like a couple of teenagers. We waved good-bye as the van chugged down Grace Street and disappeared around the corner.

"Well, that's another problem solved," I said.

"How about a celebratory round of iced tea?" Kary asked.

"That sounds good," I said, "and ten points for 'celebratory.'"

Camden and I took our seats on the porch. Ellin, of course, had gone to check on the fair. Camden looked out across the shady front yard. The sun was bright, and the cicadas had started their buzz-saw chirping. "I can't believe I took all those pills."

"I let Nancy Piper have my phone. We have both successfully passed the Idiot Test and become Self-Aware."

He looked back at me, his eyes their usual deep blue. "You were right. That wasn't the life I want. I'm still not real happy to be psychic, but it's better than being so drugged out I can't function."

"Requests from Beyond will start pouring in." Something had been bothering me. "Can you tell what's going to happen to Leslie Piper?"

"She'll stay with her dad. She'll be all right."

"Let's hope he has a better moral code." My phone rang and I looked at the caller ID. "It's Reg. I didn't think he roused himself from his beauty sleep on Sundays."

"I should've sensed that."

I answered the phone. "What's the trouble, Reg? Are you protecting the fort all by yourself today?"

"I'm at the fair," he said. "Ellin wanted me to talk to potential audience members."

"He's at the fair," I told Camden. "How are things going there? Ellin was worried all the commotion yesterday might keep people away."

"Are you kidding? There are tons of people here. After that story in the *Herald* this morning, the free publicity is going to keep the fair running another week."

Saved from the Wrath of Ellin. "Good news."

"You think that's good news, let me tell you something else."

"She's agreed to the Psychic Olympics?"

He made a huffing sound. "I know you have a low opinion of me, Randall, but this time, I can save the day."

"I'd like to see that, Reg."

"I've been worried about my girlfriend, and I found out what's she's been up to. She's been seeing another man behind my back."

"This is not startling news."

"It's Matt Graber."

"What?"

"It seems she's fascinated by his so-called psychic power and she's got a thing for snakes. I'd been wondering why she was at the studio so much. I thought it was because she wanted to be with me. Then I find her snuggling with Graber in his office. Graber said, 'Oh, too bad. Honey would rather be with someone who has brains and talent as well as psychic ability.' I said, 'Oh, too bad. She's sixteen.'"

I started laughing. "So for once, your preference for under-age girls is going to be useful." Since this remark made Camden look at me wide-eyed, I had to pause and explain. "Matt Graber stole Reg's girlfriend, who happens to be sixteen."

Reg's tone was defensive. "I just found out myself. I told you I thought she was twenty-one."

"What did Graber say?"

"He asked Honey if this was true, and when she said yes, he turned an odd shade of gray. By then, I had my phone out."

"Damn, Reg, I'm impressed."

"Thought you would be. I told Graber if he leaves the PSN, I'll delete the pictures and won't say a word to his sponsors or his fans."

"Is he going to leave?"

"Yes, he is."

I gave Camden a thumbs-up. "Have you told Ellin?"

"I'm waiting for the right moment. Tell Cam to let me handle it. I don't often have this kind of leverage."

I laughed. "See you at the Olympics." I ended the call. "Reg Haverson to the rescue."

"Something I never would've foreseen," Camden said.

"Graber's out and gone. Reg wants to be the one to tell Ellin, so let him have his moment. He'll be able to create any show he wants after this."

When the screen door opened, I thought it was Kary return-ing with the tea, but Kit stuck his head out. "Snakes on the way, Cam."

"Oh, Lord," he said. "Do you suppose they want to live here now?"

"Meet you in the backyard," Kit called over his shoulder.

I swung my arm around to guide Camden along. "They can have Vermillion's room."

I was glad to see the return of his very best "go to hell" look. "They can have *your* room."

●●●●●

Slim and Jim only wanted to say they liked the idea of being in a rock band and planned to sneak out that night and join Runaway Truck Ramp in concert.

"We can't miss that," I said.

Rufus and Angie had other plans, and Ellin opted out, so Camden, Kary, and I piled into the Parkland Arena with a couple thousand of our closest friends for "Battle of the Bands." We had to endure The Scars, Zero Tolerance, and The Stick Boys before it was Runaway Truck Ramp's turn to take the stage.

The snakes were an immediate sensation. Slim let Kit wear him draped around his neck, while Jim sat in a fat coil by the drums. I swear I saw him tapping his tail along with the beat, occasionally hitting the bass drum. The spotlights caught every glint of their scales and golden eyes. Each band was allowed to play three songs. Runaway Truck Ramp sang all their potential-to-become-hit-songs, "You Hate Yourself," the Lily Wilkes-inspired "Embrace the Oddness," and of course, "Hit Me Like a Lightning Bolt." Every time Kit banged out a chord, Slim flicked out his tongue. The crowd loved it and at one point chanted, "Snakes! Snakes! Snakes!"

After Runaway Truck Ramp's set, we left the arena, ears ringing, and waited outside until the concert was over. Kit came out to meet us, his eyes shining. He was still wearing Slim.

"Hey, guys! Wasn't that the most awesome thing ever?"

"Did you win?" I asked.

"We came in second to the Razor Claws, but who cares? An agent from Starmaker Productions offered us a spot as opening act for Iron Hammer on their five-state tour! Slim and Jim are real excited."

Kary carefully reached around Slim to give Kit a quick hug. "Congratulations!"

"That's great news," Camden said.

Kit patted Slim's head. "I always knew I needed a gimmick. The snakes sold it. We're changing the name of the band to Runaway Snakes, which is what they're gonna be for real, right, Slim?" Slim opened his mouth in what appeared to be a silent laugh. Kit turned to Camden. "The only thing is, I'm gonna be gone for months, Cam. If you need to rent the room, go ahead. This tour is just the beginning."

Here was the solution Camden was looking for, a chance to settle his own visions and take back control. "That won't be a problem," he said. "You'll always have a place at 302 Grace, if you need it. You, too, Slim, and your brother."

Slim gave a pleased hiss.

"Where is Jim?" I asked.

"Oh, he and my drummer have bonded. It's good for Ace to have something else in his life to look after. Misses his sister, you know." He gave Slim another pat. "We're family now, right, buddy?"

• ● ● ● ●

That night, I didn't have any trouble falling asleep and soon dreamed. The flowers in Lindsey's playground swayed in the breeze I could not feel, and I caught a glimpse of butterflies dancing in and out among the colorful blossoms. Then Lindsey appeared, carrying a bouquet of the flowers.

Thank you for helping Isabelle, Daddy. She wasn't sure about talking to you, but now she's glad she did.

"Is she all right? Did finding the dragonfly help her?"

Yes, she's moved on.

"What about Delores? Have you heard from her?"

Delores came by and told me about Norma and Samuel. She said they don't need to talk to you. She said it's because they have each other now. They don't want anything else. They don't have anything more they need to say or do. Delores said they've moved on, too, which is what people do when they're happy here.

"But you're happy there, too, aren't you, baby? It looks like a beautiful place."

Oh, yes. But there are even more beautiful places to go.

As much as I wanted her to be with me, I didn't want to keep her from anything she deserved on The Other Side. "If there's a more wonderful place than your playground, you could move on, too, couldn't you?"

I could. She smiled her sweetest smile and then said what deep down in my heart I realized was my truest wish, to keep my family together. *But I want to stay with you, Daddy.*

To see more Poisoned Pen Press titles:

Visit our website:
poisonedpenpress.com
Request a digital catalog:
info@poisonedpenpress.com